LAST RIGHTS

Also by Tim Sebastian

The Spy in Question

Spy Shadow

Saviour's Gate

The Memory Church

A NOVEL

Tim Sebastian

William Morrow and Company, Inc.
New York

It is the policy of William Morrow and Company, Inc., and its imprints and affiliates, recognizing the importance of preserving what has been written, to print the books we publish on acid-free paper, and we exert our best efforts to that end.

Library of Congress Cataloging-in-Publication Data

Sebastian, Tim.
Last rights / Timothy Sebastian.
p. cm.
ISBN 0-688-11448-2
1. Political crimes and offenses—Europe—Fiction. 2. Mothers and sons—Europe—Fiction. 3. Russians—England—Fiction. I. Title.
PR6069.E197L37 1994
823'.914—dc20 93-22922
CIP

Printed in the United States of America

First Edition

1 2 3 4 5 6 7 8 9 10

For Clare

LAST RIGHTS

Last Rights
Prologue

Most of us never cross the line. We walk the safe way, on well-lit streets, never late, never in the darkness. When the wind comes up, we hurry back to the warm.

Others go on—because something drives them forward. They want the knowledge, or the gamble, or they take a step into the danger zone and can't get back. And there's no one to save them, no one to hear their shouts.

I suspect he felt that way, sitting early evening in that vast room, quite alone, deep under Moscow. That steady infiltration of fear. I can feel it myself as I piece together his story.

A damp August day had brought showers of rain and kept people off the streets, but there were other reasons as well. A bungled, hopeless, ill-conceived coup was failing in another part of the city. And just for a few hours the great Soviet edifice was rudderless and drifting.

He knew it, watching the petty officials hurry out of their sacred offices and take to the streets, bundling papers into their bags, shredding and destroying whatever they could, crying out that the world they'd known and loved was ending.

But they couldn't destroy seventy years of history; they

couldn't wash away seventy years of blood. And he knew where it came from, where it was stored. The dirt—the *"Kompromat."* Dynamite that could blow the world out of its orbit.

It was so simple and so awful. Like the birth of a deformed child.

He had taken the stairs into the specially air-conditioned archive, passing through the double doors, once guarded by internal troops from the KGB, now unmanned. And then he looked around him. There was the cool stillness of a cathedral. Even here—in this temple of deceivers.

Gone were the officers who manned the central console, the electronic levers that could open the gray metal cabinets, stacked in rows, side by side, like gravestones.

In an hour, maybe two, the new masters would take over, searching through the filth, on their knees in it, digging and scrabbling as never before. In the months to follow, there'd be show trials and secret trials—and worst of all would come the blackmail and the suicides, bodies turning up by the dozen in alleys and courtyards right across the cities of Russia. And then—the door would close again.

For you couldn't open these files to the world—the world would never allow it. Everyone had been involved—here, there. In every system, in every capital, Moscow had possessed its men and its means. Each had a stake in burying the truth, stifling it, before it could walk and talk.

So he didn't have long. At the control desk, he entered the codes. Instantly, from across the hall came the electronic clatter as the gray cabinets swung apart, revealing the folders inside, shelf by shelf, illuminated by soft, pale lighting, all in perfect order.

He had brought two airline bags for the purpose, wide black leather containers, and he began to load them, sometimes removing folders complete, or simply detaching a single page. Names, he wanted. Live names. The players, the participants. Those who had served the Soviet Union out of sight—and right across the world.

And then a file caught his eye—quite unlike the others. A personal file, a case history, medical records, an address, in Britain. How did it fit together? He took it all, determined to read it later. He liked jigsaws. Russia had been full of them.

From far in the distance, he could hear the sirens of the military and riot police—the shouts of a crowd.

This Moscow day, unlike any other in history.

He took to the stairs now, moving fast along the carpeted corridors with the high ceilings. Maybe he had waited for dark, maybe it was dark already. He crossed into the modern glass building, then took the lift to the ground floor. A quick glance confirmed the control point was unmanned, the entrance to the general department—the one that had served the president himself and then thrown him to the dogs. Honor on every staircase, at every turn.

And then he would have moved swiftly into an anteroom, inserted his personal card into the lock, and watched another lift door swing open and outward toward him.

This was the most secret of exits from the building. A dozen people had access, a dozen cards; no more were ever made or issued. The lift moved smooth and silent, not like the usual rattletraps that the proletariat traveled in. This one had a mind and a brain and took him down seven stories underground. From there a corridor, two lights, a door, and he would have found himself on a railway platform, with just a single bench—the most secret transport system in the world, the tiny rail link reserved for the Soviet leadership, the private network that moved them from office to office, out of sight, and deep beneath the streets of their own capital.

He wouldn't have expected a train, and he wouldn't have waited. Not that day, when the system in all its glorious intricacy broke apart. Instead, he got down along the track, still in his suit, walking maybe one kilometer, maybe more, till he found the concrete staircase.

It can't have been an easy climb, with the airline bags and the summer heat, and the stifling atmosphere below ground. But he made it, into a labyrinth of tunnels and staircases and finally to an exit in the metro station at Revolution Square.

From there, it must be assumed, he was lost to public view. A man like that can have been of no importance, not even passing importance, in the midst of the cataclysm that was breaking around him.

So look at him now, before we lose him again. The fifty-year lines on his forehead, the features flat and wide like the endless landscape of Russia. He was tall with thick, curly hair, permanent stubble, a face with patchy, reddened skin, scratched and uneven, like a street cat that has fought too many battles.

As he ran on that summer evening, he must have known it was over. He couldn't live long, carrying what he held in his hands. Like sweating gelignite, it was too unstable, too delicate. It touched too many lives in too many countries.

The fear in his heart would have told him that, as he made his way out of the city.

Part One

Chapter One

And now we can color in the gray. We know he bought an airline ticket, we know they wished him a pleasant flight. We know he took on an identity quite unlike his own. He made a safe and final landing in London, three-and-three-quarter hours after leaving Russia.

To the airport officials who looked him over, he was New Moscow man. Money in his pocket, tailored suit from God knew where. None of the visible baggage of repression they'd carried around with them all those years.

He told them he was a businessman. Joint ventures, he said. Give us money, tell us what to do—and we'll get rich together. He had the phrases, had the patter.

But somehow they weren't buying. Not all of it. Little traces of doubt over this one.

To those who met him along the way, he was George. Never Georgi. Not with a long name attached that no one could pronounce. "It's George from Moscow," he would say. "My mother had two kids—one was clever, the other was me."

—It was part of his routine.

Remember, those were the days when Russia was in.

Walls down, borders open, love and welcome on every face from Murmansk to Vladivostok. They sold us any rubbish they wanted, and we hadn't the heart to turn them down.

—George smiled a lot. Always smiling. He had about him the air of an amiable sinner, unkempt in his dress, unrestricted in his morals. George would go all the way. That's the picture they painted.

And yet I think he showed restraint. He invited out the hotel receptionist, the tiny blond one, and didn't try anything on till she let him. Just in the taxi home. A kiss and that. Nothing else.

—They talked to her afterward, you see, made sure they had the facts.

So George was the new exotic—a Russian who looked like a human being, not one of those buttock-clenching bureaucrats that we'd all got used to. He carried a firm, dry hand, knew how to hold a knife and fork. The little things they'd never had before.

You might have thought he'd go to ground once he hit London, stay in his hotel, make the calls, do the business, whatever it was. But he seems to have decided to play it differently. Went out, looked at the sights, Tower of London—ceremony of the Keys.

—Look at the picture. Look at the cover. George, the respectable. George, the honest. Made in Moscow.

He was three days in London before he put a foot wrong.

Maybe it was all too much for him—the heady Western diet—or maybe he wasn't getting anywhere with his plans. But he drank himself very silly in a bar off Piccadilly, where he tried to dance with a girl who wouldn't dance back.

She had a friend and he had a friend, and when it came to the fight, George had none.

They watched him throughout—but they didn't step in, didn't help. Even when he was down and the boot went into his neck, scraping off the outer levels of skin, they stayed where they were.

A social worker put him in a taxi about four hours later. But not before he'd seen the inside of a police van, and Casualty at St. Thomas's Hospital.

And still they watched him. Random surveillance, they

said. Haven't got the staff to do it properly anymore. Part-time security—that's all Britain had these days. You got what you paid for.

Final detail now. It seemed they watched outside his hotel for an hour or two, concluding that if he couldn't even behave in a pub, he was probably genuine.

They therefore pronounced George "a good boy" and went off in search of a more credible threat to the British way of life.

By the sound of things, I don't think I'd have cared much for George. Not my kind of Russian. Too glib, too easy. A little too much at home in a strange place. I'd got used to them being dark and complicated.

Underneath, I suspect George himself was pretty dark and complicated. Only he arrived in a different wrapper.

I try not to look on him as a bad man. Somehow in Russia there isn't such a sharp division between good and evil. People can be angels one day, devils the next. They cross and recross the line many times. Who's to say I might not have been like him, if I'd grown up there myself?

From his age, George would have been a child during those lively days of Stalin. He'd have known about fear. He'd have known how to betray his friends and his family in order to save himself. Those would have been his values—his ideals.

Bright as he was, he'd have allowed himself to get sucked into one of those special schools for special children. Accelerated promotion through the party ranks, ties with the KGB, friends who matter. I'm only guessing though . . . I don't know for sure.

And then, when the whole system went to hell, he made a break for it, didn't he? Took out a slice of the most expensive insurance in the world and went looking to sell it. I'm only guessing . . . piecing it together . . . I told you.

But I still don't want to imagine what happened then, how George was found sitting in a red Volkswagen in a street in Docklands, near a pub, so popular with the up and coming, so far away from all things Russian.

George, the smiler from Moscow. George, crossing my path.

Did you console yourself with a drink? Did you limp

along the embankment, nursing your wounds? Your fears I can imagine, but what about your hopes? Speak to me, George, from anywhere you can.

He had been killed quietly, they said, if that's the word. No blood. No horrendous instruments. Helped on his way, if you want to be kindly about the thing. Probably a sharp blow to the carotid artery, or any of those other pressure points. I gather it's easy if you're an expert. And George was very fragile. At any rate, he was sitting there quite peacefully, looking out over the river, no sign of concern in his final expression.

And yet I don't want to think about who took him there, whom he spoke to, the final minutes.

I just want to find out why he was left in my mother's car, and why she herself had disappeared.

Chapter Two

She should have forgotten Russia. Long, long ago she should have got up, screamed, and run away from it—the people, the music, the twin burdens of culture and history. Mother of mine.

To me she could have sat in her English garden, rainy day after rainy day, growing giant apples and tomatoes, looking anywhere she liked except to the past. Should have been enough.

Some afternoons we used to stroll together in the park, when I finished early. And instead of recognizing people—she would greet the animals.

"You see that squirrel. He has only half a tail. Look at that bird. He's been in the same nest for three weeks. Never goes out. How does he feed the babies?"

I told her once that she knew the city only by its wildlife.

"Much nicer than the people," she replied.

Of course she had regressed with the years. Enter the little house, and you could feel Russia squeezing down on you—from paintings and oversized books and the photographs of faces, made very much elsewhere.

As a child, I remember her trying to be English. I remember days when her gate-creaking accent was held in check, when she even achieved a kind of languid stability, when she met mothers at my school, or my friends came over, or we ventured out into London for tea.

And yet the attempts were cosmetic. She always insisted English colors were too pale, English characters too dull, and the climate never delivered. In summer there was insufficient heat, in winter insufficient cold. Annual disappointment.

But you couldn't be indifferent to that woman. Not to the way she jumbled in and out of her moods, not to the emotional marshland, not to the sharp, spiky, often uncomfortable character she was.

And to the eye? A tall, top-heavy figure that must have spoken eloquently of afternoons in bed, of love and fun. Can I talk like that about my mother? Red hair that curved close to the face—legs that were "good"—not "wonderful"—wrinkles that lost themselves in her smile.

People didn't turn away easily from such a package. They looked again and again, to see if it contained something for them. A rich mixture of life enjoyed, life suffered, life seen and exposed well beyond safe borders.

Mother was still beautiful and dangerous, and the smile said so. I can count thirty years since she had left the Soviet Union, a political firebrand, a troublemaker, a role model for far too many—released as a vaunted gesture of goodwill, before a summit. She had been a name on a table, a statistic exchanged between East and West. She came to England and perhaps in celebration, or in need of comfort, or for the joy of the moment, had decided to have a child.

So there was Dad.

I never thought of him as a real father until he'd gone. The man who entered our house with cold hands in winter and warm hands in summer and seemed to live, like a butterfly, for just a single evening.

And yet he left marks I could never forget.

It was thanks to Dad that I was ever called Edward Bell. He had found the name in a book shortly before I was born and decided it was so totally English that he would bestow it on me.

"He always wanted you to be English," Mother told me.

"English school, English traditions, English breakfasts—all of it. 'What's the good of him being Russian?' he would say. 'This is no such great favor to the boy. No favor at all.' "

When I look back, I see so many of the little things about him. The giant striped handkerchiefs with which he battered his nose. The way he would take off his winter coat and jacket as one garment, sitting in his shirtsleeves, his face all red and his hair close-cropped. I see his shiny, polished shoes, with the leather old and cracked. I can feel the limitless strength of those arms.

Above all, though, I recall the long absences, stretching like a fault line along the surface of our lives. Dad was a gap—not a presence.

Mother always said it was his work that took him away. He, too, was of Russian origin, something of a scientist by all accounts, who'd come to London on a conference and decided he didn't want to go back. Apparently it was a huge scandal at the time, but it was long forgotten by the time I was born.

And yet Dad couldn't hack it in the West. He worked only intermittently, as a government adviser. He taught intermittently in various parts of the country. There were no real jobs; there were engagements. "Little here, little there," he used to say.

In a way, though, I think he was caught in quicksand, midway between what he wanted and what he'd left behind. Neither was any longer attainable. No route forward and no route back. And when you realize that, as he must have done, then the sinking has already begun.

Even so, I don't like to think about what happened that grimy autumn Friday, soon after I was twelve, when he wouldn't stay for dinner, wouldn't kiss Mum, wouldn't look at us.

He sat us down, but he couldn't speak; and only now can I hear the silent good-byes.

Tears were in Dad's eyes. I remember looking at them quite dispassionately, wondering how they'd got there. I think he held my arm for a while, and I could feel his heart beating double time, his leg quivering from nerves under the kitchen table.

"Sorry I can't stay."

Mum's anxious expression, flustered gestures. "Won't you have something to eat?" As if that would make it all better. "Won't you tell us anything?"

And his answer was to hold us tight, each of us, one by one for a precious minute of silence. His rough hands clamping us to his body. And Dad was so scared. Like a fox chased onto open land, and he'd stopped running and come in here for a moment of comfort or reassurance, or something else. I couldn't bear to see him scared, for it went against the natural order of things. Dads don't scare, don't run, don't cry.

I remember him going. He never said "See you next week" or "I'll call you later" or anything that spoke of future intent or commitment. So I assume he knew what would happen.

As I said, it wasn't till he'd left that I felt his presence.

For years afterward, I would question him in my mind—did you care? I would ask. Did you care at all? Why did you go?

He had gone, of course, back to Russia—some kind of deal, Mother said, where he got his old job back with no retaliation for running away. Why? Because he was learned and valuable and they needed him back.

Only I needed him too.

Somehow, the effect of Dad's departure was to distance my mother even further from life in Britain. She returned to being a foreigner, went to foreign shops, met foreign people, emigrated inside. To her, England became nothing more than the view from the front window.

And yet there was plenty of work. She was an interpreter of peculiar mental agility, much loved, I gathered, by all kinds of delegations, and trade unions, and businessmen—never averse to injecting her own comments and thoughts into sensitive discussions.

"My dear, they are all so boring," she would say. "Half the time they talk about having lunch or who is to sit where. Pigs—you wouldn't believe. It's as if none of them ever had a meal. Soup, they spill down their fronts, crumbs everywhere. Always they are wearing their food, instead of eating it. Complete animals. Complete."

And that was her outside world. She came and went at all hours and from early in my life, so did I.

She never fussed over me, never told me to wear a scarf in winter or look out across the road. I brought myself up, and she was my companion. I suppose, in the accepted sense, I never had a mother at all.

There were always visitors to the house—men and women with wind-reddened faces and rough coats and suitcases fastened with string. They would bring out books and creased old clothes and fling them all over the place as if they were camping. They seemed to collect every free handout the world had ever known—packets of sugar and toothpicks, hotel towels and crockery, pens and bags and wrappers galore. But then they were Russian.

They would drink a lot—and instead of laughing the way we do in company, they would weep their tears, individually and collectively: Russian tears and Russian vodka—blended by time and suffering.

But I remember one visitor more than the others.

An old woman who arrived at the house with nothing—no bags, no boxes. Just a single black dress that she wore each day and washed on Sundays. I recall it hanging like a quarantine flag on the clothesline in the garden.

I was to call her Maria, and sometimes we would walk up the road hand in hand to the park or the newsagent's on the corner. I remember the hairclip, the whiteness of her skin, the gold in her teeth—but the face eludes me. I no longer see the expression or the eyes.

At any rate, she left without saying good-bye to me. I simply woke up one morning to find she had gone back behind the wall.

From there came the occasional faded postcard. Covered in stamps and pencil marks—cheap, rough envelopes—the smell, the texture of sixties Russia. And then came nothing at all.

I had the impression of a black hole into which people disappeared and rarely, if ever, reemerged.

So there was nothing ordinary about Mother's background. It was all strange, and—to the people I grew up with—faintly suspicious.

Remember, postwar Britain didn't like foreigners. You could never be sure that a foreign accent wasn't really German. And being British, they were too strung-up to ask.

Mother's policy was to tell everyone she met—which only made them more suspicious. Why was she so forthcoming? What had she to hide? Who cared, anyway?

In the end, she learned, as we all do, right across the numbered postal districts of Britain, not to bother. The worst thing was to appear keen—on work, or friends, or life in general. Just muddle along and be rude, offhand, and unfriendly. The British, she used to say, respect that sort of thing.

She got the idea in the end. As I said, she simply lived as a Russian in London—and that was eccentric enough for everyone's taste.

Eventually I moved away. Eventually was my twenty-fifth birthday, the day after the party. She always gave me a birthday party, said it was the only thing she could still celebrate with no regrets.

So right through my life, she would find me and take me out for the ritual feed—from school, from university, from the clutches of girlfriends, whom she would often ridicule and belittle.

"Look at the creature," she would say. "No breasts at all. Like a piece of wood. And that laugh. Have you heard it? Doesn't it drive you completely insane?"

My birthday, though, was truce day—the acknowledged link that bound us both. The fleeting constant that neither of us ever forgot.

And so it was on that November day, still knowing nothing of George the Russian, that I took a bus out toward the contours of North London, assured of a bilingual evening with guests and drink, and plenty of Russian tears to baptize the occasion.

I found instead that the street had been cordoned off—white Ford Sierras at both ends, groups of neighbors, standing talking on the corner, pointing and whispering. Men in raincoats stood around dejectedly, holding their pocket communicators, looking as if the main event had somehow ended early.

And as I walked farther, I could see that the epicenter was Mother's bungalow. That jolted me. I started to run—and so did they. I reached the front gate, now clearly the center of attention, to be met with four or five raincoats barring my way, and the face of a woman so cold and so expressionless that a vital part of her had either died or never been born.

"Are you the son?" she asked.

I nodded. Somehow it was like confessing a sin to a priest.

Chapter Three

I SUPPOSE WE recognized each other at the same moment.

"Jane Card?"

"Edward Bell, oh God!" And that said almost everything about our meeting after such a long time.

Plenty of hurt, plenty of embarrassment, and for me, the sudden sense of an old wound being torn open. But "Oh my God" seemed to sum it up quite well. Jane Card, standing there in her raincoat, with all the flunkies looking on. A name I haven't said to myself in so many years. I remember you very well. "Card, as in Christmas," she used to say. "Not Coward, the way some people pronounce it."

"What the hell's going on, Jane?"

The introduction took place as we entered the front room. She hadn't wanted to let me in—but I wasn't having that.

And yet I could understand her reluctance. Two men in overalls were lifting up floorboards; the chairs had been taken out to the garden. Paintings were down from the walls; books and papers lay in a heap by the fireside.

"What the bloody hell d'you think you're doing?"

"Sit down." She gestured to a stool.

"For fuck's sake . . ." I couldn't control the anger, even

though she'd been a friend, and more, even though we had once shared time.

"I'm sorry, Jane." But I didn't feel sorry, moving closer to her, catching the perfume, near enough to touch the lacquered brown hair.

She sat on the stool and gestured to the demolition squad to leave. She was forty by now and desperately unexciting—clothes pale and colorless, face okay. You see people like her on the train, only you don't look at them. No landmarks. No places of interest. Nobody would ever fall for Jane Card. Not anymore.

"We don't know where your mother is." She said it coyly, as if she really did.

"We?"

"My department . . ."

"Which is?" I was losing it rapidly. "Come on, let's have it—speak in sentences, Jane. The last time we met, you were a diplomat in Prague. . . ."

"You don't have to remind me. . . ."

"A second secretary, Jane, married to a first secretary. . . ."

"I'm not a second secretary anymore, Edward. I work in the home office."

"You mean security. . . ."

"It's called the home office." She shrugged. "I won't play games with you. . . ."

"You did once."

She gave a big sigh, not of impatience, or annoyance, but much as one might do at the start of a long climb. She told me about George the Russian, about watching him, and losing him, and finding him again, very dead by the water's edge, in Mum's car.

She said they didn't really know who he was, "bit of a spiv," but what did that mean? Was he genuine? Was he a plant? Did he belong to the new Russian security service, or was he a problem from the past?

She threw out the questions, maybe hoping I'd catch one of them, but they all passed me by.

"I want to know what you're going to do about this," I demanded.

She didn't reply.

We sat in silence for a while as the suburban darkness took hold. Orange streetlights came on, and skeletal trees appeared, and the orderly front gardens sank away into the shadows. And I thought of Card as I had known her once—with that great expanse of unmarked, unlined skin, and the kind of expression in her eyes that married people aren't supposed to have. Remember, Jane?

"I'll give you a lift home," she said, "and we'll do some more talking." She smiled, rather like a head girl, dishing out school assignments. And that was new.

I didn't argue.

We went out to her car, and the "little friends" were there, acting sullen and tight-lipped and refusing to answer any neighbors' questions. As we left, they went in and started turning off lights and shutting the windows.

"We'll look after things for a while," said Jane.

It was clearly her car. A red hatchback thing, with a child's scarf on the backseat, a handful of chocolate wrappers stuffed into the door pockets.

"No official car these days?" I asked.

"We lost them after the cold war," she replied, and held out a Fox's Glacier Mint. "Besides, we're all a bit more normal these days. I have a house in Barnes and two little girls. I'm normal. And after we're finished with you tonight, I'll go home and cook them dinner and tell them what a nice day I've had."

"Have you?"

"Of course I haven't."

"So how will any of this help my mother?"

She swore loudly as a car pulled in front of her. We pulled up at the lights.

"Something frightened your mother." She turned to face me. "Something she saw or heard. Maybe a ghost from the past. But something that so terrified her that she had to run. That's what I think."

And I remember her question so well. I remember the color of the car next to us, the song on the car radio, a couple kissing on a bus.

I remember her asking, "Just how well do you know your mother?"

Chapter Four

When I thought of my mother in that moment, I could see a woman wearing her history in the darkness of her eyes.

I see her slurping tea from a twisted spoon, her hand so shaky that she would spill it many times on the stone floor. I see her back in Russia.

She wasn't old. Maybe twenty. Not old enough to be in prison and make the decisions she did.

I see her on the night she was arrested—stripped of her clothes and her humanity, locked in a cell for crimes against the state, sobbing, out of control.

I see the wardress, banging on the door, yelling at her to shut up . . . because crying was forbidden. I see her pulling a blanket across her shoulders, sinking to the floor, willing her life to end.

Only sometime before dawn a new resolve was born inside her—the resolve to fight, to live and survive. Whatever it took, whatever the length of time, whatever the cruelty.

And I see her slowly wiping away the tears, forcing herself to be calm, waiting for daylight to enter the cell. She had seized back her fate into her own hands.

I see her transferred to a camp of former human beings, a thousand miles north of Moscow. I see days of fear and hunger, endless as the steppe itself—but she never wavered, never gave up hope, willed herself to live on.

And then six months later on a dark October morning, the sleet turned to snow, and the winter lay down over the countryside, and she was brought by train back to Moscow.

They took her in handcuffs to an empty house. She remembered passing a sloucher, leaning against the wall. His eyes followed her, and he muttered to himself and kicked at the ground in anger and frustration. To him she was neither victim nor friend. She had nothing to give and nothing to take. And therefore in the Russia of those days, she was of no value.

For several minutes, she stood alone in a dingy room, not understanding, and suddenly there was a figure in the doorway—bearded, sickly, and yet with eyes, she once said, like beacons on a hillside. In her words—"the man I had offered my life."

I have no knowledge of what they said to each other. She never told me. I know only that he was a doctor from Leningrad. A researcher, a man with impeccable qualifications, ten years her senior. And yet he must have had connections, must have used them to buy a final meeting. For that's what it was—no room for doubt. In those days, Russia was full of farewells. They both knew the codes, the inevitability, the requirement of sacrifice.

And then she was led out to a car—only something caught her eye in an upstairs window, and as she glanced up, the moon sat there, clearer, larger than she had seen it before.

It was the last time she saw a Russian moon. For they led her to the airport, took her past the uniforms and the barriers, down staircases and under the runways, where the noise of the planes seemed to explode in her ears.

She recalls coming into the open, under the wings of a jet, and no one pausing to say good-bye. A hostess strapped her in—a strap with a locked clasp, or maybe it wasn't a hostess—and a boiled sweet pushed into her hand—last gift, last taste. . . .

She reached out to grab the seat in front, and something jolted her body, deep down, a spasm of pain, her own nails, gouging the skin of her hands, the blood gushing onto her coat and the seat. . . .

My takeoff, she used to say. New life. New start.

And yet all she could think of was the man she had left behind. How she had been released and robbed at the same time. A final slap in her face, another dagger in the chest. Because everything hurt in Russia. You couldn't bypass the pain. It was all around you, in the trees, in the wind. It followed you, disappearing and reappearing, lest you think it should ever depart.

Even on that flight, she seemed to realize that Russia would never release her. It wasn't just a country or a culture—it was a seed planted inside its people, pulling them, drawing them back.

My mother had been out of her country for thirty years—my lifetime and most of hers. And yet that absence, that new life, seemed suddenly to count for nothing. When Russia had wanted her, it had simply taken her back.

"Have another mint," Card said, and pulled up her handbrake.

We had stopped outside the building where I lived.

"We're here," she announced pointlessly, and got out and stood on the pavement.

It didn't seem as though we were anywhere at all.

Chapter Five

She has a bloody nerve, coming here uninvited. It's not like the old days. She's become a lot more assertive.

We're in the lift now. My lift. Third floor in my converted warehouse deep in the London Docklands, with all the big rooms and views across the river. I'm choosy whom I bring here.

"Do we have something to talk about?" I ask.

"Depends on you, really." She goes into my kitchen and starts making coffee. "You could do with this," she says.

For the first time, I can see her as the little housewife, the little mother. "Take your coat off, Tina, wash your hands, Gilly, let me see them" . . . and yet she's as cold as the day outside. There wouldn't be much sitting on her knee or cuddling in bed. And the husband? "Oh, put it away, Jim, not now, for Gawd's sake." Funny the little segments of her life that I seem to hear across that desk.

The strap is broken on her handbag, and I notice she's fixed it with black tape.

"Sugar?" she asks.

"No thanks. Look, Jane, I'd love to talk. You know that. . . ." Only when I get to thinking about it, I don't really want to talk at all. It's not the passing of the years, or Mother's disappearance, it's just that this lady and I said good-bye to each other a long time ago and shouldn't be meeting again. We're a bad combination. Some people are like that. I shake my head. "Isn't there anyone else I could see?"

"I'm sorry." Card scrapes the two brown locks behind her ears. "I'm on this one." There's a twang in the voice that hadn't been there before. It's probably put on—a leveling kind of twang, a sort of run-down regional thing, to show she's not stuck-up, or overeducated, or anything special. Home-office Jane.

"Edward," she says, "I want to take you back in time, for what it's worth. . . ."

"I'd rather go forward. . . ."

"Bear with me," she says impatiently. And she has the facts about Mum in Moscow, the leaving, the lover left behind. I'd never told her any of it. So many things I hadn't thought about in years. The dissection of my life and hers—the way they intercut. Her job, my boarding school, a holiday or two. Why? Why have they been watching the bungalow in Stanley Road for so many years—the two of us inside, growing up?

"You've been busy," I observe.

But she takes no notice, gets up, smooths down the back of the blue skirt that seems to have stuck in her bottom.

"D'you know why your mother was allowed to leave Moscow?"

"This was all a long time ago. Does it matter?"

"Do you know?"

I clench my hands together. "Look—I don't think you and I ever discussed this, so I'll tell you once and that's it. She was a dissident, okay? Good one, I imagine, upset all the right people, really pissed them off. Anyway, they let her out of Russia, on condition she cease political activity—forget about the country, forget about communism. Just shut up and pretend it never happened. She didn't have much choice. Why go over all this?"

"I'm trying to discover if anything from her past suddenly sat up and bit her. It happens, you know?"

"I *don't* know."

"Is there anything in your past, Edward?"

"You're in my past, Jane. Let's leave it like that, shall we?"

She walks nonchalantly out of the kitchen and goes into the sitting room. It's my favorite room, with a view of the river and a balcony. I don't like the way she wanders around as if she owns half of it.

"Twenty-nine years ago, Edward, your mother was very carefully vetted. You and I were in primary school at the time. You in North London, me in South. You joined a gang, and I cut the head off my teddy bear with a kitchen knife, to see if he'd bleed." She looks hard at me. "If you want facts."

A thin line of moisture appears on her forehead. The voice acquires urgency. Card is moved by something.

"Anyway," she tells me, "we vetted her again when your father went back to Russia. Bit of a loss for us—that."

"It was a bigger loss for me, Jane."

She flushed. "I know, I'm sorry. Shouldn't have said that." For a moment, she's at a loss for words. "Did she never talk about anyone from Russia?"

"Only one person—the doctor she left behind. Sergei."

"No current contacts?"

"Not anymore. They all died off over the years."

"We believe that someone wanted to get a message to her, and George was the messenger. What could that have been? Or maybe it was blackmail." She runs her tongue over her lower teeth, as if there's some food caught in them. "At any rate, he isn't here to ask—dear George, is he?"

"Nor is my mother."

"Nor is your mother," she repeats.

"Jane . . . I need to know what's going on."

"I don't think anyone does," she says. "Not where this case is concerned." She gets up and opens the door to the balcony. The wind is blowing hard off the water. I somehow feel obliged to join her. "How's business?" she asks, staring into the middle distance.

"I'm a consultant," I hear my voice saying. I don't know why I'm talking to her about this.

"Eastern Europe," she says. "Yes, I know. You were when I met you."

"Recession and all that . . ."

"One last question, Edward. You may not like this, but do you think your mother could have killed George?"

I look at her in disbelief. "I'll try to forget you said that."

"Edward, she grew up in a violent world. . . ."

"I think you should go now. We have nothing to say to each other."

"Please yourself." She's changed tone again, still looking at the river.

Who are you these days, Jane Card? I'm starting to see a lot of different faces.

One more glance around, and she's heading for the door. "I'll be in touch tomorrow," she says, and in that instant, without even the tiniest warning, she leans toward me and runs her index finger across my lips—so softly—the merest, lightest of touches, tracing a promise. I can't tell you how shocked I am, because the gesture is so out of place for her, for me, so inappropriate to the circumstances.

No one ever did that before—not even she. I'm stunned by the sensuality of that finger, by the tenderness, stunned by the motive and intention it seems to reflect. Jane Card in her blue suit and beige mac, and the two brown locks, folded safely behind her ears. Safely?

As she closes the door, I recall her saying . . . "I'm normal. I have a house in Barnes, and two daughters, and I'm going to make them supper."

She has to be insane.

Chapter Six

Why should it matter what she did?

But it does.

I sit awake for hours, ashamed that I'm reliving the movement of her finger.

An act of possession.

For I can remember so well when she filled the open spaces in my life. I knew every part of that face—the tiny crow's-foot under the left eye, a mole above the mouth, the cleft chin, the eyes that could hold still for hours, daring you to look away. She was confident and committed, and once upon a wonderful time, committed to me.

When I think back, it took a long time to disconnect her from my daily world, to fade the pictures and drown out the sounds.

And now Jane Card has touched me, to show she still could. Whether I want it or not. Touched me for reasons I can't even begin to guess, touched my body, touched a distant desire.

My mother would have laughed. "Little bitch," she'd say. "Playing with you. The world is full of little bitches. What's so special about that?"

But something is, because my mother doesn't disappear

every day, doesn't meet little bitches like this, doesn't get investigated by them and suspected of murder. This doesn't happen where I live.

Take it slow, I say to myself. One thought at a time. Like footsteps.

This day was to have been so different.

I would have left on a tour through Eastern Europe, guiding businessmen into deals with the new democracies. Except they weren't. Everything was run the way it always had been. Names had changed, and the slogans had been chucked away, but power was the same blunt instrument it always had been. Take Yugoslavia and the start of another Hundred Years' War. Take Poland, Czechoslovakia, Romania—a wedge of bitter mediocrity, lodged across the European continent.

I had studied East European languages, spent time in the dark, gray cities, learned what a movable feast the truth had been and still was.

To the clients, I called them "the lands of the piecrust promise." Pick it up and it crumbles. And so it did.

My business began nearly ten years ago, but it hasn't exactly grown. I make the deals, the coffee, and the excuses. In the early days, the last two were handled by an assistant—a young lady just out of university, who had graduated successfully in petty theft. I was her first victim and unwittingly paid for her flight to Australia, from where, I understand, she has not returned.

Similar luck befell me with the cleaner—a former wardress at Holloway Prison, where she is now an inmate. She was stupid enough to steal the few checks I got and pay them into her own account.

So these days I do the brushwork; I don't subsidize air travel. I am, as they say, between people.

But I still attend to my clients as nurse and guide, confidant, little brother—or anything else they want. I give up my evenings to those traders in suits as they drone into their beers about wives or lovers, regretting or cherishing the trips away, racked by their doubts and their debts.

You're paid, of course, to suffer. *They* don't want to suffer. They pay you to take it away. And for that reason you must never sleep, unless it's with someone who gives you information, never take vacations, unless it's with a named government source, never take strong drink, unless it's to get someone else drunk and loosen his tongue.

And you shake their hands, strongly and dryly, and look them straight in the eye with an expression that says, "I'm there anytime you need me, Phil or Dave or Harry. Count on it." And they do.

Sometimes they ring you just to make sure you mean it. Saturday night, and you'll get a conversation like this.

"Hi, Edward, it's Harry."

"Hi, Harry."

There's a moment of silence while he verifies that I'm not the answering machine.

"Just wanted to see what was going on," says Harry.

"I'm right on top of it," I reply. "Was there something on your mind?"

"Don't think so. . . ."

"Well, in that case, I've got a couple of hours left on the laptop tonight. I'll call you the moment I have some news."

I replace the receiver. I'm always amazed Harry can manage a piss without assistance. But they're all the same. At best I'm a comforter. At worst just a number to call when their hands are idle. I sometimes feel London is built on my back.

Outside the window, an early river bus is hauling its way toward Westminster.

There are orange lights on the water, moving diamonds, currents, pulling and drawing. But this morning only the boat has purpose, forcing its way through the darkness of the capital.

Where are you, Mother?

Harry goes to work on this boat. Harry, leading the delegation to Eastern Europe, dressing now in white Oxford shirt and red power tie, and about to phone me to see if "we're all on course."

Well, we're not, are we, Harry? And I'll just sit for a few more seconds before I lift the receiver and tell him.

But I wanted this trip. I needed this trip. For so many reasons. I dial Harry's number.

"Just about to call you, fella," he says. Harry isn't American, but he'd like to be.

"You'll have to go without me," I tell him. "Something's happened."

"I don't like the sound of this. . . ."

"My mother's gone missing."

"Shit, Edward, I'm so sorry."

"That's all right, Harry."

"Jesus, that's awful." He pauses a couple of seconds for reasons of good taste. "What about the trip?"

"I'll join you later. Promise."

"It's three weeks, Edward."

"I know, Harry. I set it up."

"All right, I suppose. It won't be the same though." He sighs audibly. "Hope you find your mum okay."

"Thanks, Harry."

So it's lighter now. A tug is pulling yellow container barges, low in the water, seagulls squawking behind them. A jogger flogs himself along the embankment. Across the river a tramp stretches his arms in an overcoat, patterned with holes. Cities don't burst awake. They rise in fits, unevenly, coughing themselves and their machines into life.

Wherever she was, I knew Mum would be sleeping. She didn't do mornings. "Not in my repertoire, darling," not for anyone, not since her time in the camps, where the siren had sounded at 3:00 A.M., and the prisoners had been herded out into the Siberian darkness to pay their socialist dues.

"Ten years was for nothing," she would say. "If you really did something, you got fifteen, twenty. Ten just opened the bidding." Sometimes she would tell me of the fights, engineered by the prison guards, setting one captive against another. Sometimes the guards would steal food rations and let it be known that a prisoner had taken them. Just a rumor, just a word in a few frostbitten ears, was enough. And like every rumor, it would burn through the camp until the named prisoner was knifed, or, if lucky, beaten senseless. It was entertainment for the commandant.

Once, she said, they had turned on her, and she had fought off three women and then a fourth, rolling like bears in the mud, as the guards looked on. And then her hand had closed on a shard of glass, and she had gripped the woman around the neck and offered to slit her throat.

"Shall I kill her?" she'd shouted, and her voice had echoed out over the dawn wilderness. "Tell me to kill her, pigs."

And they had stayed silent, too stunned, too miserable, to respond. Such a macabre little scene—a bunch of half-humans, playing games of life and death on the fringes of the world.

In the end, Mother said, she had thrown the woman to the ground, and the crowd had stood aside, making a path for her, as she hurled the glass away. No one had ever touched her again.

A fighter, my mother. Vicious, when provoked, ruthless. But not a killer. Not that.

Only Jane Card wouldn't know. Card with her finger across my lips, cutting into my world.

She would know nothing of the mother's hand, reaching out to me in the night.

She would not have seen the hurt in my mother's eyes, when I was sick, the anxiety when I was in trouble.

Oh, Mum could kill, but only with her tongue. And on that front she was an executioner without equal. Her victims were dispatched daily, garroted, strangled, left bleeding where they lay.

For Mother never tolerated indifference, or rudeness, had little time for boredom and those who caused it. Patience was a concept that had never interested her.

Standing in lines, waiting for food in a restaurant, receiving poor service—all this could touch off a sudden, violent storm.

And yet you could always disarm her with a smile and a kind word. Two commodities so alien to her childhood, so irresistible in her later life.

But would Jane Card know anything of that? With her two little girls and her safe upbringing in a safe world.

I'll prove you wrong, Jane. Be certain of it. And I'll find out why you're back in my life.

Chapter Seven

When I look back on that morning, I can feel my own desperation—the clamminess on my clothes and in the apartment—the dull focus from a night without sleep.

I suppose I went outside to clear my head. The boardwalk was empty; only a slight mist had blown in across the water.

The wind puckered little waves beside the riverbank. The air was cold and moist.

I know why it reminded me of Dad; another patch of water, another country, but the mist was the same and the feeling of drift and hopelessness.

You see, it wasn't the end of Dad, when he returned to Russia.

For a long time afterward, there were letters from him, scraps of tatty paper, as if from a child's exercise book. Mother said they had taken months to arrive. Often they'd been opened, and on occasions lines were crossed out in thick blue pencil.

"What does he say?" I used to ask. And she'd always reply . . . "He says he's fine."

* * *

To this day, I don't know how the journey was arranged. It was shortly before Christmas, just after my ninth birthday, when she announced we were going away.

"Where?" I demanded.

"The seaside," she said.

But it wasn't like the seaside I'd known. We traveled by train for three endless days and nights. The carriages were filthy and cold, and we spent much time sitting silent in the compartment, waiting at borders, waiting for searches, waiting for one country to let us out and another to let us in.

Christ, you forget what a hassle it was, going East. Anyone would think I had been declaring war on the Communists single-handed, the way they searched my tiny suitcase, and under my blanket, poring over our passports and jabbering away to each other in whispers.

And then we were there. And there was Poland. The port city of Gdansk shrouded by cranes—where the trams rattled and crashed over the cobbled streets, full of smoke, with piles of coal in the streets.

I remember the hotel unkindly. Bare walls and a bed with a blanket—a single pillow, cold floorboards, and people who stared and scowled and refused to speak when Mother tried talking to them in Russian.

On the first night, we went for a walk in the darkness. Few people about. I remember the sense that there wasn't much of anything in this place. If there had been, it had gone. The lights were dim and scattered. No friendly voices or laughter or music. Maybe, I thought, you were sent here if you'd done something wrong. Poland was punishment.

We stopped in a square, and Mother told me suddenly, "You're going to see your father tomorrow. That's why we've come here. They're allowing him to spend three days with us. It's his holiday."

I recall we both cried at the same moment, standing, hugging each other, and I don't think I'd ever felt such sudden elation.

We sat up all night, talking about him and wondering how he'd look and behave, and what he'd be wearing. We had both stored so many tiny snapshots; how he would sometimes take us along the Bayswater Road past the Sunday picture sellers, stopping for coffees and ice creams and bars of chocolate—the little things of life, the only things he could afford. The bus trips into the country, the walks, the image of three wet and freezing holidaymakers, alone on an English beach in August.

It was those times that I remember with the greatest affection. For Dad became like an old coat, warm and familiar and a little more tatty as the years went by.

I thought back to the time he had once come home around dawn, just as I was rising. He was so tired that his great hands hung lifeless at his side. Standing in the hall, he shook his head and breathed a little sigh into the English air—and from deep inside him came a poetry of Slavic phrases that seemed to encompass the sufferings and trials of daily life and somehow ease the pain.

Yes, you, Dad.

As the sun came up over the Lenin Shipyard all those years ago, I wondered if he still cared and whether he was still my dad.

We weren't to meet until the afternoon, and by then the clouds had blown in from the sea and the cold Baltic wind filled the streets. Neither of us ate that morning; the rolls had an air of antiquity, as if someone had dusted them.

To kill time, we walked by the port. I'd never seen anywhere so busy, never heard such deafening noise. It seemed they were smashing ships, not building them.

Eventually we moved into the old town, in among the tall German houses and the church spires and the smell of a once-prosperous city. Along a canal and Mother was snapping at me for not keeping up, for having dirty hands, for being rude. . . .

And without the slightest of warnings there was a face in front of me, like an old photograph, half-forgotten, faded and creased—part of a life moved on, moved away. And I looked at the figure himself with his clothes hanging loose and his face a mass of tears.

Dad made whole.

The memory come to life.

To a young boy—nothing short of a resurrection.

Somehow his expression contained the sense of time lost, time spent elsewhere. He smelled different, he talked in short gasps, he was nervous and frightened, not as he was on the day he left Britain, but because he had grown to live that way. Although I didn't know it then, the fear was permanent. I just remember standing back a few feet and looking at him, trying to take in all the things he had become.

He was, after all, my dad.

We held each other, and he took away my doubts.

There were two men who followed him throughout the visit. I like to think of them now as Stalin's dirty little children—mindless, graceless creatures, with hats and raincoats and expressions of distaste that never varied.

They had clearly never possessed anything resembling a personality—or else medical science had already claimed it from them.

Dad only mentioned them once as we walked away from the canal—"They are my guarantee," he said simply, but he never explained what that meant. So perhaps he used the wrong word.

Strangely, I have the barest recollections of those days with Dad. The three of us hugging in one cold bed, long afternoon walks on my own, talks about nothing, because we had to stay away from the past and bypass completely the future. The present left us so little to go on.

How, you may wonder, can a child not ask the questions he so badly needs answered? And I have asked myself the same thing.

But whether it was from Mother's sharp looks, or Father's fearful eyes, I kept my thoughts to myself.

Looking back, I'm acutely aware of Dad's fears. Only now I see them as the legacy of the Communist system—the intrusion of state terror into the lives of ordinary people. Like everyone else, we were prevented from leading normal lives, with normal relationships.

Political boundaries were one thing, but they didn't stop there. In each human being who lived there, they erected mental walls and barriers, with which I have been obliged to live for so long.

And then came the last day. No signposting. No train at 2:00 P.M. Or six. Or midnight. Nothing to look forward to, or dread. Nothing so concrete.

I can't forget that departure in the hotel room, where my parents severed their lives, hugged each other until they both whimpered from the pain, and waved their hearts out of sight, as the fear and the foreboding gathered around them.

It's a picture that dogs my life. Each time I retrieve it from my memory, I hear sounds and see visions that I have tried for so many years to disown.

"Yekaterina, come with me . . . both of you."

"I can't."

"You must . . . I beg you . . . we have to start again. . . ."

And Dad was shaking his head and jumbling his words in piles that seemed to repeat over and over again and finally make no sense at all.

With supreme effort, I can recall him sitting on the bed, holding a hand from each of us, giving us his blessing and his farewell.

Eventually Mother forced herself to smile.

"It is like wartime," she whispered, "only I know you will be safe and one day maybe. . . ." And she had left that day unmentioned, unpredicted, left it to happen by itself, if ever it would.

Chapter Eight

Standing by the Thames that morning, I could hear those words so clearly, as if they were carried in on the morning tide.

I walked for a while, not fast, but I wasn't an easy target. I mean they had to have set it up very carefully, worked at it, got the right position, brought in professionals. . . .

And you look back for warning signs, for the moment you could have changed course and avoided all the pain. But I still don't know where it came from, and I probably never will, the body goes so rapidly into shock.

I recall, simply, the feeling of a battering ram in my left shoulder. There was fresh blood on my jacket, and as I lost consciousness, my thoughts turned strangely to the pirates of old, who were brought to this same place for execution, not two hundred years before—and how so little seemed to have changed.

Time is like the mist along the river, out of reach, patchy. I can hear the water so clearly, and the voices. I can feel the movement over rough roads. And yet my mind is jumbling the present with the past, making no sense of either.

A figure sits beside my bed. Why should that be? He

doesn't say anything, doesn't move. I question him time and again, but he continues to sit silent.

When my eyes open, I ask why he hasn't replied, and he tells me I never made a sound.

For God's sake engage.

I'm trying to move, only some of the pieces aren't responding. My left arm seems tied. A plastic wire protrudes from it. I can't identify specific pain, just a general impression that damage has been sustained across a broad front. Somewhere in the white-gray ceiling I can see the sun.

When I wake again, the figure is much clearer, and the pain has edged away.

I should be surprised to see him, but I'm not. For Edgar Coffin is like the summer furniture, stored in a garden shed. You may not see him for months and months, he may lose his color and his shine. But you know he's there, you can dust him down and display him again at any time. He won't have changed.

Why is he here?

Coffin is Mother's best friend—or was. He used to remind me of an Afghan hound, with his long, thin hands and legs and the narrow body and the tail he kept wagging at Mother. And now he sits silent and staring. Such a comfort to the sick.

And yet Coffin was always wrong-footed. He could always be relied on to take people's coats and tear them, to blow his nose over his tie, to drop keys and tickets down drains, or lock himself in and out of places like a lunatic. I once saw Coffin turn the paradise of a hotel swimming pool into a wasteland by knocking over the buffet table and diving after it.

It was a useful disguise, for behind the facade of a genial idiot there stalked a wakeful mind.

I'm wandering now. I can feel it. Why is he here?

He used to say he'd left behind him a whole string of Coffins—farmers who had spread themselves across the bitter-cold plains of Iowa, in the South-Central United States. This Coffin, though, had got himself last-posted to England as a U.S. diplomat, because someone had said it was an odd, eccentric kind of place, and he thought he might fit in.

Look at you. I grew up with you, Coffin, sat up with you,

listened to your stories, and told you mine. I've known you a quarter-century. Why are you here?

He moves over to sit on the bed, which annoys me intensely. There's a perfectly good chair by the window. We look at each other while I wait for him to say it's good to see me, just as he always does.

From a space close to my feet, the deep, baying voice recites its opening line.

"Why is it good to see me?" I reply.

He removes his glasses. "You're still in one piece. How d'you feel?"

"Lousy." I lie back, suddenly aware that I don't feel anything at all.

"You're in the papers," he says conversationally. "Business consultant, Edward Bell, shot in Docklands, motive unknown. Taken to Guy's hospital, critical condition." He swallows hard, and I think . . . Coffin, you're looking old . . . old as the plains you left behind. People are like tides—some coming in, others going out. Coffin is going out.

Of course, when I look back, he's been going out for years. This elderly and so amiable American.

"Coffin, d'you mind sitting on the chair?"

He gets up, and his bulk follows him.

A nurse comes in, followed by a doctor. Coffin is ushered out. For two or three minutes, they fiddle around with my shoulder, lifting up the bandages, replacing them, worrying away as if it's their wound, instead of mine.

Then the doctor sits down on the bed—another one who doesn't know what a chair is for.

"My job," he tells me, "is to delay the inevitable. In your case, Mr. Bell, I think we've succeeded."

I look back down at the bandages. I can feel my bad temper burning away, but I control it. "You're very kind," I say. "I'm so sorry for the trouble."

"Surface wound," he says, not listening. "Bullet didn't even enter. It'll ache for a while, but there's nothing else we need to do. Should heal fine. You can go tomorrow and get shot again if you like. Your cousin says he'll look after you."

I can't help smiling. The thought of Coffin passing himself off as my cousin is patently absurd. He's old enough to be my father.

"What exactly happened?" I ask pathetically.

"You know what happened, Mr. Bell," he says. "You were shot. Either very well or very badly. A miss or a warning. How can one tell? They don't put that in the textbooks. Well, then." He pats the bed and says he'll be seeing me, which means I'm no longer of interest.

Coffin shuffles back in, only I've decided to get rid of him and get myself out of here. Except it's a different Coffin this time, out of breath, worried.

"Can you walk?" he asks.

"Since I was two."

He makes a face, pulls back the covers, and half lifts me, for God's sake, into the air. . . .

"What the hell . . ."

That's when I feel dizzy, when I know I've met a bullet.

"No time to play the invalid," he remarks. "We have to talk."

He eases open the door and peers out. I feel myself maneuvered like a parcel into the corridor, toward the fire exit. Lunch is doing the rounds. Trays and trolleys clatter past us. Part of me very much wants to eat. But Coffin kicks open the fire door, and we're standing on a cold concrete staircase—the one place where you can be certain lunch *won't* be served.

"I just saw something I don't much like." He puts his foot against the door. "Surveillance on you—which is normal enough, except it's not the police. Looks like security. A lot of it. The entrances, the lifts. The worst thing is that a couple of our people are here as well. I know them. They're not the kind to go out, visiting the sick. Why are you suddenly so important?"

"Christ, you don't know, do you?"

"What?"

I unhook myself from the wall and tell him how life has attacked me: Mother's disappearance, the murder of George the Russian, Jane Card's attempts to breathe down my neck and beyond.

I can see a nerve begin to flicker in his eye. He shouldn't be in this anymore, should have gone back to Iowa, back to all the other Coffins. And yet he sits there shifting bits of furniture around his brain. "It fits," he says. " 'Course it does. You were supposed to act as bait to bring your mother into the open. That's why they gave out details of the shooting. It's probably why you were shot in the first place."

"What is this about, Coffin?"

"I don't know."

"You have to know."

He sits down on the steps and shakes his head.

"We don't have time for this. But I'll tell you anyway. Your mother and I weren't just friends; we did some work together. Confidential. Okay, secret. Nothing world-shattering." He wipes his brow with a ridiculously large handkerchief. . . .

"Coffin, I need to ask you something. Is Mum capable of killing anyone?"

"How do I know?" He doesn't like being interrupted.

"That's not the answer I wanted. This is important."

"No, it's not. If she killed, she had good reason."

"For God's sake, that's my mother you're talking about."

"Oh, grow up!"

We look unkindly at each other. Far away down the staircase, doors are slamming shut.

"Straight answer, Coffin. You knew her better than anyone."

"No one knew her, Edward. She wasn't for knowing. That was the fascination about her. A moving target. Never there, where you thought she was. Permanent transit. Journeying, journeying, never seeming to arrive. . . ."

"What was she involved in?"

He gave a sharp little laugh. "What wasn't she involved in? Everything. Nothing. She's Russian, Edward. That's a secret society in itself. It's as if they're all born on the same side of the same street, in the same remote, fucked-up little town. They all know each other, went to school together, screwed each other, I don't know. . . ." He drew in his breath and released it slowly. "They never seemed to blame each other for all the killing and the cruelty—just the system. Your mother was the same, even after the things she suffered. One moment she'd be talking to the dissidents, the next to the KGB. I couldn't keep track—maybe she couldn't either. Uh? Thought of that? Look at it this way. . . . Judging by the boys lounging around this place, a lot of people want to see her. That's too much wanting for a lady who just worked as an interpreter. . . ."

Thanks, Coffin. That really helps. Thanks for pissing in my water. Thanks for making it so fucking complicated.

He brings his face to within a couple of inches of mine, and his voice is barely audible. "I won't say this again, and maybe I won't get the chance to. But I'm almost certain your mother's in Moscow. That's not a guess. She used to say it was the safest place when you were in trouble, and I didn't know what she meant, till now. My advice—get yourself on a plane soon as possible, and get out there. She's going to need help. I'll do what I can."

I look at him blankly. "Coffin, what the hell are you talking about? She hasn't set foot in Russia in thirty years" . . . . but he's already loping down the stairs at frightening speed.

If I'm honest, Coffin has always managed to scare me. When I was a child, he'd come into my room in the dark, playing the monster, with a rag over his head and noises like a gurgling drainpipe. He would throw me over his shoulder and carry me off to what he called "his lair" while I screamed the house down.

At other times, he'd come up silently behind me, gag my mouth, and tell me he was a mass murderer and today wasn't my lucky day. Often I would hide in the attic when I knew he was coming.

Looking back, though, none of his antics scared me half as much as our exchange on the staircase, when it became clear that the games of make-believe were finally over, and Coffin was just as terrified as I was.

Chapter Nine

I was bloody angry with Coffin. With all of them. And I couldn't afford to be lying in hospital with my shoulder bandaged and my mind mangled by fear.

Forty-eight hours ago, they were in their place, and I was in mine, and that was the way it should have stayed. Now we're all caught up in the wrong life. And I'm learning things about Mum that I'm not sure I like.

I don't mean her affair with Coffin. That was common knowledge. In the early eighties, they wet-kissed and cuddled their way right across the South of England—dinners, parties, hotels. Mother was living the youth she'd never had. Coffin was networking for the American embassy, groping his way along the outskirts of British society. Burrowing into their navels, he called it.

And yet it was Mother who got him noticed. She alone could address them in their language and in hers. She could be charmingly obscene, she could be rude and obsequious, she was the coquette and the demure, adoring companion. Half Russian, half anything they wanted. She was Coffin's smile and his eyes. She was invited. He went with her.

I am sure she knew her strength, and his weakness, and for a while they could feed from each other. She was needed.

He was carried. Why not? Two social animals, smelling the same scent, "not too much talking, darling," life anchored in the present, with nothing promised and nothing expected for the future.

For Mother it was a transformation. By the time Coffin came along, she had acquired the cachet of a thing unattainable—a confirmed widow, her shutters drawn, her door slammed, vitriolic in her dismissal of male advances. Only as she once put it—"Coffin didn't advance, he sort of tripped in front of me."

Quite literally, he fell over her feet in a restaurant, banged his head on the floor, and suffered mild concussion. Mother, who immediately shrieked and made a great show of feeling responsible, took him to hospital and brought him out the next day.

They built from there. No foundations, of course. They never bothered with them. But they constructed something.

For a few years, he became the man in Mother's life, but he never became the man in mine. Coffin was too introverted to play the role of father, too frivolous, too superficial.

He was a wonderful companion but never a guide. He could share, but he couldn't give, and as the two of them fell gradually out of love, Mother got tired of the parties and the late nights, and everything else.

I remember asking her once if she'd ever really loved Coffin.

"I only ever loved two men," she replied. "The man I left in Russia and your father. I would marry them both if they were here now."

"And Coffin?" I asked.

"We reached the point, darling, where we would rather eat lunch than go for a fuck," she said. "And when that happens, you know it's over."

Only it wasn't. Not completely. If Coffin was telling the truth, they had discovered a professional bond—and that worried me even more.

I think I realized then that Mother was a player as much as a victim. It didn't change my feelings, but it complicated them. Coffin didn't know if she was a killer or not. And maybe I didn't either.

Toward evening they brought me a tray of food.

"They"—I should have looked at more closely, because somehow, on eating their chicken and their cheese, and the muddy little cake and the muddy coffee, I fell asleep, at once more fitfully and more deeply than usual.

Later . . . don't ask me for the time. Minutes, hours. I don't know. There are many states and stages between the wakeful and the unconscious. There are clouds to obscure and voices to distract, and among them all are the memories that you cannot push away. You are at once an open mind and a captive, and if they know what they're doing with you, they can own your thoughts and direct them at will.

There was a face that looked at me. No detail. No expression. We may even have talked.

I remember fighting myself awake. How long had I been like that? Believe me when I say I just don't know. Time went its own way.

But I know the point at which I came awake. The white emptiness of the room, the disinfectant, and on me fresh, cold sweat against the skin. And I was alone.

I knew I had to move fast, reaching for clothes from the cupboard, steadying myself against the wall.

From outside in the corridor came the sound of footsteps on lino, whispers, the hum of electronics.

Patients might die, but the hospital lived on. The routine so quiet and so smooth. And yet in the calm of the night, the living were struggling to survive.

I moved out of the room, stumbled a moment, felt the twinge of pain in my shoulder. The lifts were to the left, the fire escape beyond them. I could hear voices from an open door somewhere much nearer, nurses, maybe, a doctor—and then a man's voice, questioning. And it didn't seem clever to pass that way, not clever in this maze of casualties. So easy to become another.

But there wasn't time to think it through. At any minute, a nurse might emerge, or someone from that room. And don't think about it—just count yourself lucky you can move at all, not wired up to a machine like some poor bugger in there. So do it, gently, quietly, as if you have every right in the world, walk past the room, don't look in, keep going. . . .

And even as I passed the door and began a pathetic sort of run, I could hear a shout from behind it.

But I was beside the lift now, pressing every button in sight. Fifteen, twenty yards away comes the first tangible danger since . . .

"Mr. Bell, hold it. Mr. Bell, don't move. . . ." A gray, suited figure at the edge of my vision.

Thank Christ the door was opening.

And the figure was running and talking into a radio at the same time, but he wasn't going to make it. Door closing. Press ground. Not ground, stupid. Go to first. They'll all be waiting on the ground floor, like a fucking convention.

First floor. Open and out. Not a soul. Jesus. It's radiology; they don't work at nights. A sign mentioned another wing, a bridge, and all I could see in front of me were shiny floors and dark corridors, and lights outside, scattered across the buildings.

Better still a staircase. Going down. Wait. Invest just a few seconds, and maybe after all you'll have a future. I couldn't hear anything, couldn't feel anything except the pain, eating away at my shoulder.

The stairs led into what looked like a day center, dark and deserted for now, but with glass doors under a parapet, and the world beyond the hospital.

Just push the bar, it says, just walk out.

I could feel the wall of cold, and I must have closed my eyes for a second. How else could I miss the two figures either side of the street, moving rapidly toward me, perfect shadows, reaching out into the darkness?

Of course they were good and I was sick, but you can't give it away on a plate. So I ran out into the middle of the road, not really knowing why . . .

Looking back, there were shouts coming from the hospital, two, three people in the distance, approaching fast. And in that moment, I couldn't move any farther, couldn't get my feet to respond, couldn't slow the awful rasping pain knifing me, it seemed, from every angle.

They were closing from every direction, running with radios and shouts, and me the fox, cornered on some dark stretch of ground by all those dogs. I still have no idea how the car came through them; but suddenly it was beside me, nudging me like a strange animal. I turned to find an open door and a voice above the others, shouting at me to get inside in the name of Christ, and all the things he and I had ever held dear.

I banged my head and jumped, expecting my shoulder to ignite in a fireball of pain.

But instead I blacked out for a few seconds and woke, feeling my way back into a moving world, not knowing if I wanted to be there, raising my head and vomiting all over the seat.

The man beside me cursed and moved away. I was aware we were traveling very fast along the side roads. No traffic. I saw a bridge, saw faces, a bus—but I have no idea where we were.

A towel was pressed into my hand, and I wiped my face and did what I could with the rest of me.

The driver turned and glanced briefly at me. "You don't look that bad," he said. "Try to get some rest."

It only hit me much later that he had spoken in Russian.

CHAPTER TEN

THE LANGUAGE WAS Mother's first gift—the building blocks with which she sought to mold my thoughts.

It was the only key that ever gave access to her world. For Russian sends the mind down different paths, embraces different concepts, holds out to those who speak it a sense of mankind unlike any other. Her sense. Passionate and all-involving, the full range of emotions laid out on display.

Even in the darkness of the car, I could feel myself among Russians—their clothes, haircuts, their demeanor—direct and violent. They wouldn't panic, and they wouldn't disobey—and maybe, like all the millions of others, they wouldn't mind dying if they had to.

"Russians are good at sacrifice," Mother used to say. "They have so much more experience than anyone else."

We were moving fast through the backstreets, the driver relaxed at the controls, the tension all mine.

And which lot are you? I wondered. The new boys or the old boys—or a clone we haven't seen before?

No doubt Mother would have recognized them. Hadn't she grown up in a land where they bundled people into cars and chased them along dark streets? Hadn't she grown up trying to fight it and win some justice? Wasn't it time, all in all, to give up? Maybe the thugs would survive whatever the system. Maybe powerful men and women would always need them.

Nice thought—just when you'd started believing Communism was finished and there were tickets to the Promised Land.

The time you end up in a car with armed men you've never met.

When danger tiptoes close and stands behind you.

For now we were back on the main road, hugging the river, heading west. The driver had slowed to keep pace with the late evening traffic. Good-time traffic. People going home.

Through Fulham, and we turned back south across Putney Bridge, the car lights shining back at us from shop windows, up the long hill, turn again.

I could see what they were doing, trawling the traffic, watching in the mirrors.

We pulled into a garage. Two minutes later another black car stopped behind us. A man in a raincoat got out and came over. It was a young, sallow face, which couldn't have been made in England. Too flat, too wide. They simply don't build them that way here. He leaned in, and I caught the words—*"Vsyo v poryadkye,"* "Everything in order."

So our back had been watched.

We took on petrol and moved again. This time the second car was pathfinder. Wherever we were going, they'd decided to bring us in.

I tried to get comfortable, but every part of me ached—the bits they'd shot, and the bits they'd manhandled in the ambulance and the hospital. I could feel the route they'd all taken across me—like a herd of cattle.

I think hard about all this—but I can't remember a time I was so frightened.

They pulled up without any warning to me. A row of terraced houses, cars parked along the curb. Lights in windows.

Driver opens my door, makes a mocking gesture of servitude, as if he's doing me a favor.

He leads, and I'm in the middle as we go up a garden path. This is a nice street, I tell myself, a do-you-no-harm street, where they don't beat the kids or throw litter on the ground. A well-behaved little place . . .

He rings the bell—like a bloody postman—and the next moment she's standing in the doorway in jeans and a red pullover. And she looks quite different. Or is it that a close bullet has changed my outlook? But the smile is new, I'm sure of it, and the hair looks more recently washed; the whole package neatly tied instead of bundled up like a trash bag. Is there even a dab of makeup on your eyes? Are you trying to make an impression?

"Vy pozdno priyekhali," she says without trace of an accent. "You're late."

And Jane Card, I observe, speaks Russian like the rest of us.

"You have much to explain," I tell her.

She leans against the mantelpiece, with all the photos, and it dawns on me this isn't any old house, it's hers. She's in the pictures, standing next to a couple of girls in school uniforms and a jolly-looking fellow in a donkey jacket. The normal life. The lady who ran her finger over my lips has a normal life, and this is where it's conducted.

"How are you feeling?" she asks.

"So many people want to know." I peer out of the window. The Russians have got back in their car. "It varies such a lot. I think I'd like a drink."

"Gin okay? We've got some tonic somewhere."

"We?"

She looks vaguely embarrassed. "This is my house. Sorry, I should have said."

"Think nothing of it."

She goes into the kitchen, and I get up to follow.

Oh Christ! As I reach the door, a dog throws itself at my trouser legs—one of those Labradors that has to rape you to say hallo. Somehow it gets behind me and starts licking my backside.

"Can't you teach it a more conventional greeting?"

Card laughs.

We return to the sitting room, and suddenly I don't feel amused anymore. I'm on my knees from exhaustion and fright, and the pain is needling my shoulder.

Card has enough sense to read the change of mood, for she takes up position at the dining table and opens the business.

"I'm sorry about the strange journey. But you looked as

though you could do with a lift. The men who brought you here are Russian security. They're part of the new Service. They're mandated by the new president."

This is going too fast for me. My forehead has begun to drip with sweat; my clothes feel tight and clammy. I'm in the wrong climate, the wrong place. I cough for a few seconds to try to gain time. When I can manage to speak again, I have to try the words twice.

"You're seriously telling me you're working with Russian security? Here in Britain?"

She looks at me unkindly, as if I've wet my bed. "Perhaps you could keep your voice down," she says, and then adds, "I have two young children upstairs trying to sleep."

I don't know why that takes me over the top, but it does.

"And hubby's up there, too, I suppose, in striped pajamas?"

"He's away on business."

I clasp the gin and tonic.

She looks away. "The Russians have found out more about George—the man who was murdered. Apparently he took some highly classified documents from the party archives in Moscow. They think he brought them to London. They think he showed them to your mother."

"Why would he do that?"

"No one seems to know."

"What was the file?"

"That's just the problem. It could have been anything." Card sniffs and wipes her nose with the back of her hand. "But it wasn't just some boring old dirge. We know that. Those archives contain enough explosive to blow holes in most Western governments. . . ."

"What does that mean?"

"Look . . ." She does her favorite gesture and wraps her hair curls behind her ears. "Let's just go back a few years and remember what it was like. Moscow was the grand enemy, repressor, invader—'visit the Soviet Union before the Soviet Union visits you.' Anyway, at various points in the cold war—the East-West dialogue virtually shut down. At least it looked that way. But in reality things were very different. All right the front door was locked and bolted, but everyone was doing business round the back, through the side door, even climbing in and out of the toilet. The Soviet Union was big business, cold war, hot war. It gave jobs to our arms industries, it kept armies and military planners in work, it was the rationale behind a thousand policies that had nothing to do with it."

She looks at me quizzically. "You see what I'm saying?"

"Yes, thanks, provided you stay off the long words."

She flushes. "I'm not saying this for fun . . ."

I watch her over the top of my glass. Get to the point, Jane. Shoot at the target.

She stands up and goes back over to the mantelpiece. "The point is that governments all over the world propped up the Soviet Union. They didn't want it to change, didn't want it to reform. They all needed the big bear out there to take the heat, to justify their own actions. So they did deals with Moscow—shabby deals, corrupt deals, and Moscow kept files on all of them inside the Central Committee. Only trouble is secrets aren't secrets anymore in Russia. They all have a price. They're all on the market if you can find the right seller." She takes a very deep breath. "Whatever your mother saw must be something pretty sensational—because a number of people are getting unusually exercised. That's why you were shot. That's why the strange characters were hanging round your hospital. . . ."

"They were American, for God's sake, Coffin and others. . . ."

"I know about Coffin. I know he came to see you." She shrugs. "These are uncertain days, Edward. Since the Soviet Union collapsed, there are new alignments, new allies. It was like a ship going down. It pulled a lot with it. You have to realize—the people who want to destroy these files come from every country. America, Britain, Russia itself. The truth doesn't have much of a constituency these days."

"What makes you think you can trust the new lot in Moscow? Maybe they're all implicated—how would you know?"

She shook her head. "They need to bring it all out into the open, more than anyone. It's the only way they can discredit the old system completely and publicly—and prevent it ever getting back into power. Apparently there's blood all over the files."

"And my mother?"

"Your mother's in Russia. I believe that—I just don't know why."

And Jane Card wants to draw a line there. I can see she's as tired as I am. One of her eyelids is quivering intermittently. And then she comes and sits beside me, and for a moment I try to look at her as a stranger. She's not beautiful in her jeans and red pullover. In many ways, she never was. But it's the sum of all the ingredients. It's the way she could give her mind, not just her body; the need that was stored and contained deep in those gray eyes; the physical figure that still winds and bends its way through my favorite fantasies. . . .

She touches my arm. "There's no reason why you should know this, but I may be the only one who stands a chance of unlocking your mother from the things she's involved in. It's a jungle out there, rival factions, hatreds. The old system is still half-alive, and the new system hasn't yet arrived. It's unbelievably dangerous. . . ."

And suddenly I don't want to talk about it. I know what's going to happen. I can read the intention—the moisture on her lips, the change in her breathing. I know she wants to be close.

And she kisses me even as my thoughts are forming. Jane from the old days, taking my head in her hands, moving her mouth against mine, altering the pressure . . .

"Why do you do this?" I ask her.

"I don't know. . . ."

"With your kids upstairs . . . have you done it before?"

"No."

"What?"

"I've thought about it, never done it."

"Why this time?"

"You tell me," she says.

But I don't know. What happened to us began and finished years ago. I never saw her since then, never talked to her, and yet she's holding me, as if she always has.

Chapter Eleven

In the distance, I hear the sound of a child crying, and she breaks away and runs upstairs.

Odd that in the middle of all the madness, the little things go on. Child cries, mother goes in, tells her everything's fine, knowing it isn't.

They say you shouldn't serve lies to children, but, God knows, they're too young for the truth.

How does Jane Card play it? I wonder. What does she say to her normal family?

She's taking her time. Perhaps the child had a bad dream. I know about those.

As I look around, it seems odd that this room should be hers. Lots of pale, restful colors, beiges and magnolias—like an old people's home. Comfortable and boring. No sturdy, sexy reds or deep blues, or flashy whites. Everything on a level—mild and unassuming.

What happened to you, Jane, in all those years? That wasn't part of your character. You were focused, and direct. You wanted bright colors and sharp tastes.

Only you changed your mind.

And then I see the postcard half-tucked behind the clock on the mantelpiece. The Charles Bridge in Prague, taken at night, with the black statues standing guard across the river.

Must have been in the old days. Poor Prague—the prettiest and saddest of the East bloc cities, as it was then. All it had was history. Lousy present. No future. At least not for us.

She and I had spent a few hours on that bridge. She, stepping out late, from the embassy, always fearing she was followed, making some excuses to her husband, who, she claimed, was always making excuses to her.

I often wondered what I was caught up in, all those years ago. On the face of it, of course, work was the cover. There was a new construction deal being set up—a chemical plant close to the Czech border with Austria—a major Western consortium involved, and I was consultant. Part of the team. Always on a plane to Prague, always in a hurry, driven along by the excitement of something, not quite right.

I had met Jane Card at the standard British cocktail party —in an elegant room of the elegant embassy that had dug deep into its reserves of gin and generosity for the business folk far from home. A chance to meet the wives—"And how do you manage out here?"—"And how do you like Prague?" and "Are they looking after you?" And if they weren't, who cared?

Or am I being unfair? Jane seemed to care, because she met me the next day for lunch, which became a walk, which became a drink in a teahouse, with the violinist and all the cozy chatter, and me and her. Central European seduction, I call it. Illicit encounters in a hostile environment. All the senses heightened. Even a good-night kiss seemed to mean things that it shouldn't.

Maybe it was our third meeting when we went back to my hotel. I remember thinking . . . how magnificent to go to bed in the afternoon, when the world was working.

Prague did us proud. The sheets were fresh and white, the room decorated "à la West" and Jane "custom-built" as the adverts say, "for the discerning man." She threw away the hours, till I stopped thinking of anything or anyone else—about "doing the right thing"—a notion that only arises when you're not.

We got up in the early evening and looked out over Wenceslas Square and knew exactly where the day had gone.

Later, walking her home, I made up my mind that it shouldn't happen again.

But I remember so clearly the words she used when I

told her. . . . "I'm going to leave Eric. We can't stay together anymore. It's gone on too long. We just don't share anything. You only get one chance—and you have to take it. . . ."

So we kept on meeting—until she changed her mind.

That winter in Prague, when the river froze over.

She's back in the room now, watching me, and she's noticed the postcard.

I don't like this sense of helplessness, of constant pain, of playing in a game where others decide the rules.

"We're going to get you out of here now," she says. "I made a call upstairs. You're becoming very popular around town. We've just had an official request to hand you over for questioning. . . ."

"I don't understand. . . ."

"A request from the Americans . . . which means they have some very pointed questions to ask you. . . ."

"What are you telling them?"

"We don't know where you are, thought you were in hospital. Love to help, but you're of no interest to us. That line should hold for an hour or two."

She's looking out of the window. Car's still there, Russians inside.

"Listen, Edward. You're going to leave for Moscow now. Nowhere's safe anymore. I don't know who's involved. I don't know who's with you or against you. Or me, for that matter. The journey's been worked out. The driver goes with you. Whole way. Do as he says. He's done this kind of thing before."

"What kind of thing is this, Jane?"

She doesn't answer. Instead, she hands me a wallet, and I can see a passport and money poking out from the top. And then she stands in front of me, arms loose at her side, and I remember the time I used to look at her and trust her. For a short time, she was even the engine that drove me—the motive. Does she think I'd be stupid enough to let that happen again? Does she have even the slightest idea how I feel?

After a while, she reaches for my hand, but I pull it away.

She shrugs. "Go well," she says quietly.

Upstairs, I hear the child begin crying again, as if in sympathy.

Chapter Twelve

She is drawing us to the East.

I can see my mother so clearly, back among her people in the broken city of Moscow. I see her tripping through dim courtyards, past barking dogs, past the old men who stand there with eyes tight shut, muttering soundlessly, their minds dismantled and shrunk by vodka. Around her—the epic tragedy that is Russia. Only she is once again a part of it.

She is playing the grandest of games, but she plays on her ground and her terms, reeling in the unfaithful to be shown without disguises or mannerisms or fancy titles—just the men and women, seeking to kill her.

They know she has read the files. She has looked into the common grave of Soviet history and seen the victims and the tormentors.

They can't let her live.

Do you know what you're doing, Mother? Do you see the threat? They are fresh and skilled, and you are thirty years in the West, with nothing to fight for but the mortgage and the school fees.

Will I come to Russia to watch you die?

I remember the questions, and I remember the answer I

gave myself; that I wouldn't let it happen, that I wouldn't have her hunted down like an animal in the forest, that my mother would one day return to the house in Stanley Road and talk out her days in the garden that grew and grew each year into a field of fruit and flowers. And I would bring her back.

The driver tells me his name is Yevgeny, and to sit in the car and let them get the hell away. There's no time to dream.

He possesses an overelegant name for a thug, but he's clever. You talk to him, and the light goes on. He's programmed with all the responses he'll need, and within them, he'll guard and cajole and bring me back to the fold if I stray.

For the first time, I can sense his anxieties, palpable in the hurried gestures, the staccato bites of conversation, the rapid glances.

"Where's the other car?" I ask.

"Fucked off," he replies. "We're on our own. What am I supposed to do about it?"

In the front passenger seat, his colleague is turning maps upside down. I tap his shoulder. "What's your name?"

"I don't have one," he says. "It's better that way."

Gradually we shake off the city, the traffic thins out, lights are going out all around us, and we're heading into darkness. I shut my eyes and when I reopen them, it's just us and the countryside, the headlights on full beam ranging out into the void, and this is a worried car, I think, making its way to Russia.

We drive in silence. It's what the British and the Russians have in common, traveling quietly, in taxis and trains. The British always too awkward, the Russians, by tradition, too scared.

And that is what I feel in the car—Yevgeny and colleague worried beyond the normal boundaries. They won't tell me, but it's a smell they carry with them.

Over the brow of a hill we slow down, and a lighted telephone box comes out of the darkness by the side of the road. We go past twenty yards and then reverse back.

"What is it, Yevgeny?"

"Instructions," he says. "Mrs. Card tell us to phone, report our position . . . if anything unusual . . ."

The two Russians exchange looks in silence.

"Luchay nye dyelat." The colleague shakes his head. "Better not to do it."

"Why?"

"Why?" he repeats. "Why are you an idiot? Why should we call from here or anywhere else? We have money, we have orders, and now we go. Stop for nothing. . . ."

"She ordered me to call. How do I know?—it could be important."

"Call," I tell him. I don't know why, but we can't sit here arguing in the middle of the night.

He gets out of the car, and I watch him pick up the phone and fumble in his pockets for change. He puts down the receiver, then tries a second time, and a third. And I sense the alarm in his gestures, the way he stands, tense and stooping.

To me, it is like seeing the cracks break out along a frozen river. You stand there powerless in the middle of it, knowing the danger is rushing toward you.

Yevgeny gets back in and starts the engine.

"Nu shto?"

"The line's dead," he says. "Dead, dead, dead. A fucking special line for this call that we have to make, because it's urgent and vital. And what happens—it's dead."

He's into third gear by now, right foot flat on the floor, the engine rough and screaming, and I can feel my heart, dancing wildly out of time with the rest of me, answering the call of fear.

"You shouldn't have phoned," says the colleague.

"Of course I should." Yevgeny takes his left hand off the wheel and waves it in the man's face. "Now we know that the whole thing has gone to hell and we have no one to trust. Mrs. Card is gone, the line is gone, and we're more fucked than we thought."

"Is there any way to abort this journey?" I ask.

"No abort," says Yevgeny, whose hands, I see, are clenching the steering wheel, threatening to bend it. "No abort."

"We should go a different route. Zhenya." The other Russian is pleading. "Be clever for once in your life. Read the signs. This way is too dangerous. Turn the wheel. We go somewhere else."

But Yevgeny isn't listening, and I don't know anymore if

he's right or wrong. I don't move in these circles; I don't face these kinds of decisions. What does it mean, if Jane's gone silent?

"We take the ferry as planned," Yevgeny says, and neither of us argues, because when it comes to it, we don't have another idea, and as long as we're moving somewhere, it feels safe.

I sit back, as we crawl into the outskirts of the town. There's pain in my shoulder, but otherwise I find I'm surprisingly calm. For it seems to me that this is the day I learned to walk. The day I left home, the day I graduated from school. All the important times when I cut loose from the old world and entered a new one—all of them somehow crammed together. And now I make decisions that in all probability will decide whether I survive into the glorious days ahead. It's not a bad sensation. I want you to know that. People don't usually get the chance to find out.

Even in the dark I can see the port of Dover crouching in a damp mist. There's a fine light rain blowing in from the sea and an English wind, gentle as a child's breathing.

On the jetty are tiny shapes and lights, and far away I hear the seagulls out along the coast.

The last time I came this way was on a class trip to Paris twenty years ago, and the extent of my worries was the enormous decision about whether to kiss Rosemary from the girls' school.

Funny the things your mind throws out along the way. Rosemary had curly brown hair and skin so fresh and unblemished that she might have been made that day. We did kiss, I remember, somewhat anxiously, dribbling down our chins as if overflowing with passion. We laughed a lot, and halfway across the channel I put a hand up her skirt, and she laughed again and told me I'd lost my way. I replied that I knew exactly where I was going.

Only now I think to myself, Maybe Rosemary was right, even if her timing was wrong. What would I give to be taking her to France? All the years in between have simply returned me to Dover with no one to take her place. Twenty years and a hole in my shoulder. The rest of the class has probably done better.

Yevgeny orders me out of the car, and they drive off to join the desultory line of campers and minis and German sports cars going home.

I'm to join the foot passengers, while they get the car on board. They'll watch me, and I'll watch them, and if there's anything at all suspicious. . . .

"What?" I ask him. "What do we do then?"

"Then we deal with it," he says. "Don't approach us. Just watch." Inside the reception area, the people look terrible. They loll about half-eating, half-reading, eyes open, minds closed.

The air smells as though a herd of elephants had a lousy meal, so I go outside and begin to wish I hadn't. Because I stand in the cold for ten minutes getting the sense of a few cars that are skipping the queue, of passes being held up for the vaguest of inspections, a salute or two and the growing impression that officialdom is up and active much earlier than it should be.

But maybe Dover is like that. Maybe it's a shift change.

I try not to run. I try to take deep breaths and look normal. Through the reception area, stepping over piles of sleepers, out the other side. There are three rows of cars, and I'm scanning them all for the distinguishing marks.

Ours is beige. My first glance tells me everybody has a beige car. But this one, I recall, is fitted with two aerials, and that cuts down the search.

So I stand, trying to look casual outside the lavatories, hoping no one will take me for the standard pederast, importuning harmless teenagers.

I can see our car some fifty yards away—three from the back—second row along. Inside are the two talking heads, so maybe there's nothing to worry about. "Don't approach us," Yevgeny said. I should give them credit for knowing their business.

And it's then that I freeze. The background fades and goes silent, and I'm watching two men walking down the row of cars, hands in their pockets, gray anoraks, jeans, and white sneakers. I'm taking in the details, but nothing is coming out. And I know what is going to happen, but there is nothing I can do to stop it. Please God I seem chained to the ground with my mouth gagged and my heart hammering at me to move.

Even as I watch, the two figures stoop toward the beige car in macabre unison, pulling their hands from their pockets, and I know they have guns. I know they are firing and there are two Russian heads that are turning and jerking and I turn my own away, because I cannot get my mind to comprehend it.

When I see again, the two men are sprinting toward a car, and no one is watching them, no one is trying to stop them. It's dark and children are playing and there's music from a car radio and the seagulls have begun to squawk across the jetty as if in terrible pain. For the sake of Jesus Christ, am I the only person in the world to see what is happening?

The car isn't going fast. It's driving off, slowly, as if it's lost its way or changed its mind, or it's too early for the boat. And there are killers inside, in gray anoraks, who have just killed people I knew, no more than fifty yards from where I stand.

Why can't I do anything? I've lost them. The car drove casually behind a warehouse. God only knows. But I have to pray. I haven't prayed since I was a child. I don't know who's there to hear it. But I need to pray that I can move, that my legs will take me, that my heart and my breathing will slow down for just a minute. Please, God. Lord of all life. Hear this prayer. I beseech you, I beseech you, I beseech you. . . .

And I don't know whether I'm heard, I don't know what I'm seeing, but with no warning, there is the loudest and most shattering scream that I could ever imagine on this earth. It's coming from the beige car, from a woman kneeling on the ground beside it—a cry of horror that pierces the darkness and echoes out across the water.

Awful as it is, it releases me from this terrible immobility—my legs already in motion, my eyes searching every face and every car for the danger. I know that I've witnessed a massacre. I know, with the clearest of certainties, that I'm under imminent sentence of death.

Chapter Thirteen

Fear builds a world of its own. You can't live there—I can't live there. It's a world you must pass through, where the familiar becomes strange and grotesque, where friends transform themselves into strangers, where dying is done.

I can't think about Yevgeny. Not now. But he's left me with the legacy of his final seconds.

I'm running back to the reception center because all the people are still there and I won't go alone.

And yet they look different. They've woken up, they're watching. In a corner, an old lady crosses herself. There's a low whisper of shock that's building even as I enter, and now a few of the travelers are unsticking themselves from the plastic benches, making their way to the door. . . .

I'm not waiting here.

Through the other door and the cold hits me again. A corner of the sky is lighter; the rain has stopped. Quiet though. A train is crossing railway tracks in the distance. These are good signs. I'm forming cogent thoughts, stopped running, just walking with a purpose, back out toward the town.

You wouldn't notice such a figure, surely. Man in early thirties, tall as people go, black trench coat, head down, mind on fire, leaving a murder by the quayside.

I'm a prime candidate, suspect number one—I have to be—the first person I'd stop and pull in and beat the shit out of to get an answer to a straight question. Who shuffles away from a killing?

And yet I walk freely from the port. No sirens, no convoys of police or any of the rapid-response teams that are supposed to care about things like this.

Where are the officials I saw passing into the port? Why aren't they dragging the area?

A full-scale massacre has taken place right next to the car ferry that was to have shipped us all merrily to France and beyond. For God's bloody sake! Two citizens from the new state of Russia shot down as they argued in their beige car, waiting to board, afraid . . . afraid of everything, I recall. Afraid to go on, afraid to go back.

Suddenly I have this image of Yevgeny and his friend, who wouldn't tell me his name. The two of them in their twenties, confident first, then less so, then frightened that maybe they wouldn't get back to Russia after all—and now they would go in a box, with name tags and stamps and the kinds of confidential papers that always get filed away and lost.

Out in the Moscow suburbs perhaps, in a dilapidated block of flats, a couple of families would get a short call and a long warning, and they'd fetch the boxes and spend their life's savings giving the two fellows a more dignified departure. Tears and a priest and a meal they can't afford for the friends and relatives.

Only they'd never hear about Dover, about the journey in the beige car, about a phone call along the way, or a ferry that didn't, after all, take their young men to France.

I'm into the town now, and not enjoying these thoughts. I'm not enjoying the probability that whoever killed my guardians is hanging around cherishing unkind thoughts about me.

It'll be daylight soon; some of the early risers are on the move. I ask about a bus station, and I'm told it's not too far. Over there, says a postman, pointing into a brick wall. "You can't miss it."

Within half an hour, I'm on the first bus to London, which starts off cold and damp with a gaggle of passengers, not wanting to talk, and brightens up as the sun appears.

For a little while, I let the tiredness and the horror push me under, thinking that if they killed me in my sleep, it wouldn't count—since I'd never know.

Fear is a chain reaction. Give it one outing and, almost certainly, it will seek another, leading you by the parts that hurt. It's best not to start down that road if you can help it.

For me, though, the journey began a long time ago. And now I'm rounding the corner, a young boy again, and there's a day in March that I wish I had never witnessed.

Months had gone by since Dad had written. Normally he'd send a letter every three or four weeks. No address. No dateline. He could have been in any of eleven time zones, for all we knew. And yet I waited for those letters. I counted on them. They were the emotional cement that held so many features of my life together. They told me Dad still cared. They kept alive the hope that I would see him again.

Lately, Mother had let me read them myself. For not only could I understand the Russian, I could read between the lines, all the way to a man who had trapped himself in another world far away.

Once, he wrote that he was happy. Just a bald statement, no backup, no evidence. And I knew then how desperate he was feeling. Happiness had never been a concept in Dad's life. He couldn't have expressed it, couldn't have luxuriated in it. The Slavic background dictated passion, not contentment—a dark, bleak view of man against a hostile environment. There could be hatred and light and intensity. But happiness—the state of coasting sublimely, at peace with the world—that was not my dad.

It must have been around nine in the evening when the doorbell rang. I remember running to the top of the stairs; Mother called out, "Who is it?" A voice answered in Russian.

She opened the door, and I could see a short figure in a gray raincoat. He was bald and wet through from the rain and seemed to stand there excusing himself for being alive.

Mother let him in and called me.

"This is a representative of the Soviet embassy," she said. "Mr. Modin. He wants to talk to us. . . ."

"Perhaps it would be better for the boy . . ."

"You are in my house, Mr. Modin," she interrupted. "I will decide what is better."

We stood in the dim hall, and I remember thinking it would be good to get a brighter lightbulb. Mother wasn't going to ask him to stay, so Mr. Modin drew himself up to his five feet and pulled a piece of paper from his inside pocket.

"With great regret," he read, "by the authority of the ambassador of the Union of Soviet Socialist Republics, I have to tell you of the death yesterday morning of your husband in the village of Khimki in Moscow Oblast. . . ." And there were numbers and names and titles that meant nothing at all and seemed to have been added to make the announcement less abrupt, less sharp.

Dad had died of a heart attack, went the message, confirmed by Professor So-and-so in a clinic that no one has any reason to have heard of. Formal identification papers were on their way. Notice of burial—unfortunately in an area closed to foreigners—would follow. If there was anything he, Modin, or the embassy could do . . . ?

I kept looking at the rain on the top of his head and hearing his voice but no longer taking it in. Maybe he was in the wrong house; maybe it was someone else's father.

I felt the kind of numbness in the face and around the mouth that only rapid intakes of alcohol have since reproduced. We stood looking at each other, blankly and with nothing to say, until Modin took off his glasses and rubbed his eyes.

"I am so sorry . . ." he began, and I wanted suddenly to grab him by the shoulders and say, "Don't be sorry. It's all a mistake. Dad's fine. We can celebrate after all. . . ."

He was looking at Mother. "Have you no questions, Mrs. . . . ?"

"I have many questions. . . ." And her voice seemed to crack in her throat. "But I do not think you will be able to answer them."

Modin must have found his own way out, although I don't recall him leaving. And thankfully, perhaps, I don't recall what Mother and I did or said to each other.

But I remember the rain, tapping endlessly on the roof, and the wind tearing through the garden, and a night devoid of all dreams.

* * *

I know without opening my eyes that we're in London. The traffic has set solid around the bus. And I am left here to recall a murder I did nothing to prevent. There are two voices in my head. One is mine—but the other I don't recognize.

"You were too scared to move. . . ."

"I tried to move, tried to shout, but nothing happened. . . ."

"Don't give me that. You just stood there and let it happen. The men who were trying to save you—and you just watched as their heads were blown off. . . ."

"It's part of an operation . . . I don't know anything about it. I don't know which side anyone is on. . . ."

"Think!"

"There were two killers. The men in sneakers and anoraks. Leisurely . . ."

"Why?"

"Because it was planned and premeditated. Someone knew exactly where we would be and at what time. They were tracking us, waiting for us. The scene on the quay. I remember now. There were no police anywhere in sight. No Customs officials. No crew. Now that I think about it, they were there one minute, and then they'd disappeared. The site was cleared intentionally. They all knew a murder was going to happen. For God's sake, they're all involved. Everybody. . . ."

"That's better. You're thinking at last. Now sort it. Get off your arse and start putting the pieces together. Otherwise, you'll be next."

I have no idea where this other voice is coming from.

I know only that I have to get myself out of the country and into Russia. All the other doors are closing.

CHAPTER FOURTEEN

THE WAY IN was Harry. No doubt about that. Harry Willets and his little troupe of whining, scheming businessmen, having lunch around Eastern Europe.

This was the trip I had organized before life turned round and bit me. The trip I should even now be attending.

Ironically, Harry's business was security—I mean in the small sense. Personal alarms, infrared detectors, surveillance cameras—all the gismos and gewgaws that mark you out as a perfect target for crime.

According to word on the street, the firm was doing quite well. But Harry couldn't leave it there.

One Sunday, about three months earlier, he had read an article about rising crime in Eastern Europe—and decided the people of that afflicted region needed him.

He also decided he needed me.

Harry rang me the following Monday with his simple theory. "All those years of being buggered about by the Communists, now they're buggering each other. Blackmail, robbery, murder—it's as if they've just discovered the joy of it all. But what about the ordinary people? That's what I want to know." His voice dropped as if to indicate a social conscience. "They're all terrified they're going to get biffed on the head the moment they buy a new pair of gloves. They need help. Self-defense, security systems. Deadlocks on the doors. Edward, they need us. And you're going to set it up."

Oh, Harry, Harry, Harry. It was just what I needed. He was what I needed. Harry in his white shirt and power red tie, to match his cheeks. Harry with a much better and wider view of the river than mine. Harry with complex upon complex piled inside his balding head.

Only much later did I discover what lay behind them.

In his day, Harry had been something of a con man. Nothing national. He'd worked the local businesses, offering that most sacred of gifts—protection. Of course there'd been some tears and some violence, and Harry had been unwise enough to offer his services to an undercover agent, working for the serious crime squad.

Harry went down, but they couldn't keep him there. For he never lost sight of the mountain, and never stopped wanting to climb it. He knew instinctively which way was up. He was going to make it.

As I stood like a wet plant in the traffic around Victoria Station, it seemed simple enough. Harry would be my cover. By now he'd have arrived in Berlin, then on to Warsaw and finally Moscow. It was the route I'd set up just a week ago. I'd fixed their appointments and their hotels, their restaurants, their massages, their evening concerts. Just like a school tour. All they had to do was show up.

I crossed the road to the British Airways office and booked a ticket to Berlin, bought two changes of clothes, some bandages, dressings—everything a man with a shoulder wound might need when he goes abroad. It was traveling light, the way the guide books tell you. Have a wonderful trip, said the ticket lady. Good-bye, good-bye, take care.

Don't get killed.

And yet I must tell you it's good to go light. There's a certain freedom in having no friends or ties, no one to trust and therefore no trust to break, no feelings to heed, no worries of hurting anyone, except yourself.

I sat on a bench beside a little green triangle and thought about Jane Card. For someone who led what she called a normal life, things were going badly wrong. She gets two

Russians to call her from a phone box, but the line is dead. Three hours later, so are they. And I'm on my own.

A few pigeons stared at me expectantly. And I couldn't help wondering who else was doing the same thing.

I was being used to find my mother—and when I'd done that, someone would attempt to kill us.

So it was a safe journey to Berlin. We landed in something very close to darkness, with the sun left firmly back in the West and low clouds obscuring the stars.

I decided to leave Harry till dinnertime, so I rented a car and drove around the city looking up old landmarks. At the former frontier crossings, it seemed hard to grasp the idea of reunification. No unfed Alsatians eyeing you over the fences, no fat-pig border guards letting the rain trickle down your passport, no long stares of suspicion as you knock on that shabby Eastern door. In its way, Berlin was just as strange without a wall as it was with it.

After an hour or two, I was looking forward to seeing Harry. There was something infinitely reassuring about his duplicity. The yellow-toothed smile, the laughter, the backslapping—but in there, somewhere, was always Harry on the make. Eyes that didn't quite look at you, a hand that didn't quite grip hard enough, promises you couldn't quite believe.

And yet after the events of the last forty-eight hours, Harry was Mr. Fair Play himself.

I found him and his two colleagues where I'd told them to eat—the Café Paris on the Ku-Damm. He seemed unsurprised to see me.

"Found your mum, eh? How's it all going? Glad you made it."

I said my greetings and sat at the table, and in the general commotion I didn't need to answer Harry's questions.

His two sidekicks were with him. Costa, once from Cyprus, now "dark and horrible" as Harry used to describe him, and smiling little Arthur—once a pickpocket and therefore the perfect man to advise on security. He made a big show of pouring me a glass of champagne—"Not that there's anything to celebrate," said Costa.

And yet this odd gathering was a breath of normality. No one in the restaurant was being attacked, nobody skulked behind the hat stand. I was in Berlin on a business trip. Everyone believed that.

"Look, old son," said Harry, and I could see from his reddened face that this wasn't his first bottle of champagne. "Before the evening runs away with us, shall we just put down a few markers?"

I nodded. Elbows on table. Look of wide-eyed attention. The please-the-client pose.

"We were over in the East this morning. Quite a good little run, though I must say some of the people you fixed us up with are a bit odd. Not many laughs. Not much conversation about anything, really. I tried saying how nice and free it all was. One fellow just looked at me like an armadillo without the charm. Who are they all?"

"Ex-security." What did Harry expect?

"I see. Is that wise?"

"Yes, Harry, it is wise. And you know why? Because the people who had power before are going to be the ones who have it now. Okay? They just wear different suits."

He looked bewildered. It was time to remind him of the rules. "Look, Harry. Berlin is freer than it used to be, okay? But it's got a lot of memories, and it's not too happy about one or two of them. You know what I mean? They don't sit easily with the current realities."

"I think I understand that, Edward."

"I do hope so, Harry. Because, as I said before, you don't come barging in here asking people for their life histories, as if it's some kind of polite conversation and part of your sales pitch. They don't take kindly to that. Most of them don't want to think about the past, and those that can't help it are not in a generous frame of mind and might just cut up nasty. I thought I made this clear in London."

I looked at them all in turn. At this rate, I stood a very good chance of ruining their evening. But I've made a study of this kind of thing. Lots of businessmen like rough talking, on the grounds that if it isn't hurting, it isn't doing any good. Also, they get to understand that if I'm hard on them, I can be even harder on their opposition. A little exercise in stick-waving, that's all. Shows you mean business.

Harry was beginning to smile. One further kick in the arse would do it. "So next time you're pushing the product, don't ask questions, don't remind them who they were. Just tell them how bloody good you are, state your terms, and fuck off. Got it?"

"Point taken, Edward, and thanks for the reminder." Harry patted me on the back. "Give him a refill, Costa."

Costa made a face.

"Thought you ought to know," Harry went on, "that we seem to be close to clinching something quite reasonable here. That new firm you found us is starting up a home-security network—they want to link a whole bunch of flats to a central control. Panic buttons, burglar alarms, that kind of thing. They all know how it's done." Harry reached for the bottle and filled his own glass. "Thing is, we weren't really getting very far until this afternoon."

I sat back and had the distinct feeling I would remember this conversation.

A waitress arrived with steak for Harry and the boys, and I told her I'd have the same. And then I asked him why things had improved.

"They'd been a bit upset you weren't with us. After all, you told them you'd be there. You were the one who set it up. . . ."

"I know that, Harry. . . ."

"Well, when your mum rang us to say you were on the way, we told them the good news, and they brightened up like nothing on earth and said they were sure we could do business."

And now I knew why I'd remember it. I could already feel the sickness climbing inside my throat.

"My mother rang you?"

"Of course she did, Edward. Said there'd been a mix-up, but everything was fine now. And you'd meet us at the hotel."

I looked hard at the three of them to see if it was a joke. But I knew it wasn't. After that Harry ordered another bottle. Said it was all a good sign, whatever "all" meant. Said we'd get a great deal. Said we'd go out afterward and have some fun. "Some of the dirty stuff," and Costa and Arthur leered and nudged each other a couple of times.

And I felt as if the sky itself were pushing down on me, forcing me into my grave before I was ready to go.

* * *

I don't know how I got through that evening. We did three clubs. There were shows that showed and shows that didn't. Girls who wanted champagne to sit with you in the smoke and darkness.

But what I really needed was somewhere to sit and make sense of it all.

I didn't need a dusky hand down my crotch, or a few pert bosoms in my face, although God knows there've been times . . .

Around two in the morning—we had finished up at a place called the Thai-Sauna-Erotik, inaccurate on all three counts—I announced that we ought to be leaving. They'd all lost something in addition to their dignity—a sock, a tie, Harry had his shirttail caught in his zip—it was hardly the finest hour for British business, as we flagged a taxi and returned to the hotel.

I lay on the bed fully clothed, as if making a private protest at the evening's activities. What was it Harry had heard? A message from Mother? A sign she was still in charge? That seemed hard to believe.

And if it were someone else, then my every step had been followed, and Berlin was fast becoming another cage.

Chapter Fifteen

I know what it's like, feeling trapped.

When I was fifteen, Mother sent me to Paris to practice my Russian. That's not as odd as it sounds. The city was home to many thousands of people from the White Russian diaspora, refugees from the Revolution—whole families who'd escaped with their bodies but had left their property and their lives behind.

They often became taxi drivers, just as they do these days in New York. Men and women from Odessa and Omsk would drive to Montparnasse and Saint-Michel and drop you at Maxim's or the Louvre, and after a while think nothing of it.

The trip itself came out of an unexpected postcard from one of Mother's old Russian friends—Sasha Levitch, once an actor on the Leningrad stage. It transpired he had been living in France for nearly twenty years before summoning the energy to write.

"I have been so busy," he said. "But now things are quieter."

In fact they were quieter because he hadn't had any work for the last six years. But, in any case, he and Mother seemed to get on well enough.

They talked for hours by telephone and eventually decided I'd go over in my summer holiday to speak Russian—and nothing else.

"Why don't I go to Moscow, instead?" I suggested.

"You're not going there," Mother replied. "So it'll have to be Paris. It'll be good for you. They have their own community, they marry a lot, die a lot—always something going on. Sasha has a family—it will be wonderful fun."

I was British enough to have serious doubts on that score. It was a year since the news of Dad's death, and the memory remained a dull, intermittent ache.

And yet I found myself increasingly interested in his background, the city of Moscow where he'd lived, the events he'd witnessed, the personalities that might have shaped his life.

Books helped, but I needed to talk to people who'd grown up there. Perhaps there was somebody who'd lived in the neighborhood, attended Dad's school, even played football with him. Perhaps such a person could be found.

I didn't tell Mother. If I had, she might not have sanctioned the trip. She often said she didn't believe in the past. You couldn't fight the past, she insisted. The past was not a battle you could win.

And yet she knew its dangers.

She took me to the airport on a fine August day, wishing me safe travel and a safe return. But I remember her holding me longer than was usual.

"Be careful, Edward."

"Of what?"

"Just be careful. If I knew why, I wouldn't say so." She looked around. "You will be meeting plenty of Russians. . . ."

"That's the idea. . . ."

"Don't be rude and listen to me, otherwise maybe I stop you going."

We sat in the airport café—she ordering coffee, and I considering the seriousness of the threat.

"Listen, Edward. I don't know what kind of people Sasha has for friends. Maybe there are those who will claim to know you, or me, or your father. You should tell them nothing."

"Why?"

"Because they can't be trusted. No one can. Look at

you"—she pointed a finger—"I can't even trust you to do as I ask."

She put a hand on my arm. "Some people play games, political games. Maybe we still have enemies in Russia—how do I know? These are crazy times; in Russia they have always been crazy times. Someone might use you, to try to make trouble for me. One can never be careful enough. Okay? Okay!" She got up. "You go away now; here's your ticket. Call me tonight and tell me you've arrived." She laughed. "After that, I don't want to hear from you."

I remember raising my eyebrows and thinking no more about Mother's unspecified "trouble." It wasn't the first time she had given vent to her rich imagination. What I didn't know then was how far it had been fed on facts.

Paris did nothing for my Russian.

Sasha's "family" couldn't speak the language at all. His wife was in fact his mistress—and French. The son, in his early twenties, stayed in bed most of the day and refused to talk to me. They lived in a large, dusty apartment beside Emile Zola métro station. And I disliked them more or less on sight.

Sasha and his blond lady, Eloise, fought each other from the time they got out of bed—which was late—to the time they returned to bed, also late. It proved to me that hatred was just as much a basis for lasting relationships as anything else. They argued about politics, about wine, about whether and where to go out. At any hour of the day or night, the damp, cool atmosphere was full of complaints and recriminations, of slamming doors, of people speaking and not speaking, of awkward and petty silences.

I wouldn't have minded so much, but they swore in French, and when they made up, it was also in French, ever searching, said Sasha, for *"le mot juste,"* which didn't exist in that "boorish, peasant tongue" I was pleased to call Russian.

Occasionally he could be led by the back door into the language—a reference to that "dear" Aleksandr Pushkin would help, so would the street names of Moscow and Petersburg. If lucky, we would get a half hour of flowery Russian, spattered with French adjectives—but mostly the effort was fruitless.

He was a pompous creature—unaccountably proud of the deep, booming voice that had so conspicuously failed to get him work on the Paris stage. Instead, he sang Russian songs in a bar near St.-Germain—and from that, I assume, he paid his bills.

I visited him there one night and found his reddened, bearded face, dead to the world in a backroom, and an empty bottle of wine, lying beside him like a suicide note—which, in the end, I suspect it became.

So with no help from Sasha or his "family," I took to wandering the local streets for diversion, and was befriended by the most unlikely of characters. Each day I would pass along the embankment toward Notre Dame and the Latin Quarter—and most times I would see the same face in a café.

It belonged to a young man, dark-skinned, short, with an enormous stomach that seemed to rest on the chair beside him. He had a quick smile, wide-open eyes, and a pile of books and papers on his table. He was also, I noticed, a priest.

So when he waved for the fifth morning in succession and gestured to me to join him, I did so without hesitation. He offered Coke, and we labored briefly over the weather and Paris, and the where-do-you-come-from routine—and discovered that we both got on better in English.

"I'm from Italy," he said. "Angelino. My church three streets from here. Nice to meet you."

We ate lunch after that. He had a bowl of spaghetti, and I ordered a cheese sandwich. I'm not sure why, but it was a relief when he didn't offer to pay. Perhaps it was his way of saying, "You're an equal."

We met for several days after that—always at lunch. Sometimes we simply walked or sat on a park bench. He told me about his childhood and the reasons for becoming a priest. "Not easy," he kept repeating. "Not easy." And I wondered if he meant then or now.

Of course I told him about Dad's death and Mum's background. But he offered little comment or insight.

Mostly we talked about the future. Angelino said the church would have to play a greater role in politics. Its influence was waning. All he did, these days, was funerals. "We are like doctor, who gets to see patient after he died," he told me. "We need to say things about his life—while there is still time."

I suppose he had a point, but it seemed pretty irrelevant to me, and to be honest, after a week of metaphysical wanderings, I was thinking of bypassing Angelino—taking a different route at lunchtime, finding a different companion.

Maybe he sensed it—for as we walked that day through the Latin Quarter, the conversation took a different route.

"Listen, Edward, something new come up in my parish. We have lot of foreigners arriving—they don't know anyone, never been in Paris before—that kind of thing. A couple from Russia just visiting—maybe you'd like to meet them. We having little party at the church tomorrow afternoon—you want to come?"

But it wasn't the church.

"Sorry, Edward, they doing some painting there. Better we go to my place."

I remember standing on the church steps, wondering if this were a clever idea. And yet Angelino was a priest, and a friend (more or less)—and this was Paris on a bright summer day—so what was the problem?

Looking back, it seems odd that the couple were already in the flat—just two rooms that faced onto a courtyard, narrow and tall as French apartments often are. The man was in his forties, the woman slightly older, both dressed in winter shoes and sad gray pullovers. Their faces seemed strangely unmarked. No laughter lines—as Mother used to say. It wasn't hard to believe they came from Russia.

I sipped orange juice, and they had wine, and we all looked at Angelino to start the conversation.

"Edward, these people have come from a village outside Moscow. Apparently it is a secret place with some scientific installations. I do not understand such things, but they will tell you themselves. . . ."

"Why do they want to tell me?"

But Angelino put a finger to his lips, and the man began to speak.

He had the look of what I have since come to recognize as the party functionary—anxious little movements, busy eyes, bags of disingenuous enthusiasm; and when he opens his mouth—the well-worn meaningless phrases of introduction, the winding, circular discourse, the inability to get to a point, and the ability to disguise it once he has. Such was the figure that sat before me.

"Viktor," he said, and I leaned over and shook his hand.

He told me a lot about his life. Yes, he had been in the party; yes, he had believed. Yes, he still did.

But the party wasn't just a prison camp, and he wasn't a guard, and the time would surely come when the gates would open and Russians would welcome the West with kisses on all their cheeks. Surely.

I listened, but I think I'd already decided Viktor was no use to me. Maybe good man, maybe bad man—maybe just a bore. I resolved to give it another five minutes and leave.

Viktor was midway through a treatise on the local collective farm, when Angelino interrupted him.

"Viktor"—and he raised both his hands like a Stop sign. "Viktor, just tell the boy—there is no need to give history of whole country."

I remember the Russian placing his hands on his knees, turning a mental page. There was a moment of silence, as if we were setting out on a long journey, saying our prayers. And maybe we should have been. Outside, I could hear a woman calling out a name—again and again, but there was no reply.

When it came, it was Viktor's wife who spoke.

"He will find it difficult to do this"—she pointed at him—"so I will say what must be said. Forgive us please for any trouble, but this will not take long." Her face was red from embarrassment. She wasn't used to this. "Six years ago, we worked at the Khimki Institute near Moscow. It was secret work—satellite pictures, reconnaissance. . . ." She looked toward Viktor for reassurance. "Anyway, we met a man there—brilliant mathematician, liked by everyone. Big man, but dark, lonely man—always tortured by fears. He and I would talk for hours. 'Lena,' he would say, 'Lena, at night I close my eyes with anxiety and utter unconfidence. Deep inside I anticipate that through pain I will find strength—but sometimes the pain is too great.' " She paused. "This is how he would talk to me. Sometimes we would sit in the woods and the tears would descend his face and I would hold his big head in my hands until it passed."

She stopped and looked around at each of us in turn. "That man, Edward, was your father. He is still alive."

I fought for air and couldn't find it. I simply remember rushing, stumbling, hurling myself at the door, half falling down the stairs—out into the street, hitting people and running faster than I had ever run in my life. Maybe three miles, maybe four or five, through a market, down side streets, main streets, my heart like an engine out of control. And when I stopped, it was with the terrible fear that something unknown and dangerous was reaching out to me. Not my father, but something I had never encountered—a power, a force that had to be resisted.

I found a phone box and filled it with all the coins in my pocket, and when I spoke to Mother the instructions were clear and precise.

"You know the Arc de Triomphe?"

"Yes."

"Go there now. Mingle with the tourists, stay there, and don't move whatever should happen. Wait for me. I will be there tonight. Do you understand? Don't leave that point, whatever happens."

Yes, yes, yes.

She must have caught the last plane to Paris. Four hours later, with the city lights now on, I saw her crossing the jungle of traffic in a white summer blouse, looking cool and in control.

Somehow, I don't think any of this surprised her. We checked into a hotel close by and sat in her room, as I told her the story.

In the end, she put out a hand to me, but I didn't take it.

"Is is true, any of this?" I asked.

"Of course not. Don't even think so for a second. Someone has been cruel and devious. . . ."

"Why would anyone say this if it wasn't true?"

"I don't know. As a way to get to me. Sometimes the KGB checks up on people years later. You're still on their books—they shake you. I don't know, Edward. Russia is full of don't knows—little straws that mean things and little straws that don't. But you leave them alone, you understand, you walk away from them. When they invade your mind and manipulate you, you switch off. . . ."

"I can't do that."

"You have to."

She got up and went over to the basin, turning on the water, splashing it on her face. "Bloody hot," she whispered, "bloody hot."

I watched her back. "Supposing Dad is alive?"

"He isn't. We had the certificate, the identification. . . ."

"They could have been lying. They lied about everything else."

"Not about this. I made my own inquiries. It is one hundred percent. Believe me, Edward. Would I not follow this, if there were any chance of it being true?"

"I don't know. I can't put it all together. I don't understand. . . ."

Many months went by before I allowed myself to shelve the subject. Often my mind would return to worry it, of its own accord. And yet that night Mother and I stayed away from the questions, she armed with her certainties, and I beset by doubts. We could take it no further.

The next day we went back to London. Mother didn't say much about anything. But two days later she informed me she had changed our telephone number, and a month afterward the house was on the market.

By the end of October we moved to Stanley Road. Mother sent no change-of-address cards and placed no adverts. She never spoke again to Sasha. To him and to many of those who knew us, we simply disappeared.

Chapter Sixteen

I WOKE AT FIVE. Berlin was already moving around me. Across the street, people were trickling out of the old buildings, the light of the night turning to dawn.

And now there was a feeling of purpose and direction. I picked up the phone, dialed Harry's client in the East, and told him we were coming round.

In Britain, they'd curse you to hell and back for ringing so early. Here in Germany, it was a sign you were serious. Not only did you get up earlier than your competitors, you didn't even appear to go to bed. You were therefore a disciple of the Great God Work—and for that alone deserved cringing respect.

"Yes, of course, Herr Bell," came the response. The man coughed himself awake. "A pleasure to see you. I will cook coffee."

I love the way the Germans translate their language. While he was cooking, I hurried round the trio, telling them plans had changed. Pack and leave. East Berlin, then Warsaw. Got to go.

When it came down to it, I didn't mind lying at all.

Harry stood in the doorway, in shirt and underpants. With hair all over his face, and a drooping jaw, he was ample proof of man's close connections to the monkey.

"You look nice," I told him.

"Fuck off, Edward. You go. That's what I pay you for." Harry could be really unpleasant when he wanted to be—a throwback, no doubt to his bad old days. "What's this about Warsaw? We're not due there till Thursday."

"New plans, Harry. That's the great thing about business. Clients suddenly make decisions. . . ."

"At five in the morning?"

"Even that. Your Herr Barsch rang me half an hour ago. He has to go away today. He wants to do business before he leaves. If we have to go East, we might as well flog on to Warsaw. We're only forty miles from the Polish border."

"Oh Christ!"

I loaded them into the rental car. The hotel had come up with coffee and rolls. Beside me on the passenger seat, I could make out Harry, trying to spread jam on a crossaint with a plastic knife.

"Bugger," he said, and I assumed he'd spread his tie as we headed East across the city into the suburbs.

When you looked around, it seemed odd that West Germany had wanted to reunify with this lot . . . rutted roads, houses peeling plaster, street lamps like tiny candles in the gloom.

To me it had always been the worst of the East bloc cities—aggressively separate from its Western counterhalf—like a poor, spiky scarecrow, armed with a big mouth and a big gun. A tough city. Easy to die in if you didn't know what you were doing.

Someone, though, knew what I was doing, and for the moment I couldn't shake them. In Poland it would be different. I'd dig in and leave Harry and the others to zip up their own pants. For now they were useful protection. Later they'd slow me down.

When I look back, I had no doubt I could lose myself in the East. They had the networks, the escape routes. They belonged to the dark continent where you could disappear and never come out. That was the real legacy of oppression. People closed their eyes and mouths and took their secrets with them to heaven or hell. Because lives depended on it, and too many had been lost already.

* * *

Mother's words.

I could hear her saying them, as we drove that morning, silent and ill-tempered. She had been sitting in the kitchen in Stanley Road, cutting stems from her roses. She laughed hollowly. "They talk about openness. You don't just open people up like shops. These people are coffins. Closed and closed for good. And once a coffin is shut, you shouldn't try opening it again. Uh?"

I had looked at her blankly.

"The underground struggle goes on, my son. It's a tradition. It's the only defense against authority. Russians will never trust their leaders—not after all the things they've done to them. Never."

She had stood up and put the flowers in water. "There's no kinder, gentler Russia. When they are tender, it is like tigers cuddling in their sleep, dreaming of another world. That's why I'm here," she told me. "That's why I'm here."

Funny the snatches of conversation you bury with the years, or cover over. And yet, something had been stored—something I could use.

Herr Barsch was waiting on the street, a Doberman chained by his side, sniffing the morning air. Both had close-cropped hair and looked lean and fit. It was safe to assume they were friends.

"Blimey, he's keen," said Harry.

We got out and shook hands. Barsch took us inside. He had indeed cooked coffee. It was thick and sweet and helped kick-start the mind. As the boys went through their pitch, I glanced around the living room. Barsch had been a policeman in his East bloc incarnation—local militia, nothing especially sinister—probably bashed up a few dissidents in the demonstrations, standard stuff. On the sideboard stood a row of merit badges, a shooting trophy, a swimming medal. Obviously he'd put himself about, joined in. I had a sudden urge to sit him down and ask what it was like to live in that smug, sanctimonious little regime, to be a hired thug for the party faithful. But it wouldn't have endeared me to Harry.

I'd got to know Barsch about three months earlier. He had written to me after I'd advertised in a Berlin paper, looking for joint ventures. Nearly all the replies had come from ex-Stasi men. Not that they were down on their luck. They simply got employed by the new lot doing much the same thing . . . or went freelance. And then God only knew whom they were working for. It didn't do to look too deeply into the pool. The waters were muddy, and there were plenty of unpleasant creatures below the surface. Like Barsch.

By this time, Harry and the others were enjoying themselves. He was explaining the merits of bugging your own office—which meant he and Barsch had found a common language.

I got up. "Mind if I look around?"

"You are my guest, Herr Bell." His teeth made a brief appearance.

Outside, I could see just how well he'd done. The cottage was a small farmhouse on the edge of a village. Two stories with window boxes and shutters. Fields rolled away behind it over flattish country. On the horizon, I could make out wedges of forest reaching out toward the sunrise.

Beyond the back door—a greenhouse, an orchard—well kept, trim, and orderly. Well done, Comrade, I thought. But what about your sins? Don't you leave litter? Is there not even a speck of dirt on that new Volkswagen, parked in the lane? Whom have you been stroking, my friend—and who has been stroking you?

Of course he could have simply fallen on his flat militia feet; could have possessed a natural talent for business, submerged all these years under Marxist claptrap. He could have got lucky, had a flutter, backed a few good horses.

In fact, I was prepared to believe all that—Barsch the innocent, new German man. East made good, made West. Hip-hip-hooray for one more Commie stooge, come in out of the cold.

But somehow he didn't fit the image. As I turned toward the house, he emerged looking altogether too professional, sliding on the balls of his feet, leading the boys in front of him, clutching one of those highly effective East bloc pistols.

I have to say I was disappointed first and scared second. A few days ago I hadn't lived in a world where guns were waved around like sparklers. Now it seemed I was consorting with people who did little else. It's odd how quickly you adapt.

"What the bloody hell's going on?" asked Harry, as much to me as to Barsch.

"A little delay, gentlemen." Barsch was herding us closer together. "A few friends, wishing to have a chat—nothing more. You will please come back to the house. Perhaps I can offer you more coffee."

I didn't think it was good to go back inside, and by the look of him nor did Harry. He seemed to be gesturing with his eyes to Costa and Arthur, and then he walked to within a few inches of Barsch, poking a finger at him.

"Listen, you. I don't expect this sort of thing. And frankly we'd just as soon be on our way out of here. If it's business you're interested in, that's one thing, but . . ."

As he spoke, I could see him moving in front of Costa, obscuring Barsch's vision. Barsch shifted position, and then several things happened at once. Costa suddenly broke into a run, deflecting the German's attention, and as he did so Harry's fist arced outward, with a lot of anger and experience behind it.

As it caught him, Barsch must have dropped the gun, for in a single movement, Harry scooped it off the ground and whipped the German hard across the face.

"The dog, Harry, the dog, watch it," Arthur was yelling as Harry turned around to confront the Doberman in full flight toward him.

And say what you like about Harry, and I've said plenty, he swiveled coolly from the hips and shot the animal in the head from a distance of about two feet. It dropped to the ground, twitched for a few seconds, and died. I think we were all mesmerized by the sight. For the dog seemed to open its jaws and visibly release its life. Not a smooth exit—but a tangible journey between the living and the dead. And I'm not sentimental about animals—no more than other Englishmen, but somehow the dog seemed to matter considerably more than Barsch. I think it shocked us all in the same way.

"Bloody hell," said Harry, and removed the ammunition clip from the butt of the pistol. "Bloody, bloody hell."

I walked over to where Barsch was crawling on all fours and kicked him hard in the head. He groaned and passed out. I wanted him unconscious—at least for a while. As much for reasons of sheer hatred as anything else. Besides, there didn't seem much point in trying to get him to talk—it would take too long, and most likely he would say nothing of interest.

"I think we'll get out of here, lads," I told them.

"What about him?" said Harry, pointing toward the inert German. "I think we should finish it."

"What . . . kill him?" My voice had risen an involuntary octave.

"Something like that," said Harry. "I don't think he would have been too worried about shooting you."

"Harry's right," said Costa.

Harry may have been right. But I wasn't in the mood to induce another dead body.

"Your funeral," said Harry, and shook his head. The three of them collected their things from inside and stowed them in the car.

"Nice places you bring us to," said Arthur, as we took a last look around. Barsch was lying face downward in the mud.

"Another satisfied client," murmured Costa.

I turned the ignition and moved the car into the lane. By my reckoning there were twenty-five miles to the frontier at Frankfurt an der Oder. We'd get on to the old Transit route, skirting Fulda, and join the traffic to the East. The sooner we hit the main road, the safer I'd feel.

"You did a nice job back there," I told Harry.

"Yeah." He leaned back in his seat. "Sometime you'll have to tell me what it was all about. Anyway, we haven't had so much fun"—he glanced behind him and grinned at the boys—"since last night."

I watched the road and didn't feel much like laughing. As far as I was concerned, Barsch was only the first account settled.

Chapter Seventeen

Look at it any way you like, but there's always been violence on the road to Russia. All through the ages, people killed in their thousands to get there—and then had to kill again to stay alive. In fact, the disposal of vast quantities of human beings is just about the only dynamic the country has ever known.

So Barsch was lucky we hadn't disposed of him.

But whom was he working for? There wasn't any shortage of interested parties. Russians, Americans, British—they all wanted a chat with Mother, and therefore a chat with me too. It wouldn't have been clever to hang around for them.

I pulled into the side of the road and turned the car in the opposite direction. I think it was the sudden memory of Yevgeny that made me head back toward Berlin. Just two days ago, on the road to Dover, we'd kept on driving, and he had died. We didn't have to go to the ferry terminal. We could have taken dozens of different routes. And he and his partner would be alive today. Doubts should be read as warnings, and I was hearing them from all directions.

Barsch himself was a warning and had to be heeded. I wasn't at all sure we'd get another.

"Change of plan?" asked Harry lazily as we came to a

sign for Berlin. "I'm not complaining," he added, "just asking."

"Bit like the old days, this rough stuff," said Costa enthusiastically from the backseat, and Harry turned around and shot him a dirty look.

"We're catching a train," I told them. "Time to go missing."

When Mother and I disappeared all those years ago, we took no more than a few tiny steps across the city of London. The scenery changed. The accents changed—so did the prejudices and eccentricities. But the neighborhoods all had one thing in common. They were separate little Londons, isolated from each other, noncommunicative, fiercely private. Tailor-made for disappearing.

And the great thing about Britain is that disappearing is perfectly understood and rarely, if ever, questioned. You have only to go to a bank manager, or doctor, or the landlord of your flat, armed with a little gift to be told, "I quite understand. Of course, we all need to get away from time to time. Wish I were coming with you. Naturally I won't say a thing to anyone. Absolutely. See you in about ten years then. Jolly good."

We got the new house from a lady who'd done a bunk so successfully that she'd been gone a year before anyone noticed. A thin old crab in a worn cardigan, said the estate agent, colonial type, who'd hidden her "fifty-thou" under the bed and gone back to Africa to reinvent childhood.

"Not my cup of tea," I remember him saying. And I kept wondering why not. What did he prefer to do—go down the pub, sink a handful, then stagger home blotto? No, who the hell would want to go to Africa when a good pub was beckoning instead?

Soon after the move, I went to a new school, and for the first time I could remember, Mother used her maiden name, and no one seemed to question it. We had moved to the north of the city where they were used to foreigners—Greeks, Israelis, and the incessantly argumentative East Europeans, who, it has to be said, imagine that London was built solely, but unsuccessfully, for their convenience. At any rate, it was getting fashionable to speak with an accent.

Of course, we didn't manage to escape from Coffin. He always seemed to know where Mother was, even long after their affair had finished, and he'd gone to fish in other waters.

When I think back, I have covered over so many incidents in which he featured. As a child, you accept so easily, and as an adult you forget with equal facility. But I'm finding the memories returning to me, and I don't like them.

I see the house in Stanley Road, on a summer evening, closing early, the darkness hovering nearby. I'm supposed to have gone to bed by now, because Mother has invited guests.

"Can I come downstairs?"

"Not this time."

"Why not?"

"Not, how shall I say, very nice people." Mother was full of "how shall I says," especially when she knew perfectly well how to say them.

"Why invite these bods?"

"Sometimes it's necessary. Please do as I say."

About ten o'clock two cars drew up outside the house. I'd been watching for them from my bedroom window. I always did. Why? Because Mother wasn't like any other mother. She didn't have a routine—she didn't enjoy any of the regularities of life. She used to read me stories, and I'd wonder more about her than them. I never knew if she was the damsel in distress or the wicked witch.

The cars were black. Coffin got out and looked up and down the street. More doors opened, men and faces appeared, and there was one in particular—a fellow who didn't fit. His clothes were borrowed or stolen—they were far too big. He looked at the ground, and they flanked him, the way sheepdogs herd in a farm animal that's gone astray.

I thought to myself, If they untied him, he might run away down the street.

Yes, that's what I saw. His hands tied behind his back, only I couldn't make out if it were handcuffs or rope, for the little group was already through the garden gate and up the tiny path and the voices in the hall were muffled and whispered and then switched off altogether as the downstairs doors were shut.

But where I watched, I also listened.

An hour went by, maybe two, and I could have gone to sleep. I was tired enough. The evening had become progressively less entertaining. Someone had gone to the lavatory; someone had shouted. The kettle whistled on the gas stove. My mother began to lecture. These were the moves, this was the game.

I was about to switch off my light when I heard the voice. It was deep and Russian, cutting through the flimsy walls of our thirties house. There were tears between the words. I could hear those, too—the rhythm of a monologue, rising and falling, telling a tale of suffering or fear. Even though the words were muffled, the message was clear.

And I think of this man, brought into my home, tethered, I assume in the kitchen, weeping his story for my mother and all the rest. I knew nothing of his life, but he left in the house the traces of his pain. For days afterward, they still clung to the walls.

Much later that evening, the voice quieted and finally ceased altogether.

By now I was crouching on the carpet beside the bedroom door, and I heard them moving in the hall. This time, no one was talking. There were no good-byes.

I could barely see them from the window, because it was dark and they were dark and moving, if anything, more rapidly than before. Doors slammed, headlights ranged across the street, and in a moment the cars had gone. It was then that a voice behind me asked in Russian, "Have you seen enough?"

Mother came into the room and almost lifted me onto the bed. She held me, not in a childish way, just an arm around my shoulder, almost in friendship, woman to man, and we sat there for a while, drawing our own thoughts together from the day that had passed.

Eventually she said good night and went to the door.

"You heard nothing," she whispered.

"I heard nothing," I replied.

In the quiet backwater of Stanley Road, we transplanted and grew like two seeds on wild ground. Together, though, we had sealed a pact.

And now I was to disappear again—only this time our lives depended on it.

The road led back into the dismal dilapidation of East Berlin—past empty buildings, new bright hoardings, foreign cars—bits of the West bolted on to a people who'd been bought and sold for the last fifty years and never had a say in it.

We left the luggage in lockers at the Lichtenburg station, bought tickets, and dumped the car in a side street beside the Alexanderplatz. Harry and the boys were hungry and attacked one of the new food kiosks.

Why am I still amazed by all this? But I am. Look at the fruit, the choice, look at the quality. Maybe the cold war has been about lemons and bananas? We had them, and they didn't. We had to protect them because God only knew what the other side would do if they got their filthy Commie hands on them. Lemons and bananas. The old system wouldn't allow them. The new one does. Is that what divided Europe all these years? Lord help us if it did.

The trouble is that I remember the old days. The times when I tried to do business while they broke up demonstrations on the street outside or threatened and intimidated children for watching Western television.

But it's over—don't think about it.

Don't think about the way they painted the eastern side of the wall in bright clear white to give their marksmen a better silhouette. Don't think about it. It's over.

I sit by the fountain, crude and angular, its multispouted arms offering water to the sky. People walk by in bright clothes, with currency in their pockets and permission to go where they want . . . and a single light flashes like a warning in the darkened building across the square.

So I killed time, and the darkness came to Berlin, and Harry and the boys were getting nervous.

I took them to the U-Bahn and told them how to get back to Lichtenburg. The train left at nine. Buy beer, buy some sandwiches, and I'll meet you there.

"Wait a minute," said Harry, "you're not ducking out on us, are you?"

"Of course not, Harry." As if I'd tell him.

They treated me to an unfriendly stare, and I hurried off toward the Stadt Berlin Hotel, without looking back. Once out of sight, I flagged a taxi to the Friedrichstrasse. We stopped beside the old checkpoint Charlie, now just a straight road through the city with a few of the old guard-posts left for the tourists.

On the western side, there was a gaggle of street sellers, Turks and Russians, Romanians, selling off the final chattels of the old Soviet empire—military caps and watches, flags and dolls and party cards.

I found the man I needed, squatting on a stool, beside his stand. He had the largest collection of military souvenirs—thick leather belts with the red star buckle and all kinds of documents.

He had the right haircut, the right demeanor, maybe a supply sergeant, or some deeply untrustworthy private in a big Russian army that no longer even had a name. He was in a hurry, maybe the MPs were out that night, or there was a purge on corruption.

"Can we talk for a moment?" I asked in Russian, adding a deliberate mistake.

He winced visibly. Where he came from, talk had a nasty habit of presaging a bullet or a few years in exile. But he left his stool and took me into the shadows beside what used to be the "house by the wall."

He kept his hands in his pockets and looked around incessantly.

We were very focused that night in Berlin—both of us—and very scared.

Chapter Eighteen

"I can't get it," he said. "Impossible. Tomorrow maybe."

"Tomorrow's too late."

He shrugged the kind of shrug that closes doors right across Russia. Told you, don't have it, get lost.

I pulled out three $100 bills from my pocket and held them up to the light. He looked from them to me, and I could see him weighing up the possibility of beating me senseless then and there, taking the money, running. But maybe I was just that bit too tall.

"Two hours," he said.

"Half an hour."

He nodded, and I watched the thin, slouching figure move away.

"Oi, Sash." He yelled to a partner I hadn't noticed, and something small and nasty called Sasha came out from beside the beer bar and sat on the stool, minding the shop.

He was back in twenty minutes, and I could only guess at the deal he'd done. The dash to a secret store in East Berlin, a bribe here, a promise there, dollars changing hands, trust and mistrust. And at the end of it all, a gray paper package in his right hand.

He beckoned me back into the shadows, but I stayed

where I was. I wanted light and people around me, in case his natural-born dishonesty got the better of him.

"You got it then."

He grinned—flash of pride, excitement. Three hundred dollars going his way—or a decent cut. He couldn't have been more than twenty, pale face, sprinkled heavily with acne, one of the glorious half-million they'd billeted in East Germany to bring us to our knees.

"Does it work?" I asked.

"You want me to shoot you?"

Why don't I find that funny? He grinned again and offered me another version of Russia's shrug—get moving, you don't talk and I don't talk.

That's why they shrug.

Back East on the U-Bahn. It's still early evening, and the carriage is littered with beer cans, an Alsatian lies in a puddle, its face muzzled against evil intentions. Schillingstrasse, Strausberger Platz—we're really on the dark side now, platforms still dimly lit, a few adverts and pictures, but they haven't shaken it off. Two passengers are talking about visiting the "former GDR." Not their land. No-man's-land, really. They don't like what they were, and they don't yet know what they've become. The same identity problem they were born with, ever since man put a wall around them and called it a country.

And I have a gun in my pocket—first time, I tell you—because this journey leads me East where the old bets are off and the rules are changing by the hour. Jane Card had told me she didn't know who was on which side, nor did I.

I reached the Lichtenburg station in the middle of a row. Harry appeared to be leading it, standing on the platform gesticulating at a group of conductors and car attendants.

"Bloody hell." He turned toward me, and I could see the veins sticking out of his forehead. Thing about Harry was that he always put everything into it. There was a dog lying in the mud twenty-five miles from there to back that up.

"Listen"—he waved a ticket in my face—"carriage number three ninety-five. Okay? Beds forty-four–forty-eight. Okay? Stamped, paid for. What happens? There isn't a bloody car three ninety-five, doesn't exist, wasn't built, took the fucking day off. How do I know?" He threw the ticket on the floor and marched up toward the other end of the platform. So much for a quiet disappearance, I thought. And yet it was hard not to laugh.

The Polish conductor sidled up to me. There was the semblance of a Central European bow. "It is most regrettable," he said. "The carriage was not operationally ready."

"Is that so?" We British can be very offhand when we want to be.

"But if you come with me," he added, "we have places in another carriage. It is almost empty. Each gentleman can have a compartment to be alone."

I told him that with gentlemen like that, I'd rather take another train. And he smiled forgivingly, as if I didn't really mean it, and we'd all get on in the end.

Somewhere around its appointed time, the train slouched out of the station, and Harry stood in the doorway of my compartment.

"Are we going to have an argument, Harry?"

"Looks like it," he replied. "I have to tell you, I'm less than happy with the trip so far. What I want to know is . . . are we going to do some business or just go from one shithole to another getting attacked? I don't want to be offensive, you understand, but we were doing okay till you showed up."

"Business, Harry. From now on, it's all business."

He rubbed his eyes with both hands and sat down on the bench beside the window.

"So what happened back there with Barsch?"

"I'm not sure."

"I need more than that, Edward. I'm threatened with a gun by a business associate you've introduced us to. This may be normal practice in the circles where you move—but for me and my friends . . ." He stopped for a moment, and I imagined him trying to push the past back where it belonged. "Let's just say we've left that sort of thing behind."

"Listen, Harry. It's possible Barsch had some friends who wanted us out of their territory; maybe we stumbled into a deal we know nothing about. Maybe they thought they could lean on us. I'll make some enquiries. I'm sorry it happened. I can't say more than that."

And I couldn't.

Harry stared out of the window. His lugubrious expression reflected in the glass, as the city lights got sparser and we rattled East toward Poland. To him, Barsch would have meant unfinished business—and whether you're bashing heads in the East End or the fields of Germany, the theory is the same. You don't leave things to chance. No comebacks.

"We'll talk again," he said, and got up. "How long till the border?"

"About an hour."

I moved out into the corridor and leaned against the window, watching nothing. Harry was right to be concerned. If he knew the reasons, he'd probably jump off the train while it was moving.

Or would he? All right, he wore his shirts well starched and lived with a magnificent view of the Thames, but Harry had spent plenty of time where the view came with bars in front of it—and an exercise yard, and a visitor once a month if he hadn't upset anyone and lost his privileges.

I hadn't asked him about those times, but I'd asked around. Harry, went the word, had liked to get things done. He'd liked to end each day feeling he had accomplished something. And if he got home and had nothing to write in his diary, he felt sore and peevish, and had tended to take it out on people.

You might argue that if you're fencing stolen cars around Hackney and Stratford, there's plenty of room for sore feelings. One uncareful day Harry had hit someone just a little too hard—and instead of "persuasion" there was a jury that decided it was called "grievous, bodily harm," and Harry went down a second time—and went down hard.

Since then, he had promised himself, he'd live with the law in mind—never breaking it, only bending it when no one was looking. Costa and Arthur thought he'd gone soft. He knew that. "But I tell them the world has changed," he said to me one morning over coffee. "You have to be subtle these days. If people don't want your products, you can't hurl a bloody brick through their window." He grinned at me. "Not anymore."

The train pulled up and stood for a moment in the vacant darkness, panting and hissing like an animal catching its breath.

Of course Harry deserved an explanation, but then we all deserved things we weren't going to get—like Yevgeny, dying beside the Dover ferry, George in Mother's car, or me, for that matter, taking a bullet beside the Thames.

It's easy to see how it all gets out of hand, when you start playing around with the basics. Then you think nothing of handing out the danger to everyone else—because, well, it's all in a grand cause. It's what you have to do. Harry and the others will just have to take their chances. Fine.

I'd come a long way in a couple of days. I'd started to weed out the expendables—like scruples—because I didn't have room for them. Under these kinds of conditions, you can find out a lot about yourself in a short time—and you shouldn't expect to like it.

The train moved again, slowly this time, the start of the old "hate run"—the long, painful penetration of the East bloc border. Of course it had changed, but you couldn't forget. You, the little Westerner, fodder for the day for all the East German and Polish customs officials—to be humiliated, violated, and frequently robbed, as they saw fit.

And you solemnly showed the passport, with Her Majesty's secretary of state regally requesting passage without let or hindrance. What a farce—all those years in the bloc.

I was about to go back to my seat when Harry caught my arm. He must have left his compartment without my hearing. For his right hand fastened onto me with staggering strength, pushing me back against the rail. I could see his anger, right up close, in the sweat on his face and the sharp eyes like little pockets of darkness.

In that instant, I had a flash of what Harry must have been like—going round the poorer parts of East London, enforcing his little code of ethics, leaving his five-fingered imprint on faces and bodies, a slash here, a kick there in the groin as a little postscript to a wonderful day, going home to the wife he'd had then. Did you have a nice day at the office, dear, as he counted the casualties.

"You stupid bastard," he whispered. "I ask for an explanation, and you go off buying yourself toys like this. . . ." And his left hand went into my jacket pocket, and suddenly he was waving the gray paper package in my face. "You toad . . . 'I'll make enquiries,' " he mimicked, "with this? That's just bloody marvelous . . . business from now on, Harry. I've a good mind . . . Christ!" He released his grip on me and shoved the gun back into my pocket. "You don't even hide the thing properly. What d'you think Customs are going to do—wave you through the Green Channel?"

I watched him but said nothing.

"For Christ's sake, Edward—I know you won't tell me what's going on—but take some fucking precautions for your own sake." Harry wiped the sweat off his forehead. "And I'll tell you this—when you get to Warsaw, you're on your own. Me and the boys—we're going to do some business. If we see you on the way, we'll walk on the other side of the street. Got it? I am terminating our agreement." He said the words very carefully and with exaggerated precision, and I watched him return to his compartment—and slide the door shut.

I stood for a while, breathing deeply, unclenching my fists, letting the muscles relax. I was scared not by Harry but by myself. For a moment, I had been quite ready to kill him.

Chapter Nineteen

The train was pulling into the station at Frankfurt an der Oder—the new border on the old site. Light green uniforms for the Germans, dark green for the Poles—and studied disinterest in my passport.

"Quite a change here," I remarked. But they didn't reply. It's all very well for a Westerner to come along, fat and jolly, celebrating the end of Communism, but it was still their country—the only one they had. And now it had gone. Hard to admit that everything around you had been a failure.

We sat immovable under the neon lights, and there's nothing so lifeless as an empty platform in the middle of the night, with the flies circling endlessly and the world in darkness around you.

Poland was just across the river, although it could have been on another planet.

I had only ever known one Pole, but the circumstances and that time of my life stick in my mind.

I was twenty and in the second year of a Russian course at London University—the lazy man's option, or so I was told.

"You speak it already," the admissions tutor had said. "What's the point?"

"Culture," I replied. "The history, literature . . ."

"Oh God, don't give me all that crap! Why not just say you want to piss about for three years, doing bugger all?"

"I want to piss about, doing bugger all."

"Excellent. You'll fit in admirably."

The activities, of course, had been just as he had described, until one night in the spring.

I remember coming back to the house very late, choosing my floorboards carefully. I could still taste the full, moist lips of a new first-year student, I could taste the gin we'd spent hours ingesting, my right hand could still feel the alternate softness and hardness of her breasts.

Above all else, I didn't want to talk to Mother.

But she came out onto the landing, eyes half-closed, face like a dismal lightbulb.

We sat in the kitchen, and she told me to expect a visitor in the morning. A Pole named Karol, an old friend.

"You don't seem very happy about it. . . ."

"Karol can be difficult," she said. "I'm not sure what he wants."

"But I thought he was a friend. . . ."

"What difference does that make? They are often more trouble than anyone else."

There was no point in arguing; the drawbridge was up.

"Where did you meet him?"

"I don't know . . . it was a long time ago—a conference, maybe . . ."

"Why didn't you invite him before?"

"He travels a lot, always here and there. . . ."

And I suppose I stopped listening after that. I recognized the evasion procedure. Not lying, just not giving. For information was a product Mother didn't really understand. She would offer it out, as if in rations—jumbled pieces that frequently made little sense. Sometimes years would go by before you could see which of them fitted together and how.

So I left the puzzle and went to bed, thinking of my first-year student. And Mother stayed in the kitchen, waiting for Karol.

* * *

You could see he was trouble. A brick wall of Slavic arrogance and prejudice.

He sat in the kitchen, a hard, intolerant man, his gray hair close-cropped, the face lined and patterned like an old rug. Nothing pleased him, nothing satisfied him. He had done it all—and we'd done nothing.

Fifties, you'd say, but he looked both older and younger. He was fit, moved well. There was real strength in the hand that took mine, in the fist the size of a Sunday roast. And yet the eyes had seen more than they should have done for fifty. There was suffering in them, both witnessed and inflicted.

As the day went on, he expounded his theories of where the world was going, a combination of guesswork and insight, in any case now dated and irrelevant. His ruling passion was hatred, and his target was Moscow. How to bring the animal down was the exercise. How to cut off its head and bury it.

I'd heard it all before. Karol was another East bloc crank. Either they were locked up over there or they were lunatics over here. I rather hoped it was our first and last meeting.

When he'd gone, I told Mother what I thought.

She looked hesitant. "He's a good person to keep in with," she said. "I've known him for a long time. He has interesting friends."

"He's a pain in the arse."

"So are you." She smiled. "But I don't stop seeing you."

We were to run into Karol again later that week. Mother insisted I go with her to a meeting somewhere in Kensington. There was to be a talk about Russia. Food and drink. Questions. What she didn't say was that Karol would be the speaker, and the venue was his flat.

Oh, he loved himself that night. The small-town rhetoric—the meaningful and, to me, meaningless pauses. The thumping of the table. The stream of invective against the Russians and all their works. "We will win," he told the audience of six lonely women and me, "we will win but with different methods. Clever methods. Soviets are corrupt; they are always fighting each other. We have to make sure they fight each other to death."

He waited for a clap, or some sign that any of us were still breathing, and then he sat down.

Mother and I stood beside a plate of cakes, and he came over to us immediately. "Wonderful evening. Thanks for coming. Big thanks."

"It was very interesting," I said.

"Marvelous," added Mother.

"We will do it again, when I get back."

Mother looked interested for the first time. "Where are you going?"

"Just a little journey, East," he replied, and leered at us. "Just a week. I'll call you."

That was something to look forward to. And I remember hoping we could get on with our lives and forget all about him.

On the following Tuesday, as I left for the university, Mother came down into the hall to see me off. It was unusual, for she normally shouted from her bedroom or stayed fast asleep.

"Would you like to borrow my car?"

"Of course I would."

"All right, you can. But I need a lift later. Pick me up by Holland Park Tube, eight-thirty. You won't forget?" The black eyes sought to imprint the time on my brain.

"I won't forget."

As it turned out, I was early for once. A good half hour. There'd been no one to meet up with that day, and my full-breasted friend was working late in the library, "being good."

So I drove leisurely around the area, passing, as it happened, the block of flats where Karol lived. It wasn't a happy recollection, and I turned the car quickly in the forecourt and resolved to head back the mile or so toward Holland Park and wait there.

I didn't notice the van by the entrance, until the traffic forced me to wait by the roadside. Glancing in the rear mirror, I clearly saw my mother come out of the building and get into it. She was carrying a bag and seemed in a great hurry.

And somehow it wasn't appropriate to get out and greet her. She was busy, preoccupied. I could feel her tension. So

I drove back to the station and waited till 8:30, wondering whether to ask her where she'd been.

Of course I was wary of Mother. I didn't want an argument. Like an avalanche, it was always difficult to stop. Sometimes it would roll on for hours, so, as ever, she would need careful handling.

She emerged from the underground station, fifteen minutes late, flushed, slamming the door behind her.

"What are you looking at, Edward?"

"Hallo, Mum. I'm looking at you."

"I'm bloody late, aren't I?"

"It doesn't matter."

"Okay, let's go and eat."

We found a Mexican restaurant just up the hill. The food was wonderful. Mother just picked at it.

"Good day?" I asked her.

"So-so. I had to translate for some lawyers. Another joint venture with the grand CIS." She could never talk of the new Russia without some mocking adjective.

"What? Round here?"

"Embassy Row, just along the road."

The waiter asked if we wanted dessert.

"Yes, please," I replied.

"I want to go home," said Mother. "Bring the bill."

In the car, I decided to make one more try.

"When is Karol coming back?"

"What do you care? I thought you couldn't stand him."

"I just wondered when we'd have to go back there for another riveting evening."

"He's coming next Sunday."

I deliberately drove past his block.

"Doesn't he live round here?"

"Perhaps," I distinctly recall her saying. "I really can't remember."

Well . . . why do I recall this tiny incident with such clarity—and why have I sought for so long to bury it?

There's only one reason. It was the first time I knew my mother had lied.

Karol became a more or less permanent feature of our lives—a fact I never really understood. Mercifully he was more a feature of Mother's than mine. She went to dinner with him a few times, attended some more meetings and seminars.

Maybe he had been in his flat that day, and she had visited him. I don't know, and she would never have told me.

Maybe she had entered the flat while he was out. And who had been waiting for her in the red car, beside the main door?

I never solved the questions.

Karol returned to Poland nearly three years ago, once the Solidarity government came to power. He gave us his address and telephone number before leaving, and I only glanced at it, but it was the kind of number you don't easily forget. Three ones and four threes.

It was still in my mind when I looked for it, and I knew I would call him in the morning. In Poland.

CHAPTER TWENTY

COME INSIDE MY MIND. Sit down. Take your coat off. Don't worry about the mess. I tried tidying it, but the woman who did that for me has gone. Can't get good help these days—you know what it's like.

I've invited you here because I hoped you'd see things in a different light.

Sometimes I think I'm going backward—and that's not right. I keep stumbling into parts of my life that I'd put away and forgotten. And I can see why.

When you look at them now, after so many years, they're not very pleasant.

Oh, don't think I'm complaining. It's just that I have this acute sense of foreboding—and it's at times like this I'd like to be able to trust someone.

Mother? I don't seem to know her anymore. She disappeared, apparently after seeing some important papers. Everybody thinks she's gone back to Russia—which is why I'm heading that way. I need to find her before anyone else does.

Yes, she may have seen something she shouldn't have. Something extraordinary.

Oh God, I'm sorry. I should have offered you a drink.

You had something before you left home. Okay.

Where were we? Oh yes. I haven't mentioned the people who were killed. No—you noticed that straight away, didn't you?

Well, I don't like to think too much about it. Here I am trying to find Mother, and the path is starting to get crowded with bodies. I got shot, too, you know that. . . . I'm sorry I didn't mean to shout. But it's not what I'm used to, you understand.

Have I delved into my own conscience? What's that supposed to mean? I was never involved in anything Mother did. I'm only just beginning to learn what it was—stuff with Coffin and all that. You're making a big mistake if you think . . .

Let me tell you something. Whatever I did, I did for good reasons. I had no choice. None at all. They never gave me one, you understand? I did it for the family. And when you peel away all the other baggage—that's the only thing you have left.

Let's go back to Mother. All right. I prefer that line of talk. And yet, what can I tell you? She always kept everything to herself. I barely knew where she worked and had no idea at all of her contacts. She could have commanded the entire bloody Red Army, and I wouldn't have been any wiser.

Secretive? Of course she was. She's Russian.

I have to say, I thought you'd have some information, or at least some insights to offer. But you keep turning it back on me, suggesting maybe I've forgotten. . . .

You know something. . . . I thought I was getting closer to it, when I remembered Karol. Bloody suspicious that time when she came out of his block of flats and told me later she didn't even remember where he lived. What was that all about?

All right then, come out and say it. No, really. Let's put the bloody cards on the table.

You think there's something in her past we ought to explore?

Christ—I don't know. That was the thing about growing up in the Soviet Union. They got you whichever way you moved. And if they ever let you out, they put you on a long lead, like a dog.

* * *

We weren't the only ones, you know. That's the tragedy of it all. I mean, there were many other families caught up in the cold war. They turned us against each other—they blackmailed and manipulated till we didn't know whom we were working for. In the end, we did anything they asked, simply to save ourselves and the people we loved.

Whatever it was. We'll do what you want—just leave us in peace.

Only they never did. Not even when the cold war ended. Especially then.

That's enough now. I've said too much. You'd better go. It was a bad idea asking you here in the first place. Just get your coat, here it is. Now please go. It's safer this way. Go on. Who knows—maybe I'll get to live a little longer.

The lift is down there on the left. See? Don't be so helpless.

Early morning brought me to the outskirts of Warsaw.

And bad dreams, they say, are the product of a troubled mind.

Chapter Twenty-one

I LEFT THE TRAIN in the Eastern suburbs, where it took on fresh commuters, heading for the city.

An old lady got out with me, bundled in gray and black. Baskets and bags hung from her like a packhorse. We stepped onto the platform and seemed to shiver at the same moment in the early frost.

I never said good-bye to Harry. And I assumed he'd be a good boy now, do his business and return home. A strange mixture of friend and thug, that one, trying to cross the bridge from evil to good—and not quite making it. There were plenty of flashes from the bad old days, and I had the strong impression that if I'd nodded my head back in Germany, he'd have finished off Barsch—because it was the thing to do.

But at least he *was* trying. Nowadays he ran a more or less legal business, with men in suits, who kept the books and rarely if ever beat anyone up.

Good luck, Harry. It would be interesting to meet in twenty years, to see if the angels had got him or the devil had reclaimed his own.

A taxi took me across town to the chimney lands, where the trams still plough up the roads and the power lines draw black across the sky.

As the sun came up, you could see the changes at street level. The places where Communism had got up and left town—bright kiosks full of food, imported cheeses, wines, and all the other things they never had.

Oranges and lemons on all sides. The cold war's over. Again, I wonder, is that what it was all about?

I had known Warsaw pretty well in the old days, watched the political circus turn somersaults through the eighties and early nineties. As soon as one lot got out of jail, they'd set about putting the others behind bars—or trying to. So the people I'd once known as dissidents were now running the place, still getting drunk—and showing all the signs of being as intolerant as those they'd replaced.

Same methods, different labels. Only this crowd liked their oranges.

I, too, had got drunk in the place, lost my memory a few nights running, and my pants. Oh, don't think Communism didn't have its moments. Doing business in the East meant you always got offered more perks than you wanted—and less hard cash. But somewhere along the line you had to realize when to say no—and they had to learn when you meant it.

The world couldn't be bought simply with blond hair and a night to remember. Not anymore.

The last time I'd passed through the city, a former government adviser had recommended an unusual place to stay. "You want protection," he said. "You want privacy—this is for you." Now I needed it.

I had asked the driver to go to the Belweder—the presidential palace. He'd looked twice in his mirror at that. And as we rolled down past the Council of Ministers, he put on a cheeky smile and asked if the president was expecting me.

I can just about manage in Polish, so I told him to drive slowly past the palace, down the hill and stop on the right. Then he could get lost.

"You are a funny man," he replied. "That's the Russian embassy." He spat out of the window. "It is you who are lost."

I got out, bag in hand, and waited on the curb till he'd driven off.

He was right about the embassy, standing on a grassy

hill behind high wrought-iron gates. The Poles had hated it for generations, crowding outside the grounds and daubing slogans on the walls at the height of the troubles. But it wasn't what I wanted.

Across the road, a single soldier stood guard behind a steel fence. It was the entrance to a very private road, edged with parkland and leading to a modern stone building.

As I approached, he left his hut and asked for identification.

"I'm hoping a reservation has been made for me."

He examined my passport and read the name into a telephone.

"There's no reservation, but they say they can take you."

And suddenly there was a smile and an unlocked gate in front of me and the old Polish Army salute with the index and middle finger extended. In theory I was now safer than I had been for days. For this was nothing less than protected government territory, the site of the former Communist party guest house, now open to the public for the first time ever. And since old habits die *so* hard in the East, no one had thought to announce the fact, and therefore almost no one knew about it.

Almost.

I was glad of the luxury. I was glad of the marble floors and the fine wooden furniture in the rooms, the satellite television, the linen sheets—and the receptionist who gave the impression of being glad to see me, even if she wasn't.

I'm sure they'd removed the microphones from the walls and the telephone. I'm sure they disconnected the monitors and the tape recorders and got rid of the tiny transmitters in the dining room and the army of SB Security men who had to listen to all the trivia, transcribe it, and work out if any further action was needed.

I'm sure of it. And if they haven't done so—it's probably next on their list of priorities.

But you see, I had grown very untrusting in a short space of time. I was a convert to the school of suspicion.

And as I walked up the hill and turned onto Bagatela, past the British ambassador's big-box residence, I realized that with this call, I couldn't afford to take the chance.

* * *

Three ones and four threes.

Answer the phone, Karol.

Long, slow rings.

Answer the bloody phone.

It began to rain, and unless things had really changed, that would wreck the telephone system for most of the day.

I dialed again. But now the line had dissolved into crackles and rhythmic thumps—more like short-wave radio than a local call.

Along the street was a café promoting "food from China." So I decided to sit out the rain there. I still didn't know what to tell Karol, because I still wasn't sure who he was.

The memories of him with Mother were curious. She had called him a friend and protected him from most of my insults, but there seemed little friendship between them. They never went out together; still less, stayed in. Mother insisted Karol wasn't interested in "that kind of thing." So in my eyes he was decidedly odd. I suppose both had their anti-Communism to share, though in Mother's case it took a different form.

Whatever she was, she wasn't a fanatic. She never joined all the fighters for a free Russia, because she said there was no such thing. Russia had never been about freedom—it was a jungle where animals of different stripes fought each other for absolute power. Always the same jungle and the same rules. Sometimes just a few got killed, at other times the casualties were many. There would always be killing in a jungle, because the inhabitants knew no other way to get things done.

And Karol? Which tree was he hiding in? Had he displayed his real ambitions, or simply dug a hole in the ground and abandoned them?

I could recall the time when he returned to Poland. The new Solidarity government was in power. He sold his London flat in a great hurry and for very little money, bought a ticket, and flew back in a snowstorm.

The night before, there had been drinks and plenty of those awful insincere toasts—to the wonderful future and the new dawn—and the end of that blackest of all nights. Somebody even sang "Come into the Garden, Maud," which shows you the kind of gathering it was.

Karol, we heard later, had acquired a beautiful apartment in the Old Town, rebuilt after the war, with its winding cobbled streets and gas lamps. Somehow they found enough artisans left alive and enough records undynamited—and from the rubble you could once again hear the sound of violins late into the night and the tripping of hooves as the cart horses pulled blanketed tourists around the city walls.

But the ghosts planted long memories in the minds of the people, so they were never at peace, never happy, living in times they barely remembered, locked in by the past and the scale of its tragedies. Karol had gone back to see if there was a slice of power for him. Mother's friend Karol.

It was that thought that took hold of me, like a sharp blade reaching into my mind, piercing the nerves. Suddenly each tiny sound in the café seemed magnified, each action accelerated. People at neighboring tables were shouting. The noise level was rising out of control.

And it wasn't because I'd liked Karol, or cared about him, or even known him that well.

But I could sense his danger.

Mother's friend. Not at all the thing to be these days—not a safe thing to be, when half the thugs in Europe are looking for her. Would they know to look for him? Would they know where to find him?

Not another one, please God.

I ran back down the street to the call box. The line was clearer. I counted the rings. Ten, eleven, twelve. And you're not there, my friend. You've gone out, gone away, and I hope to hell you have. . . .

But I had to find him.

I flagged a taxi to the Central Post Office, and the rain began again, hard and violent, banging down on the roof of the car and the people as if to cleanse the sins of the city.

Karol Adamski. In a telephone directory. And that is the march of progress in a country where numbers and addresses were forever secret—always someone else's secret, never yours.

Outside now there was no taxi. And so I ran, through the rain, past the natty umbrellas and sheltering bodies. After fifty yards, my clothes stuck to me, after a hundred they weighed me down, and my hair washed over my soaking, sweating face, no longer seeing the puddles, feet and shoes dredging the mud from the pavements.

The numbers blurred, streets blurred. I could hear myself shouting out to people, my voice echoing back in the narrow streets.

Past bad old King Zygmunt with the curved sword in one hand and the cross in the other, stooping low in the Warsaw sky.

And a hand pointed to the corridor and the staircase, and suddenly the rain had stopped. I leaned against the wall for a few moments, feeling the chill come in with me from the street. A narrow corridor, plain walls, wooden staircase. I heard nothing but the sound of my own breathing.

I lurched up the stairs, tiny numbers on the doors, so hard to read. Third floor, someone had said. Karol Adamski, the old Pole from London, who I'd somehow got into my stupid head was in some sort of danger . . . and he'd stand there looking at a half-drowned rat from Britain that he hadn't seen for years . . . and what do I say to him? . . . such a pleasant surprise . . . just thought I'd soak myself in this lovely rain . . . you don't have a towel, do you . . . ?

This is it. Twenty-six. Open the door, Karol.

I knocked maybe three times, distrusting the bell. Loud, rapid blows on the door.

And it was the face of Edgar Coffin that came to stare at me across the threshold, Coffin's hand holding open the door, Coffin's words, so short and so impossible to misunderstand.

"Karol's dead."

He took a step back and looked me over. "Don't suppose you did it—did you?"

Chapter Twenty-two

He was filling up space between the sofa and a glass coffee table, asleep, a touch effeminately, it looked, his cheek resting on his left hand. An odd sort of presence that seemed at no time to have had the slightest connection with the living. And I haven't seen too many corpses up close, but it struck me that when you go, you take your whole past with you. The remains of Karol Adamski filled an old pair of trousers, a red pullover, and tweed jacket—and I suspect little else.

"I got a call half an hour ago," said Coffin.

"What, all the way from London?"

"Don't be funny, Edward. We have just about managed to follow your progress across the Continent—albeit a little late—but we found your road map in the end."

"And the bodies?"

"Them too."

"Thanks for helping." I bent down to examine Karol. No obvious sign of violence, but then I don't know what to look for. The eyes were tightly closed. Could it be that Karol had died in prayer?

"You're well versed in bodies," I said to Coffin. "What happened?"

"It's winter, Edward. Old people die."

"Not Karol. He could have gone on forever."

"He had nothing to live for. The cold war's over. . . ."

"If he had nothing to live for—why bother killing him?"

"We don't know that anyone did. Anyway, I have some people coming in to take a look at him." Coffin went to the window, as if in search of them, and looked out across the old town. Lights were coming on, and the darkness was settling fast across the city. "We won't know till later."

"What is this 'we,' Coffin? What the hell are you doing here, and who was it that called you half an hour ago?"

Coffin led me to the door. He wasn't the same person I used to know, but then the world wasn't the same either. I had simply never encountered professional Coffin—just the good-time boy, lover, game-for-a-joke sort of fellow. Not this Coffin—with his people coming in.

He was wearing a raincoat and swinging one of those dinky umbrellas people carry in their briefcases. He hadn't come out in a hurry.

As we walked downstairs, I shivered from the wet clothes.

"Let's get you into something warm," he said.

"I think we'll talk first."

It was good that Warsaw had some new cafés—somewhere to sit and soak. By the time the waitress brought coffee, there was a puddle of rainwater beside my chair. The coffee, I recall, was much improved, but I couldn't say the same for the company.

"My government wants to see your mother, urgently. That's why I'm here." Coffin leaned across the table and shrugged. "Nothing sinister. They want to know what she's seen. Moscow may have had a number of *our* secrets in its vaults—along with their own."

"You make it sound like a very disinterested little inquiry. Why not send it in the post with a second-class stamp? You're going to have to give a little, Coffin. As you used to say . . . 'work the room.' "

"A call came through to the embassy"—he looked at his watch—"over an hour ago now. Female voice. Anonymous. To me, incidentally, although no one's supposed to know I'm here. Said simply that Karol was dead."

"And you knew who Karol was?"

"I knew all your mother's friends. That was the way we operated."

"What way?"

"Oh, for Chrissake, Edward. Your mother and I had business together. I told you that. From time to time, she would assess the defectors who came over. We even brought one to your place. The safe house was busy that night. Nowhere else to go."

"I know."

"Thought you might." He looked up as if recalling an old encounter. "So I knew about her life. Had to. Karol was a good friend of hers, gave her a lot of information. She trusted him."

"Really? She always said he had a big mouth. Typical Slav. Small-town mentality. You find something out, you run and tell the whole block. . . ."

"They met years ago," said Coffin. "We never knew where—and your mother never said. I suspect the friendship was cemented in Russia—God knows what circumstances. But she was always fiercely loyal to her friends." He laughed. "It was the lovers she couldn't stand."

I finished my coffee and pushed it away. "I'm leaving."

"Where are you staying?"

"That's my business."

"I can find out. . . ."

"Then find out."

Coffin made a face. "We've known each other quite a while, Edward. Plenty of games, plenty of fun. I watched you grow up. You know that—the house in Stanley Road, all the dinners we ate, and going to the movies. . . ."

"What does it count for now, Coffin?"

"I'm trying to help. You have to believe that."

I didn't answer him. I remember thinking that the years, by themselves, make little difference to a relationship. It's what you do with them that counts. And Coffin and I had used them to travel very different paths.

We walked out into the cobbled street. It was closed to traffic but full of pedestrians. There was a new rhythm to the city. People had places to go, meals to eat, profits to spend. There weren't the aimless strollers around anymore.

"Taxis are up by the Zygmunt statue," he said.

"Thank you."

"Edward, there is something here you should know. My people are quite determined to reach your mother. Quite determined. We will find her—in Russia, where I think she is, or anywhere else. But you might save everyone a lot of trouble if you helped."

"I hear you, Coffin."

As I walked away, he shouted out, "See you at the funeral"—and several people in the crowd turned and looked and wondered, as well they might.

Coffin had influence. For in Warsaw that night, Karol's death became an instant public issue. They made him into a war hero, wrote him a glittering biography, put him in battles as far apart as El Alamein and the Normandy landings—and ran it in the evening news and the next day's papers.

I knew it was nonsense. Karol had passed a decent enough war, but most of it had been spent in Britain with a brief tour in RAF Fighter Command.

Now, though, Coffin was stoking the fires, announcing a public funeral, turning those fires into a beacon, hoping Mother would see them.

He would have no scruples, using Karol's death and Mother's loyalty to an old friend.

Of course, she was too clever to be drawn that easily. She would know the funeral was staged under the tightest surveillance. But even with that knowledge—something else would pull her. The challenge of it, the risk, the thrill of trying to beat the combined intelligence services at their own game. Mother's streak of vanity—her compulsion to be first and best. And then there was the loyalty. Perhaps she had learned it in the camps, where you trusted your life to a friend, where a friend could be the only thing that stood between you and starvation. Not a person to ring up once a week, not a person to eat out with. Nothing casual about this kind of friendship—born at the fringes of life itself. And when the friend dies, you go to him, with your arms outstretched, your prayers and your memories laid out as a tribute by the graveside. You cannot pass by on the other side of the street. You cannot send flowers. You have to be there at the end.

Coffin knew my mother better than I had thought.

She would be there.

* * *

The storm died away at dawn. I was watching from the guest-house window, unable to sleep. Beside the gate the soldier, in winter cape and helmet, stamped the ground like an anxious horse, trying to keep warm. Over in the park, I could hear the crows cawing in the trees. I opened the window and listened to the drops of last night's rain, falling to the ground.

The radio said the funeral would be in the Powazki Cemetery—a huge city graveyard, and a memorial not just to the dead, but to all the shattered hopes of twentieth-century Poland—the massacres, the murders, the injustice.

Walk through the center of Warsaw, and you still come across lighted candles on street corners, plaques, tiny bouquets of flowers, marking the site of public killings by the Nazis.

When the Communists seized power, they encouraged remembrance of the wartime tragedies—but they developed critical amnesia when it came to the victims of Stalinism, to the killing of Polish officers by the Red Army, to the destruction of Warsaw, unopposed by Soviet forces that sat across the Vistula River and watched.

Nothing so dangerous as the past in Poland—nothing, they used to say, so hard to predict.

I reached the cemetery at two—an hour before the service was due to begin. And maybe it was simply superstition that sent me to the shop across the road to buy a candle.

The sky had darkened perceptibly since the morning, and a light mist settled in the trees. As I watched, a long line of heavily coated people picked their way through the hundred rows of headstones, past the pictures of the dead and the symbols of their life. Beside one grave—the propellor from an airplane and the face of a pilot, hardly old enough to have known combat.

It was damp and dismal—and I had a sudden feeling that it was we who were really dead: the mourners, tramping the cemetery, as winter closed in around us and cut us off from the outside world.

Are you here, Mother? Are you really here?

I couldn't help looking around, searching the faces, feeling the sweat break out on my forehead.

Tell me, Mother, did you kill back in London? Who are you? How many more have to die on your road to Russia?

It was easy to think such thoughts. For in this place death was the business—humanized, ritualized—made manageable.

And what about my own conscience?

Were there other paths I could have taken?

I passed an old woman kneeling at the grave of her father.

"Dad, Dad," she was saying, "I'm back in Warsaw, come to see the family, I miss you such a lot these days. . . ."

The voice droned on as I went by, but it struck me as strange and unnatural to hear a grandmother talking to her father, trying to bridge the worlds of life and death, refusing to accept them as final. And maybe it took courage to do that—and strength, to kneel in the mud on a dim, dark day—and call out across time, with no answer, no sign of recognition.

It's no good for me, standing in a freezing cemetery, waiting for a murdered man to be lowered into the ground.

We had formed a vague semicircle, sixty or seventy people, and you could tell that Coffin's security had arrived. Mostly you go to funerals with friends or family—you knew the person, you knew his world. But no one seemed to know anyone else in this crowd. A few had probably heard the announcement, the rest would be the guard dogs and the hit men and whoever else the American embassy had co-opted for the occasion.

Coffin was suddenly at my side.

"I'm glad you could find time to come."

"I never like to miss a cold, wet funeral."

He wasn't listening. Professional Coffin was watching the people, coming as close as anyone to having his eyes move in opposite directions.

A priest had pushed his way to the front of us, behind him four grave-diggers bore the casket.

"Who organized all this?" I asked.

"We did," Coffin replied. "Besides, there was no one else."

I closed my mind to the prayers. You can take hypocrisy

only so far, and I couldn't really find it in my heart to wish Karol eternal life—since I'd so clearly passed up my own chance.

And what were my excuses? You make accommodations, along the way, you make compromises, and one, unfine day you wake up to discover you've made too many. You're like a boat cast loose on a lake. You cut away from your principles, you went out deeper and deeper—and you can't get back. It only takes one wrong move, and you're gone for good. Sold a good life for a bad one. And when I look back, it's not the fact that's so bad. It's knowing it. Like the patient in a doctor's waiting room—you're not a dying man until they tell you.

They were lowering the casket with some difficulty. The ground was so wet that the pallbearers were slipping and sliding, and there was a short, sharp clump as Karol finished his descent in free flight. Just a few spadefuls of earth now on top, and more prayers that I couldn't really follow.

I suppose it was much the same as our service—all about living for a short time in misery and cut down like a flower. And how right they are.

Coffin and I were standing at the back of the group, and I turned around as another funeral party waded past in the mud. In among the faces, my eye was suddenly drawn to the old woman who'd been kneeling beside her father's grave. She was just a few feet away, stooping badly, muttering to herself as she walked.

And then when I could almost have reached out and touched her, the head turned—and the black eyes looked straight at me, the same black eyes that had watched over me, live and urgent, as a child, eyes that could love and hate so intensely, eyes that were quite unforgettable.

The sudden shock made me lose my footing for a second, and I must have stumbled against Coffin, for he looked around sharply.

"Cold, Edward?"

"I'm fine."

But I wasn't—because there was sudden alarm, screaming inside my head. Mother, you came. The woman with mud on her coat and a stooping spine and a bun of gray hair that she had never owned. What the hell are you doing?

When I looked again, the procession had moved on, and she was lost from view. Steady yourself, Edward. Don't make a move; otherwise, she'll never make it out of here.

I coughed loudly. My hands started to shake, so I shoved them into my pockets. Slow it down, Edward. Not too many movements . . .

The prayers had ended. The priest was thanking us for coming. I could see Coffin exchanging looks with a man in the crowd. What now? The group dribbled toward the entrance. No one said anything. Coffin seemed disconsolate, but it wasn't my job to cheer him up.

"You'll come back for a drink," he said.

We drove to Karol's flat, and the rain followed us, slow and insistent through the early evening traffic. But I hardly noticed it. Mother was alive and operating. She'd been in the cemetery, almost tweaking their noses. She'd crossed borders and barriers to stand at the grave of her friend. She had delivered when it counted. Alive. I kept saying the word over to myself. Mother was in business.

By the time we reached the apartment, I needed that drink—and so, apparently, did most of the others.

I had been wrong—Karol had one relative: a female cousin who looked remarkably like him. She would have put on a good face whatever had happened. She only had a good face—short gray hair, the childlike smile of a spinster, never subjected to the pain of a close relationship, soft-spoken, busy, always doing for others. She looked the type that promises themselves a life of denial and sacrifice and promptly has her wishes fulfilled. She was cutting flowers in the little kitchen, and as I looked around, I could see how the whole place had changed. Papers in neat piles, books dusted, carpet vacuumed, and the glass coffee table under which Karol had lain was pushed against the wall.

So nice the way everyone cleans up after you.

For about an hour, a dozen of us stood around with not much to say. There was an RAF veteran whom Karol had served with—a lady of about fifty who said she'd known him and then blushed in front of all of us—a man from the Mayor's Office, probably wanting an excuse for a day off, and a handful of others who looked as though they belonged to Coffin.

When I left, light-headed from the alcohol and the sight of Mother, he came downstairs to see me out.

"So she didn't show after all." He made a great show of sighing, as if thinking how to write the cable to Washington.

And I remember savoring that moment, standing in the doorway, turning toward him from the old town square and the evening lights and looking straight into his lined, disappointed face. Listen to this, Coffin, with all your "people," and your mission so holy and vital.

"She was there all right," I told him. "You just never saw her. . . ."

CHAPTER TWENTY-THREE

I HAD MADE an enemy of Coffin. The look in his face said so—and now he would act against me—without hesitation or delay.

Dear Coffin, dear childhood friend, family friend, only trying to help.

Better I find out today. Better I know what to look for. But get in my way, Coffin, and I'll kill you.

You'd be surprised if you heard my thoughts.

In the end, I was certain he'd try to pull me in, ransom me to Mother. But that was risky. He couldn't be sure if she'd come looking for me first—or tell the world what she'd seen.

Nor could I.

None of this made for a restful evening.

For the first time in Warsaw, I checked the gun—a Browning nine-millimeter automatic—and laid it in my shoe beside the bed. I'm a heavy sleeper—people can stage firework parties around my pillow, and I don't hear them. Inside my shoe, it might just be some use.

There was no doubt I had been followed back to the hotel. Coffin would have been castrated by now with a rusty penknife if he couldn't arrange that.

And Mother? Most likely she had crossed back over the

border and was heading for Moscow. And if that were so, who was guarding her—who was clearing her path?

I lay on my back and recalled the black eyes in the cemetery. Eyes that had locked onto me for just a second, boring through the mist, past the mourners and the gravestones—a look of sadness but a look of purpose. Nothing could deflect those eyes, once they'd identified their target.

It reminded me of the time she had waited outside the university hall to see if I'd survived finals. A yellow-bright summer day and she was in dark glasses and a hat she had never worn before—hated hats, my mother. I hadn't seen her at first, hadn't been looking for her, and as we all stood around in the street exploding champagne corks, she tapped me on the shoulder, smiled, and said simply, "Hope it went well. See you later," and disappeared into the crowds. "Who was that?" someone asked, and I don't know why, but I didn't tell, didn't give her away.

I must have fallen asleep with the memory, for I woke up, realizing suddenly the room was dark. I slid my hand down the side of the bed and reached for my shoe. It was where I'd left it, gun inside.

I tried the bedside light. Dead. Through the window, I could see the streetlights were out way into the distance. Must have been the storm. The power system and the telephones were always the first victims. You couldn't help thinking that with just a week of concerted rain, the good Lord could have brought Communism to its knees much earlier.

And then something shifted by the door. Not clear enough to be a shape—but the passage of a living creature, a gentle draft of movement that sent me diving for the gun, falling on top of it—twisting painfully on a shoulder wound that I'd long ago forgotten.

There are seconds of your life where you wait for the guillotine to fall. Your prayers unanswered. Your head on the block. I held my breath, and a voice said, "Quiet, Edward," and the hand of Jane Card reached out and held mine until my breathing had slowed and the tightness in my chest had eased.

"I could have killed you."

"You're not that good," she said. "Put on some clothes.

You have to get out of here. The power is out for another ten minutes, maximum. That means no lights and no microphones."

"Just a moment, Jane . . ."

"We don't have a moment."

I grabbed the first things that came to hand—jacket, pullover, trousers—the gun I transferred from my shoe to the waistband. Because I didn't trust Jane Card, didn't know her motives—and her track record was lousy.

As my eyes became used to the darkness, I could see her opening the door, checking the passage. She had a new style—this Jane, in charge, in control, knowing what to do.

"Ready?" She ran back into the room. "You picked a good hotel, this time."

"What do you mean?"

"It's got entrances and exits you wouldn't dream of. It was built for the party, who were suffering from chronic insecurity. There's a whole labyrinth underneath—in case they needed a quick exit. But we don't have time for this. . . ."

We stood for a moment in the corridor, listening. From a neighboring room came the sound of snoring.

Jane beckoned me to the staircase. I watched her movements, silent, skillful. You have changed, Mrs. Card, I thought. Grown up—got a secret job.

In the lobby, she crossed to a door beside Reception and took a flashlight from her pocket. We descended wooden stairs into a modern laundry room. The thin beam of light picked out plenty of machines, a service table, baskets—one way in through the door and no other exit.

"Very nice, Jane. I'll wash my shirt while you work out what to do next."

I think I heard her laugh, for the next moment she had crossed to the wall, searching with her hands by the skirting board. After a few seconds, part of it fell away, and I could see that two of the washing machines were dummies—no pipes or drainage—simply a makeshift door in the wall. Beyond it the beginnings of a passage.

"Where does this go?"

"Out," she replied. "It goes out. Come on, hurry. The city'll get its lights working again in a minute, and we have to be away by then."

She went first, and I pulled the door back behind us. On both sides, the wall was bare brick—the passage about three feet wide. Card was hurrying now, as the path dipped down and turned to the left.

"Where does it come out?" I asked.

"Nowhere, if you don't shut up," she replied.

I never thought of claustrophobia, but I began to think of it that night under the city of Warsaw. Card seemed to know what she was doing—but how could she? Who had explained the route and told her where to find it? This woman had a lot of questions to answer—when we finally got out.

And then I could feel cold air—and smell the dampness of water. It meant we had gone under the wall into Lazieki Park, probably heading for the lake. Suddenly I had this image of summer walks on shady avenues and Chopin concerts in the open air, an art gallery, a café—pieces of an old life that I seemed to have left behind for good.

Just ahead of me Card had stopped, and so had the path. As she shone the flashlight, I could see a wooden door at the end of the passage—nothing fancy, but some planks, fastened together along a central beam. She pulled at it, and there was a creak of resistance—she pulled again, and it came away.

A corridor now. More steps. Life's little journey, half-light and half-dark and no guarantees at all of where it will take you.

She was running now, forging upward, and I could sense her fear, as I followed, but fear that was used and channeled, fear that could get us out.

It was a wide room with long windows and high ceilings, where we found ourselves. A dining hall, with chairs stacked on tables, a bar, shelves with glasses and plates—the park café, for God's sake—and way beyond outside, I glimpsed the moon on the lake, the shadows of trees. A bird flapped its wings in a tree and then flew low over the water, its form silhouetted for a split second against the night sky.

I forced the lock on the outside door, and we were out on the stone balustrade.

"Main gate," said Jane.

And I knew where that was—from the old days, when the park had been a place to relax and stroll—where you didn't worry if someone was about to kill you. Why is all that so hard to remember?

We had to climb the iron railings, but even as we did so, I could see the car. A tiny Fiat almost buried under piles of autumn leaves, a strange foreign animal, stiff and cold in the darkness. I felt the bonnet. It must have been there for hours. Card had come another way.

She got in and started the ignition.

"Isn't anyone supposed to be here?" I asked.

"Be grateful no one is. This stretch—we're on our own, but we haven't got far to go."

I didn't like the sound of that. Card put in the clutch, and we clattered down the hill toward the main highway. The roads were still damp but deserted, the street lamps dead, and the car sounded like an angry sewing machine, attacking the silence of the city. I held the gun tight in my jacket pocket, certain I'd need it.

For the first time, I took a good look at Card. She was wearing black overalls, a hairband, constantly glancing in the mirror. I could see her hands clamped tight on the steering wheel. She was losing confidence fast.

We crossed the Vistula, and I looked back toward the center and the old town. As I watched, the streetlights came on again, no carnival of light but as dim and ineffectual as before, returning the city to its orange hue.

You don't just shrug off a half-century of dreariness. Not here. There are too many unhappy ghosts in this city. Too many that had died from unnatural causes; and I had no wish to join them.

Card had served a purpose in getting me out of the hotel. It was time to change roles.

"Stop the car, Jane."

"What the hell are you talking about?" She kept her hands on the wheel and shot me a furious glance.

"You heard me—pull up. Or I'll force the car off the road."

She came off the bridge and stopped at the bottom of the slip road.

"Get out," I said. "I'm going to drive. You forget that the last journey you arranged for me left some unfortunate side effects. Two of them. Russians. Very dead."

She got out, and I slid over into the driver's seat. She crossed in front of the car and sat in the place I'd vacated.

"You're crazy, Edward. I had nothing to do with that murder. I told you before you left that the whole thing was out of control. I didn't know whom I could trust." She turned to face me. "I still don't."

"Your weapon, Jane."

"I don't have one."

"Give it to me. . . ." And I removed the gun from my jacket and rested it on my thigh, pointing straight at her. She reached into her tunic and produced an automatic, from what looked like a shoulder holster. I laid it on the floor near the pedals.

"Where did you get this?"

"The embassy," she said. "That's where I've come from." She looked around quickly. "We can't just sit here. We have to get moving. There are people looking for you even now."

"Who?"

"Your friend Coffin, for one. We started monitoring traffic from the U.S. embassy this morning. A lot of it—high-speed, state-of-the-art stuff, bouncing frequencies all over the dial. But our computers broke it this afternoon, thanks to luck—and an old friend in Langley. You see, Coffin wasn't going through normal channels. He's part of some freelance operation no one seems to know anything about. Either that or it's so high priority they don't dare to tell us. Anyway, about ten this evening he was getting frantic, calling everyone, sending eyes-only telegrams all over the state of Virginia. He wanted to pull you in, sweat you, and then put out a full alert in Moscow for your mother." She paused.

"What happened?"

"He got his authorization about twenty-five minutes ago."

"Who from?"

"We don't know—and we didn't have time to ask. That's why I moved when I did."

"And you were able to get the power cut off to the whole suburb of Mokotow and find your way into the hotel and out again? Come off it, Jane."

"I called in a lot of favors. What do you think? That we never had decent networks in Poland." She laughed. "They were always the best here. And no shortage of volunteers. We had our people all over the place—the telephone exchange, power stations, the police and the party. If ever the word had come, Warsaw could have been ours inside twelve hours. They're still there. Until we know what's going to happen to Europe."

I remember looking at her in disbelief. "And you knew exactly where to find me?"

"Of course we did. The Poles can find anyone in this city—they've been doing it for decades. The fact that you were in the party hotel was just a bonus. The first, I might add."

"And now?"

"A safe house."

"How safe? Who knows about it?"

"Me and one other person in London. We bypassed the embassy on this one. It seemed the safest thing to do."

"I doubt it very much. Where is this place?"

"Saska Kepa. It's a house . . ."

"I know where Saska Kepa is. You better tell me how to get to the house. But we're going to stop before we get there."

We drove for another five minutes. Card had been right. It wasn't far. The houses were large and modern and never built for the proletariat. They belonged to the pampered diplomatic quarter—where the Communists had always concentrated the little charm they had. Presents for the good diplomats who didn't dirty their hands with Western slander. And sweeteners and plenty of persuasion to those who did. In any case—not a good place for a safe house. The area would already be crawling with security.

As we crossed a main road, she told me to pull over.

"About thirty yards up on the left—there's a turning. See it? The house is the fourth on the right."

"You've been there?"

"Of course."

"Is there a back entrance?"

"There's a garden."

"You're coming with me."

We took the second street on the left, and I counted the houses. Mostly, there were front gardens and gates, and little alleys to the rear. In the fourth house, the upstairs lights were burning. At the side, I could see high railings and an iron door. We'd have to go over the top.

Card went first. I could see she was a lot fitter. The climb was easy for her. She dropped soundlessly into the shadows of the garden. It took me longer, and I made more noise. We knelt on the ground and listened, but there was no movement.

The second fence was lower, but now there was less cover, and the moon was coming in and out of the clouds, flashing shadows along a wide grass lawn. Thirty yards from the back of the safe house, we stopped and lay on the freezing ground. There were no lights, no sign of any human presence.

We gave it five minutes, maybe more—and then, without warning, Card moved. I lay there for an extra few seconds, suddenly feeling the tiredness, shaking my head from side to side to stay alert. But even as I began to raise myself, I saw something that made me freeze—a flash of white, the movement of another figure. Card gave a shout, but there must have been a hand over her mouth, for the sound hardly carried, across the garden. And then there was silence.

The back of the house was in shadow. But I could make out a low veranda, with an entrance from a row of French windows. It seemed likely she had been grabbed as she stepped inside. I was looking hard for a light or a movement—some sign of what was happening.

And then it struck me, lying there, that I didn't need to go after Card. She could take her chances. She knew the risks. She probably defined them. And if I just turned my back and crawled away, there was a chance I'd make it to the border—I had one avenue still open. One chance. One lifeline that might still be there. Jane Card wasn't my battle.

When I have thought about it since, it was the scream that changed my mind. The pitch, the intensity, the primeval cry of fear and pain—and I couldn't let that go, whatever else I had done. In the nights to come, I could not have found peace of mind, or purpose, had I run away and left her. A young woman I had once known, and once loved, calling out from a house in Warsaw.

So I ran to the veranda, quietly, the gun in my hand—and I felt the kind of sharp, intense focus that you rarely if ever experience in normal life. All thought and energy and instinct channeled into one purpose. And something extra—the feel of stepping outside your own limits, becoming someone else. Hard to shake once you know it.

The screaming had stopped, but in my mind it still jangled. I went in through the French windows and stood for a moment, listening. The room was dark and comfortable; there was soft carpet. A doorway into the kitchen. It smelled clean and bare. Beyond—the dining room, a hall, and the stairs—and from the landing I could see a light.

I have never moved so carefully. I felt each step, and if once or twice I wavered, it was the gun that led me on—outstretched—like a pathfinder.

At the top step, I knelt and eased myself on my knees toward the source of light. As I turned into the corridor, I could see through the door into a bedroom. Card was sitting in a chair. She had her back to me, so I had no idea of her expression. But she was quite motionless and seemed to be staring toward her attacker on the far side of the room.

There wasn't time to think this through. I edged my way toward the door, then threw it open, hurled myself onto my stomach, and prepared to fire.

And it wasn't that I knew the man that prevented me from pulling the trigger. Nor was it his expression of surprise. To be honest—it was simply the knife sticking out of his white shirt, round about the breast pocket, and the fact that to all the world, and to me in particular, he was already dead.

Chapter Twenty-four

When I think back to that moment, I conclude she must have thrown the knife from some distance, for there was no blood visible on her clothes or hands—as she stood in the middle of the room.

I looked around, trying to understand what I was seeing. There was soft, yellow light from a bedside lamp, full-length curtains, fine sheets and covers—and in the chair a fattish, middle-aged interloper from another world. And yet, in that first instant, nothing fitted together. There were disjointed little pieces of life and death in that room—no common thread.

"Edward? I just killed this man. I never did anything like that. For God's sake, say something!"

I shook my head. It's one thing to offer comfort to the dying, quite another to try to console a killer.

I took a closer look at the figure in the chair. There was more blood than I'd have expected. And you think living is a messy business until you see someone like that—dying in violence, with the life skewered out of him, washing away over the chair and the carpet. This body had offered no dignified exits, hidden no secrets, shut down its functions for all the world to see. And he would have been Coffin's man—in some shape or form. Large bet on that. Someone who was to pick us up and wait—and not be too fussy about the methods he used. I could ration my sympathy.

"Jane!"

She had slumped against the wall. And I went across and shook her.

"I'm okay," she said. "Really."

I led her out to the car. The sky had lightened, and there was a dampness in the air. And her face had gone very pale. For a second, I wondered . . . how did you do this, Jane? You had to be trained for it. Had to have practiced. You can't just chuck around a carving knife and hope to kill someone.

We crossed the river, slowly this time. Then the back roads, up the cobbled hill toward the old town. Quiet. No one on the streets. By then I was already planning the route east, out through the gray suburbs and the dormitory lands, the poor peasant hamlets, the little horse-drawn communities—and the crossing point into Russia. Three hours to Lublin—and then we'd go over near Chelm—if I made the call. If there was someone to hear it.

Only a few lights were burning in the Main Post Office. As we entered, the night ladies were gossiping behind the glass partitions. One was cutting her nails with a giant pair of scissors. And I paid for a call to London and recorded a message in Russian on an answering machine I had never believed I'd use.

I was coming back to Russia. I needed a contact. I needed them to bring me in.

As we left the box, I said to Jane, "You knew, didn't you?"

"No," she replied. "But it doesn't seem to matter anymore, does it?"

The countryside came out of the shadows as we drove, and the sun appeared briefly over Russia.

She fell asleep, a hand wedged between her cheek and the window. She had always lain on her hand. I kept glancing at her because, even in moments of chaos, you don't forget you've loved someone. She would always be Jane from the days in Prague. We're not strangers, never strangers. Whatever we did had a meaning built in from the past. I couldn't leave her in danger. Even the Jane who killed. I couldn't leave her, the way she once left me. Now when she knew who I'd become.

For me, it began to feel like the road to Russia. Not the country so much as the old stirrings of fear, the tension in the gut, the foreboding that lies like a deadweight across your life. Russia was close. Russia was coming.

It's a fear of the unknown and unpredictable—even to those who know it. It's the extremes of cold and heat, of passion and cruelty. There will always be a danger in Russia. There will always be brilliant men and women who will light up the universe with ideas and discoveries and then go and murder their next-door neighbors or ax their children. Always a point in Russia where reason snaps, where the nerve goes, where the lifeline breaks. That's who they are.

There were many reasons why I had wanted to make this journey. For it brought to a head the conflict that has dominated my life for so many years. A conflict between duty to my family and duty to the state in which I lived.

I welcomed the chance to face it, to bring all the memories out of the drawer and lay them in the light. And really, when I thought about it, I didn't regret what I had done. I regretted the cost of it. I regretted the necessity.

For a number of years, you see, I was obliged to cooperate. Yes, I could have refused. But I didn't. A life depended on me. Not a country, or a system or a set of values. But a single human life, that I felt compelled to try to save. The only way open to me.

Now at last, with all the political changes, there was a choice. The accepted rules no longer applied, walls had come down, systems had shifted, and the old warlords would be running for cover, shedding their clothes, their positions and disguises, digging in where they might never be found.

Before they did, I would break their hold on me once and for all time. If not I would die in the attempt—and in that, too, would find some justice.

Part Two

Chapter Twenty-five

I SUPPOSE IT was my tutor at university who began it. Such an amiable man, with nothing too complicated to impart—a cultivated laziness about him that blended well with his students, who didn't need to cultivate it.

We had gone to the pub on a winter evening after our weekly tutorial. It was one of his favorites—the Ship and Shovel, under the arches at Charing Cross. I well remember the place because the trains would rattle overhead every few minutes and drown out the conversation. I must have missed at least half of what he said. But I heard enough.

"You should go to Russia sometime," he said, swilling his beer and ordering us both another. His name was Michael Dillon, and he had a penchant for those dreadful hipster trousers we used to buy from Harry Fenton all those years ago. They only did them in red and blue. And he had the red ones.

I took the beer and shook my head. "Two things," I told him. "My mother would have a heart attack, or at the very least, feign one—and second, it's too expensive."

Dillon upended his glass and turned the conversation to other things.

He was, I recall, a pretty good tutor. Young enough and

single enough to be one of us—but with an intellect and knowledge that stood out even among his colleagues. He had spent a year in Russia on a research fellowship, studied the female population, he claimed, lain back a lot and thought of Britain.

"I mean, you're half Russian," he said to me. "You ought to know. Except it's not good to be hanging around with emigrés the whole time. The language is changing, the outlook's changing. The things they talk about. You know, you get the kind of conversation in Moscow that you don't get anywhere else. Sharp, right down to the wire. The basics of life, laid out and dissected. Do we die or get fucked? Do we fight or give in? . . ."

"Heady stuff."

He nodded. "Now especially."

We left the pub and walked slowly toward the bus stop. "If you can get round your mother," he said. "There's a cheap scheme going, sort of language course we could get you on. That's if you're interested. You wouldn't have to sit through boring lessons, but you might get to talk to some people."

My bus came first, and I climbed to the top deck and watched him, standing there in his hipsters, canvas bag on the shoulder and thick curly hair. Michael Dillon could help me get to Russia—but he had no idea why I wanted to go.

You see—I hadn't made any announcements about my father. Dad was for me alone. My loss, my dream, the piece of my childhood that had never lain still.

Many times, I would see him again on that weekend in Gdansk—like a prisoner on parole, Dad on a chain, and we putting our arms around him, because he was still ours, trying to pull him back, hold on to him for the little time we could. The man who gave us life and then took his own somewhere else.

And for me there was often real agony in those memories. Years later they would float in front of me, and my pulse would quicken and the sweat break out on my hands and face.

I could never leave the memory alone, and the final sight of Dad, walking out of that Polish hotel room, the two minders way down the corridor, standing in silhouette against the dirty windows. What a cheap country and what a cheap and tatty system it had been—and I could see his face turning as they ushered him down the stairs. What was in his expression—an appeal, a farewell? I wasn't close enough to see—and Mother was holding me in case I ran after him. Dad, Dad. Don't go!

Are you still alive?

None of this would I tell to Michael Dillon—or anyone else. So no one would know why I wanted to see Russia. Not Mother. Not my fellow students. Not a single soul. That's what I believed in that far-off winter term—in my youth and my perfect stupidity.

I told Mother I was going to Switzerland. "Camping with some friends" was the phrase.

She had raised an eyebrow. "Camping with a girl, I suppose."

My smile had been answer enough.

And I had gone away and packed my bags for Moscow, light-headed in the knowledge that I had duped the world and the world had swallowed it.

I well remember the summer days that led up to my departure. The term dragged on—there were exams and meetings and parties—but I was already in Russia.

I would travel back home, imagining that I was on a tram, heading out into the Soviet suburbs. No one would know of my mission. I would bury myself in my cover, dig deep into Moscow life, and search for my father. Not until they showed me his grave, not until I had seen his personal possessions and spoken to witnesses would I believe that Dad no longer lived on this planet.

And yet there was another feeling as well—the irresistible drawing power of this country that was forever out of reach, marked gray. Right from the time I could walk, Mother had told me I would never walk in Russia. The country was quicksand. It was Sodom and Gomorrah—it was the Devil's own playground. I would not be setting foot within a hundred miles of its borders. Did I understand that and had she made herself clear?

The night before I left, I had coffee with Michael Dillon at his flat in Bayswater, with the papers all over the floor and unwashed coffee cups. I recall being disappointed at the clichéd chaos. There was the lingering smell of marijuana, the clutch of heavily indented cushions on the floor, ashtrays spilling onto the carpet—all the signs of a little gathering of the like-minded, taking their brains for a jog around the room.

"Don't forget soap," said Dillon, "and toilet paper, and a few Biros to give out as presents."

"Got them."

He sipped his coffee. His face looked cold and fragile. "I had a quick word on the phone with your course director in Moscow."

"What about?"

"Just told him what a wonderful fellow you were—and that he shouldn't piss about and waste your time practicing perfective verbs."

"How did he take it?"

"He took it, said you'd be tested for your linguistic skills and then assigned to appropriate courses."

"What does that mean?"

"Probably a bird with big tits and a book of Lenin's quotations. How should I know?"

"Well, you're the one who got me into this. . . ."

"And I shall get you out again. Don't worry, Edward, relax. Just think of it as a visit to the Third World. Don't expect too much. Upper Volta with rockets . . ."

"And tits."

"Good," said Dillon. "Nothing wrong with your priorities."

And then it was up to Aeroflot—with that straight-up, straight-down service, clumping us onto the Moscow runway.

At the gate the stewardesses said good-bye as if they hoped we'd take it to heart—and there was no one in the large German-built immigration zone to offer a welcome. Just the soldiers, pallid, ragged Caucasians, caps tilted far back on their heads, and the short, swarthy Asiatics. I knew I was abroad.

We were a group of a dozen students, from different parts of Britain. Four women, outnumbered by eight men—and none of us had ever been before.

Eric was the oldest—twenty-one—prematurely old, the

way serious people often are. He was working for a First, said he wanted to spend most of his time in the Lenin Library, hoped there wouldn't be endless lectures on friendship and meet-the-workers evenings.

Janet and Sandra had sat behind us and giggled for most of the journey. And now Janet was hunting through her rucksack, trying to find her passport.

We looked suitably proletarian, piling through passport control in our jeans and sneakers, the committed, the frivolous—and me.

Our luggage came on the carousel marked Ulan Bator—so we learned early on not to trust the printed Russian word. Customs insisted on counting all our money, making us turn out our pockets. It occurred to me that getting into the old Soviet Union was a bit like undergoing surgery.

But beyond Customs, behind the glass partition, I could make out the vision of a tiny and very beautiful woman, long brown hair swept back, colored blouse. I was aware of a flowing summer skirt and the instant reddening of my cheeks as she looked toward me. We walked through, and she stepped out of the crowd of assorted, anxious faces—and there was never any doubt that she had come for us.

Amid all the noise and shouting, she called us over, asked if we had had a good journey, and welcomed us to the USSR.

"I hope you enjoy many bright days in our homeland," she said, and laughed. And it was as if the sun had suddenly leaned out from behind a dark cloud. Moscow, it seemed to say, would be friendly and full of beautiful beings.

I have since concluded this was simply Nature's own special brand of deceit—and our illusion.

They were to feed us with zoolike regularity. That first night a bus carted us to a restaurant in town where they served the first in a series of dreadful chicken Kievs. But I scarcely noticed it. We sat alone in an auditorium the size of a circus tent and watched the crowds trudge past the net-curtained windows, as the sun fell away over the skyline.

And I couldn't remove my eyes from our guide, with the soft, tanned face and the smile and the pink lipstick. She was the contrast and yet somehow the key to this hot, dusty city, with its boulevards and crowds and vast expanses of darkness.

Bus again—and the radio played us out to the suburbs

with the balalaika and accordion, and the streetlights showed little but the shapes and shadows of the world around us.

I shared a room with Eric.

"Why you?" he asked. "I hoped it would be Sandra."

"Oh sure," I told him. "You wouldn't even know where to put it."

He went to sleep bitterly offended, and I lay awake thinking this was the most exciting day I could remember. I was alone in a hostile environment, a thousand miles from a friendly border. Dad's city. Dark and impenetrable. At about 3:00 A.M., I got up and stared out of the window. Three or four lights shone from a dismal block across a chasm of black. Without knowing why, I told myself Dad was alive.

In the morning, we rattled along the wide Leningrad Chaussée to a Romanesque building that sucked us in under its columns and into the dark stone corridors. The Moscow school of auto engineering, they said. The students were on vacation, but we, most emphatically, were not.

And there we joined a thousand people from other European countries, from Japan and the United States and Cuba, little realizing that we were the instruments of an impressive propaganda exercise. Only much later, when we were pictured on the main television news program, as the visiting world youth, thirsting for knowledge about our socialist counterparts, did we get an inkling.

But the first morning was for fun. Doughnuts, registration forms, little kits and pamphlets, books and folders—all free, free, free.

Only I couldn't help thinking they were the only things that were.

But the staff were making heroic efforts to be friendly. Go and see anything you want, ask any questions, we are simply delighted to help and assist and entertain. And there in teacher's chair was the beautiful guide from the day before, helping with the forms, giving out papers, filling the room with her smile.

"My name is Irina Semyonova," she announced. "I know who you all are from your pictures."

Eric turned to me. "What are you staring at? Have you never seen a woman before?"

"How many women have you seen like that?"

"Plenty," he said. "I'm actually going out with someone who looks very like her."

"Probably looks more like the chair she's sitting in."

Irina stood up and clapped her hands for silence, but the smile was still there.

"I think we should get started, ladies and gentlemen. Perhaps we will all read half a page from the Russian book I have given you—and then I can get an idea of your performance."

We took it in turns, but this was something I hadn't anticipated. I had assumed that by this time I'd be transferred to a different group—and I had no wish to be singled out as a fluent Russian speaker—difficult to explain away to Eric and the rest of the crowd.

I read my half-page, but I could feel the eyes of the class on me.

"Next," said Irina, when I had finished.

"Blimey," said Eric, under his breath. "Where did you learn that kind of Russian?"

By the end of the day, we had read twenty pages, studied grammar that I had known from the age of five, and carried on the kind of stilted conversation that would have had my mother crying with laughter. I was bored and frustrated.

As we left the class, I approached Irina, quietly and in Russian.

"May I talk to you?"

"Nothing would please me more, Edward." She laughed, and we waited until the other students had left the room.

Outside in the sunshine, the buses were assembling to drive us all to chicken Kiev. But here it was cool and quiet. Moscow seemed suddenly to be somewhere else.

"You speak excellent Russian." She turned from the window and stared at me. "Where did you learn it?"

"I'm sorry," I said. "There seems to have been a misunderstanding. I think I was supposed to be in another group. You see . . . I've spoken Russian all my life."

Irina went over to the desk and leafed through her papers.

"There is no mistake, Edward. You are listed in my class. I have no further information. . . ."

"I don't understand."

"Maybe it is just a question of bureaucracy. Sometimes there are details that get mislaid. By tomorrow I'm sure everything will be clear. Of course, I should be sorry to let you go. . . ." She was teasing me, and I could feel the blush spreading across my cheeks. "Perhaps we should join the others. Please, do not worry, Edward. Everything will be fine."

But I did worry. The next day Irina told me to wait behind, during the lunch break.

"Something is very strange, Edward. I myself spoke to the director this morning, and he has heard nothing about you. He says there are simply no other courses to go on. No one had any idea that you were fluent in Russian. I don't know what to suggest. . . ."

"But my tutor in London spoke to the director by telephone."

"I know nothing of this."

"Well, I must phone London then. . . ."

"It's very difficult."

"I have money. . . ."

"Edward—it's not a question of money. Sometimes you can wait thirty hours for a call. Sometimes you order it—and it doesn't come at all. It's very complicated. . . ."

Her voice trailed away . . . and I think I realized that I had met a brick wall. That was the thing about Russia—all the brick walls rising up out of nowhere, when you didn't expect them. Everything could be fine and easy and wonderful, and you round a corner and your nose is right up against the barrier. Your path blocked. No one to ask, no one at all. And in that moment, I had a sense of mounting anger and foreboding. I could see the wall, but there was nothing beyond it. Nothing to hold on to, no point of reference. There was the feeling that they can stop your life in its tracks any time they want to. A hand can reach out—and close your road. Far away I could sense the beginning of panic.

"I think I'll go back home."

"Edward, Edward . . ." She put out a hand to my shoulder. "Let us think this through calmly. Look, I have an idea. Tonight you come back to my flat for dinner, and we'll talk and see what's best to be done. Besides . . ."—and she was laughing again—"you can meet my daughter."

I remember thinking that hers was the kind of smile that could divert rivers. I looked into her eyes and breathed deeply, and the panic seemed to subside.

"You're twenty, aren't you, Edward?"

"Nearly twenty-one."

"Of course," she said. "I am thirty-three, but still really thirty-two."

We were driving in her Lada, shiny blue and ugly, standing out from the rusting, wounded hulks that shared the road with us. Some were simply dirty, others broken down, patched and plastered like invalids.

"You have to keep your car clean," said Irina. "Otherwise the militia can fine you. Don't you have that in England?"

We had left the city center behind. And for the first time, in the suburbs, I could see how they'd thrown it all together—people and concrete, power lines and chimneys, build-them-where-they-stand, and bugger the quality. No landmarks. No garages or shopping centers, no cinemas, just rows and rows of blocks, and the red slogans about the Twenty-first Party Congress, and how Soviets were the best but still had to do better.

At a crossroads, we turned off the main highway and bounced our way into the backlands, dirt-track lanes, humanized by a few trees and shrubs.

Into a dull, unnumbered block, and I followed her long summer skirt, captivated by the strangeness and the new sensations. I remember the noises of stress and strain from the lift, I remember the sharp smells and the peeling, cracking walls. Piles of rubbish in the corridors. Broken tiles and warped windows and doors. And yet, when Irina was with me, I saw little except her.

And that, I suspect, was the way they planned it.

Daughter Anna was seven. Grandmother, arthritic, bewhiskered, dressed in black, I put at about ninety-seven. And there was no husband anymore—gone, absented himself, casually dismissed by Irina as an unpleasant social tendency. "It happens a lot in our society, Edward." Not mentioned again.

She made *pelmyeni*—potfuls of it—a kind of Russian ravioli, filled with spiced meat, helped down with melted cheese. There was sharp white wine from Georgia, and when we'd eaten, the grandmother told stories about the war, and Anna tried to draw my portrait. I could feel Irina watching me—and when I looked up, she was smiling again, only there was something else in her eyes, a detachment or a distance that hadn't been there before.

Grandmother put Anna to bed, and they disappeared into the only other room in the flat and outside I could see the street lamps, stretching away in parallel lines to the edges of the city.

Irina told me about her time as a student. She talked of Moscow University in the seventies—years of passive accommodation between the rulers and the ruled. They paid people nothing, and the people did nothing in return—and along the flowery, faded wallpaper she pointed out the photographs of friends and colleagues, expectant young faces, still dreaming the Soviet dream.

She told me of the intense competition to succeed. "All of us were streamed, Edward. If we had any abilities at all, they would find them and nurture them, and try to make us the best. . . ."

"And if you didn't . . ."

"Then all you had to do was believe." Her face had set hard, and the smile had gone. "And if you had doubts, you were to keep them to yourself, bury them so far out of sight that they couldn't be seen and couldn't be heard. Smile and go on smiling and recite your lines, as if your life depended on them." She bit her lip. "And sometimes it did."

"And now?"

"Now is 1982, and the old men are still in power, and nothing will ever change."

"You believe that?"

"I don't know how to believe anything else."

Irina got up and made tea in glasses, with the leaves swirling around at the bottom. "My God, Edward!" She looked at her watch. "Do you know what time it is? We've been talking for hours!"

And we laughed at the same time because it was around one in the morning, and we both had the feeling we had crossed a small boundary. "It is better you stay here," she whispered. "I have drunk too much wine to drive, and I can't lose my license." So we made up a bed for her on the sofa, and I had a blanket and pillow on the floor. And when I turned off the light, she leaned down to me and kissed my cheek.

Only she didn't stop kissing me. And in a little while she rolled off the sofa, and I could feel her body moving along mine, quickly, urgently, as if time were running out.

I remember trying to respond in kind—but she had a momentum all her own. It was not an act of tenderness—by either of us. It was opportunity and timing, and an exploration of the unknown.

And after ten minutes, she went back to her makeshift bed, as if very little had happened.

For me, though, a lot had happened.

I didn't sleep until it was light. My mind was full of her and of Moscow—the new sensations, the stories, the sense of penetrating a life and a culture I had known only from the sidelines. For the first time, I felt something of my Russian background. For the first time, I felt I'd arrived.

I didn't go back to the hotel next day. It was Sunday, and we drove into the surrounding forests to a tiny wooden hut, which Irina called her dacha, and we lazed in a clearing in the sunshine and forgot about Moscow.

Later we ran through the woods, chasing each other and calling out, and when we returned to the hut, the grandmother had made pancakes, and we ate them with cheese and sour cream and cucumbers.

On an old radio, we listened to a concert from Moscow. The windows were open, and a warm breeze blew in from the East. We drank more wine and laughed at old Russian jokes about the food shortages; and it seemed to me that this was, after all, a place of beauty.

And the music? This was Dad's music, for, when I was a child, he would often sit listening to these melodies—his little collection of Russian records—Tchaikovsky, Rachmaninoff—and he would close his eyes in the flat in London and wander away into his other world. If you let it, he used to say, the music can take you home, it can play with you and comfort you, it can frighten you or make you sad. But you never know what it will do, he said. Not until it's happened. That is the mystery of it and the fascination.

As I listened to those same melodies that night, I believed I knew where Dad had gone.

We went to sleep—all of us in that single room. The old grandmother in the chair—I lifted her feet onto a stool and covered her with a blanket—Anna beside her mother on a sofa, and me, once again on the floor, hearing the sound of crickets, trying to imagine a landscape that would stretch out all over Asia, that bordered China and India, that reached its way well inside the Arctic Circle.

It started out as a pleasant thought, but the more I reflected, the more daunting it became. Out of all the thousands of square miles, and millions of people, I would attempt to locate a solitary, sick old man—my father. The chances of success had to be minimal.

There was a hand shaking me a long time before I awoke. Far too early. Barely light. The new day at the end of a tunnel. And Irina was telling me to get up. We had to return to the city. I was expected in class.

I staggered out to the car, and we drove toward the bleak outlines of the city.

"Edward, it is so strange spending time with you. You speak perfect Russian, and yet you are someone else. A Soviet but not a Soviet. Different responses. Different eyes."

I could feel myself tense. "You never asked me where I learned the language—did you?"

"Didn't I?" She glanced at me quickly. "No, I suppose I never did."

On the edge of the suburbs, she stopped the car beside a metro station. "Edward, you have to get the train from here. I have an appointment. Get back to the hotel, and the bus will bring you in from there with everyone else. Can you find your way?"

" 'Course. No problem." And I watched her drive away, without a wave or a smile, and it seemed that Irina was no longer the beautiful woman who had lain against me. She, too, was someone else, going somewhere else—and the brick wall that is Russia was about to rise up and confront me.

I just didn't know where or how.

The hotel was quiet when I arrived, just after 7:00 A.M., and I knew Eric would be asleep. We didn't have to leave for another hour.

I took the lift to the twelfth floor. Room 126. And even in the corridor I knew something was wrong. The old crone who kept the keys had gone, not simply to the lavatory or for a cigarette, but her little substation had been closed down, the chair put away. None of her bric-a-brac on the table. No keys at all. And in her place on the sofa was a porter in uniform, much cleaner than the other porters, creases in his trousers, shaved cheeks, a paragon of elegance and decorum.

"I'd like the key to one twenty-six," I told him, and it was the way he laughed that made me seize inside and expect the worst.

"You're with that student group, aren't you?"

"That's right."

"Well, they've gone, haven't they?"

"What do you mean gone?" And I could feel the nausea rising in me from a long way down. . . .

"Trip. Gone off on some sort of trip. How should I know?"

"Well, when are they back?"

He shrugged and laughed again. "Who knows anything in this fucking country?"

He dug into his pocket and threw me the key as if he'd been waiting for me to appear; inside the room I could see Eric had gone. His suitcase, clothes, books, the little mountain of debris that he collected and kept by his bed—all cleaned out and disappeared.

I opened the window, but there was no breath of air. Had I forgotten about a trip out of Moscow? I certainly hadn't read the brochures—because I didn't think they applied to me. Maybe this had all been planned well in advance and simply passed me by. What an idiot!

Go to the institute, I told myself. There's an explanation for everything. Has to be. You have only to ask the right person, find the right person. Simple mistake.

I almost laugh when I think about the way I comforted myself, believing I'd find answers in Moscow, believing there were "right" people, believing you could apply Western rules and logic.

You don't go to Russia for answers. You go for questions. You go for puzzles and riddles that will perplex you and challenge you now and for all time.

I didn't know anything then.

A shower and a change of clothes calmed me down, and I took the lift to the lobby and headed for the metro.

This is a place governed by rules, I told myself. Rules and laws. People behave in quite discernible patterns. I looked around at the cheap check shirts and the thick stockings and the faces that knew it all better than I ever would. Remember, I was only twenty. I could have done with a kind word.

I walked the last leg to the institute and took my time. It would be at least an hour before the staff arrived, and then the canteen would open, and there would be a small chance of something edible for breakfast. On the streets, I passed the occasional Pepsi kiosk, a bakery, supermarkets containing all the things you would never want, if you were anywhere else. Shopfronts proclaiming "shoes," "watch repairs," "flowers"—but no breakfast.

The driveway to the institute was empty. I pushed open the main door and let it slam shut, hearing the noise echo down the corridors and up the wide staircase that should have been crammed with people.

I took the staircase at a run, but I knew the classroom would be shut, the door locked. And in that moment, I could feel the brick wall, rising up out of nowhere, blocking my path. Russia was closing off one road and would now attempt to put me on another. But I couldn't just wait for it to happen. I remember standing in the corridor thinking, I'll go to the British embassy. There's nothing for it. Tell them what's happened. Get them to sort it.

It's what I would have done, if she hadn't been standing by the main door as I came down. The sun lit her back, and her face was in darkness, and for a moment we stared at each other without speaking.

She had changed her clothes and put on her makeup, but there was no smile. And just the way a flower closes at the end of the day—so Irina had closed and her beauty had gone. It wasn't by chance that she happened to be there. It wasn't by chance that everyone else had disappeared on some "trip." Nothing happens in Russia by chance. Nothing attacks you, harms you, or does you wrong unless it's meant to. Right up close to her, I could see that she was meant to.

"You better come with me, Edward."

"What's going on, Irina?"

She held the door open for me.

"I'm staying here until you tell me what's happening."

"Don't be silly—you don't understand anything."

I turned my back on her and went and sat on the staircase, in what I hoped would be taken as an act of defiance.

But she simply walked back down the stairs and out into the street, and by the time I caught up with her, she was getting into the car.

"I don't have time for nonsense," she told me. "I can take you to see someone—or you can stay here and look after yourself. Your choice."

"Don't patronize me," I told her—which sounds very strange in Russian, because they're all longing to be patronized by someone. "I'll come and see your person—then I have my own plans."

"Please yourself."

I got in, and Irina inserted the car into thick traffic.

She was silent the whole journey, but from time to time she nodded philosophically to herself as if this were somehow a meaningful journey through life—and not part of the disgraceful operation it turned out to be.

I now know that we traveled north, taking the Garden Ring and then veering off near the Kazan station. Maybe it doesn't matter, but I wanted to have the details clear in my mind.

We stopped in the courtyard of a gray block, six stories high, and I could see at once it was a hospital. White coats were passing in and out of the main door. But as we entered, there was no sharp smell of disinfectant, no sense of a clinical environment. A lot of people hurrying around between life and death—some visibly closer to one state than the other. Not much order, not much method. Belt and braces operation, because that's all they had.

Lift to the second floor. Then a corridor and a small waiting room with a section of wall covered by curtains.

Irina tells me to sit down. I ignore her.

"You may find this something of a shock," she says. "I would sit down, if I were you."

And I feel suddenly very cold, in that dry, hot room. A doctor comes in—maybe he wasn't a doctor—he wore a white coat. And then I realize suddenly that he hasn't come to talk to me; he's watching me with professional interest, sizing me up, waiting for me to react to something. Just standing by the door, hands in his pockets. Doesn't even say hallo.

There's a nod between him and Irina, and he reaches for the curtain and pulls it back.

And it's only with the passage of time that I can look at any of this dispassionately.

I'm staring now through a glass partition, and beyond it is another room, from which a strange orange light is emanating. I need a few seconds to focus.

There's a bed in there, and on it, half-sitting, half-lying, is a man with tiny wisps of gray hair on his bald head. The outlines of his face, the set of the jaw. I'm drawn to that face, because it's so thin, and without any doubt belongs to someone so sick. . . .

If it weren't for the orange light . . . and the fact that I'm shivering from the cold . . . I'd be certain . . . Only now, without any warning, something is going terribly wrong. I'm fighting for air. The floor is being wrenched away from under me and I'm falling fast and there's nothing to brake me, nothing to slow my descent, out of control, out of my mind—because in there on that bed is my father—no one else, no one else in the whole world, but the man who was dead, confirmed dead, with pieces of paper and stamps on them, somewhere in Russia, years and years ago . . . my father, mine, mine.

Even as I lie half-conscious on the floor, I keep repeating this to myself, hearing the scream of my own voice in the far distance.

* * *

And now I know why a doctor was present.

They must have lifted me onto a bed, for I couldn't have crawled there by myself.

It was a different room. First thing I looked for was the curtained window, but the walls were bare. The two of them were standing by the door—and they turned quickly as I sat up.

I've never been so angry and desperate—like a child, shouting at them, slamming my fist on the bed frame, yelling questions and accusations that I have long since forgotten. Black moment in my life. Black moment in a little white room.

Irina sat me at a table and talked calmly, and after some minutes I began to take it in—first the words, then the meaning, and finally the implication of it all. So very clear and simple when it's distilled for you by the people with the power and the knowledge—and you have none.

So their version was the only one I ever had—full of holes, as I knew it had to be, a patchwork construction of lies and truth, sewn together to keep me warm, and compliant—something to believe in and act on, in the times when I needed a faith.

Wrong and inadequate—it was all I had.

She told me it was Dad's decision to announce his "death." He wanted us to get on with our lives, not sit for years, waiting for letters, hoping for things that could never be.

"He loves you very much," Irina said. "It was an act of great sacrifice. For a long time, he was unable to take this decision. Many people counseled him against it—but in the end he did not wish to listen."

"If he loved us so much, he could have come back—or called us to live with him. We would have come to Russia. . . ."

"He wanted you to have opportunities and benefits that were not available over here. He wanted the best for you. Is that not a natural feeling?"

"And you needed his work, his brains. You didn't have anyone with the knowledge that he had." I got up and walked around the room. I didn't need Irina's editorials—bad enough that she was the only source for information.

"What's he doing here? What's the matter with him?"

"He has been sick for some time. He has prostate cancer. He needs a lot of medication. . . ."

"I must see him, speak to him. For God's sake, I need to look after him. . . ."

The doctor moved forward into the conversation.

"That would not be wise at this point. He will need to be prepared before such a meeting. Otherwise, the consequences. . . ."

"What do you care about consequences?"

"I am a doctor, trying to look after my patient. That is my only concern. . . ."

"The same way the psychiatrists look after all your dissidents."

He smiled. "There is no point repeating Western propaganda. It is not the issue here."

"What is?"

"How to help your father," said Irina. "How best to ensure that he gets the care he needs."

"I want to see him now."

"That is not possible. He has already been transferred back to a sanatorium outside Moscow. He is brought here once a week for radiation treatment, but he lives in much more comfortable surroundings."

"When can I see him?"

"Soon. Very soon." And she looked at the doctor, as if expecting him to comment. But it was a look that said, "We've got him; he's ours."

I decided the day would come when I'd ram those thoughts down their collective throat.

We returned to Irina's flat, but the daughter and grandmother had gone.

"You should stay here from now on," she said. "I will leave you a phone number where I can be found. If I'm not there, someone will take a message. I will call either around midday or at seven in the evening. At other times, you may go out and do as you wish. . . ."

"What for? What is all this for?"

"When I hear from the doctors that you can see your father, we will drive out there. I call them twice a day, and then I call you. It's logical isn't it?"

I looked around the flat. "Are you KGB?"

"Would you hate me more if I was?"

"No. You deceived me. It doesn't matter who you worked for."

"Good." She turned to the door.

"Let me ask you one thing. . . ."

"No—no, wait a minute." She raised her hand, and there was anger spreading out over the cheeks I had once thought so beautiful. "No, let me tell you one thing, Edward. You may feel cheated and deceived, and maybe you have been. But don't think you're the only one in this country. Your father is alive. There's hope—I don't know how much. But there's some. Most people I know don't have a father anymore, because of all the stupid decisions, and all the purges and killings and wars we've had to go through. Think of that, when you go to bed and condemn us all. Just think."

I listened to the lift clattering its way downstairs—a dull clunk, the squeak and the slam of the doors. And Irina was gone, taking her anger with her.

The outburst hadn't done much for me. The blurring of issues, the terrible sentimentality to which even the cruelest of Russians subscribe—the lie chain, where one lie is used to spawn and justify another—an endless cycle where the truth plays no role of any kind.

Her Russia—the Russia I faced then on my own.

I was allowed to see my father just one more time. But he didn't know me. He was sitting in a wheelchair in the garden of the sanatorium, being fed from a spoon—only his mouth must have been painful, for he kept licking his gums, and the surgeon told me there were sores from the chemotherapy.

"This is a bad period," he said. "There are good periods too. Sometimes he's in remission for weeks, months. But it is strange—there is no pattern to his illness."

Later, when Dad fell asleep, I sat in the garden and took his hand and thought us back to the life we had shared so many years before. His hair had almost gone, his cheeks were sallow and so delicate, the forehead lined by the torment of pain—but the memories of him were fresh and unspoiled by time. Dad, who had got cross with me on the beach at Bournemouth when I stepped on his foot, Dad who would sit sternly at the kitchen table and remind me of my manners, Dad who would run after all the footballs that I kicked in all the parks, on all the Sunday afternoons, in all the rain and the cold, in all the best times of my childhood. I could see his smile and hear his shouts and feel the arm once again on my shoulder.

"Do you remember?" I asked him, and watched the sleeping face, hoping he felt no pain.

What would a son not do to make his father well again?

I have posed that question to myself, over and over again, for so many years.

My suitcase was in the back of her car, and she was driving me to the airport.

"I'm not ready to leave. . . ."

"You have to," she told me.

"I want to look after him."

"We will look after him."

She pulled over to the side of the road. It was a six-lane highway outside the city limits. An endless stream of trucks droned past.

"This is as good a place as any, Edward."

"For what?"

"For what I have to tell you—the rules, the modus vivendi from now on."

"I don't understand. . . ."

"It's very simple, Edward. You want to help your father, so help us to do what we can for him. We will get him the best medical care we have, we will buy the drugs he needs for hard currency—Flutamide, it's called—we will extend and humanize his life to the best of our abilities."

She paused, and I remember looking out of the window, watching those trucks and buses grinding out of the city in the heat and the perma-dust. This may have been the airport road, the pathway out, but not to the Russians. Not to the people who should have been free to move as they pleased. Not to Dad.

However she dressed it up, this was to be a shoddy little arrangement—a dying man, given comfort, or denied it, according to a political whim. What could they get for him, as he eked out his days? What was he worth when they turned the screw?

"One day, you'll get a call, Edward, and someone will mention my name, and you will do as they ask."

I kept looking out of the window.

"We will keep to our word, and you will be given progress reports from time to time—another visit, when it can be arranged. I would not advise you to tell anyone about our understanding—especially not your mother."

She drove me to the airport, and I took my suitcase from the backseat and walked away without looking at her.

Five hours later I was in London. I remember climbing out of the taxi, opening the front door, and calling out to Mother—but she wasn't there.

I was glad of that. The house seemed cool and clean after Moscow, and somehow smaller than I remembered.

I opened my bag and in that moment took a step back from it. Right on top of my clothes were a box of Swiss chocolates and a handful of postcards from Geneva.

So they knew I had told Mother I was going to Switzerland. They knew I'd lied to her. They knew it all—and they would use it when it served their interests.

I didn't really need any reminders of that—but Fate sometimes presses home her points, just to make sure you understand them.

When the university term restarted, I went looking for my tutor, Michael Dillon. In his office was a man I hadn't met before, very un-Dillon, clean-shaven and suited, who said he had taken up a new vacancy. I visited the dean, but he was too busy to see me. I knocked at the door of the Senior Common Room and found another of the Russian tutors, who came out into the corridor and stood sorrowfully, his hands behind his back, as I asked if Dillon had really been replaced.

"I'm afraid so," he replied. "Michael was killed on a climbing holiday about four weeks ago. It was an awful shock to us. No one even knew he was a mountaineer.

"Do you want to sit down for a moment?" he asked. "You must be. . . ." He looked away and rubbed his eyes. "I'm so sorry. Michael was in Switzerland on a two-week holiday, just near Geneva. Never been there myself. Dreadful, dreadful shame. We really never knew him, you know. I mean, not properly."

I stood in the corridor, long after he'd gone away, because there didn't seem anywhere to go. There was no one to tell—and even if there had been, what in the name of God Almighty would I have said?

Chapter Twenty-six

"So now I'm telling you."

Jane Card leaned forward and wound down the passenger window. We were southeast of Warsaw in flat, wide-open country, splashing in and out of tiny dog-turd villages, overgrown with weeds.

There was no one behind us. No car for miles around. Just plenty of horses and carts and piles of coal on street corners. Poland seemed to be busily regressing into the nineteenth century.

"I think I understand a little more," she said quietly.

"I'm glad one of us does," I replied. "Look, Jane, just understand I'm doing this for my father. I want to find him and get him out. Mother's all right. Seeing her at the cemetery made me realize she can look after herself. Dad can't. Never could. I have to bring him home."

She was silent for a moment, picking her words. "That trip to Russia. They took away all the joy of finding him, didn't they?" She put a hand on my arm. "I don't blame you for making a deal."

"That's nice of you. Her Majesty's government may not feel so kindly disposed."

"Things are changing. . . ."

"Tell me about it. . . ."

"You'll tell *me,*" she said gently. "You'll tell me."

On the outskirts of Lublin, we stopped at a motorway café and took on petrol. I'd been unfair about the regression. There was no comparison with the years of Communism. Waitresses waited, food was cooked, not savaged. You were the client, instead of the inconvenience.

We sat and ordered and watched the new capitalists making money.

But Jane had little appetite. "There's so much I still want to ask you. . . ."

"Then ask. We may not get the chance again."

"I want to know about your father. Is he still alive?"

"I wish I knew. I was negotiating to bring him to the West. They said they'd let him come to London. Then came the coup attempt—and I've heard nothing since. That's why I fixed up the business trip to Moscow, with Harry and his crowd. I needed a good excuse. . . ."

"And your mother never knew?"

I shook my head.

"That must have been hard."

"Yes and no. In many ways the hardest thing was to be open with her, because *she* was always so closed up. That was her legacy. Never knowing if she was opening her mouth too wide. Afraid *of* herself and *for* herself. Some of it rubbed off on me."

We paid—Western prices—and left.

Jane took over the driving, and I thought what a long way she had come in a couple of days—from driving her Ford Escort with all the children's toys, going shopping for the family, leading that normal life.

I turned in my seat and stared at her. "What exactly are your instructions now, Jane? We haven't had much time to talk about that. But what are you going to do at the border? If we make it."

She passed a truck, and the road settled out, straight and flat in front of us. Only a few trees across the endless fields.

"I'm to stay with you and protect our interests."

"What does that mean?"

"I don't know yet, Edward. The ground has moved. Our

interests have moved. London's aware of that." She shrugged. "But one thing I do know is that you could have left me back there in Warsaw to look after myself. . . ."

"You managed pretty well. . . ."

"Instead of which you came after me, into the house. Would have been a lot safer to get in the car and drive off. . . ."

"You don't know me very well. . . ."

"I used to know you very well," she said simply.

The rain came again, and she turned on the windscreen wipers, and I watched the clouds descending low over the countryside. "To answer your question. I'm cleared to go all the way with you—to Moscow or wherever." She smiled. "I'll play your girlfriend or any other role you'd like. After all, I've done it before." She paused. "Hold the wheel for me." And I looked on in amazement as she slid the wedding ring down her finger and put it in her bag.

The farther East you go, the more you feel the presence of Russia—or was it just me?

The roads were narrower now. In some places, just a single lane. Twice we had to pull onto the verge to let through Russian trucks and juggernauts. Freer movement—only there was plenty of deep-seated dislike along this border. And it struck me that you can never live quietly next to Russia. You sleep with one eye open. You watch your back and your front—and then you watch again.

In Lublin we checked into a hotel near the Catholic University. I felt a strange jolt from the past, taking just a double room for the two of us, the way we used to, years ago.

Upstairs Jane turned out her bag, a few wash things, some underwear, a fresh shirt. "I better go out and buy a couple of things," she said, "otherwise, you won't want to be with me for very long."

And although it was a casual remark, the look she threw me wasn't casual at all. A look and a question. Did I want to be with her or not?

"I'll come with you," I said, recalling that in the old days we'd have been in bed by now. We hadn't ever wasted time, although, somehow, it had run out all the same. And now I wanted very much to trust her. The new Jane, who could kill and organize and was cleared to go with me "to Moscow or wherever." Because when you fall into quicksand, you'd better have someone by you. And she was all I had.

We kept out of that room as much as possible. We ate and drank more than either of us wanted. We walked the stone-cobbled streets of Lublin till the crowds disappeared and the lights came on and the city lay down.

It was past midnight when we returned to the hotel and took the lift to the room.

The double bed had been turned down—clean, white, and acutely embarrassing to us both.

"You take the bed," she said, and colored.

"No, you have it," I told her. "I'm used to floors."

She went out to the bathroom and changed into a T-shirt. I took a blanket and pillow and lay down by the window.

When she came back, she didn't say anything, just slid between the covers, and I watched her in the darkness, lying on her back, looking up at the ceiling.

"We should leave in about three hours. . . ." I reminded her.

"You said that earlier."

"Just making sure . . ."

"Edward . . ."

"What?"

"I'm sorry for what happened back in Prague. I never had the chance to tell you that. I was very young. I didn't know anything then."

"It doesn't matter. . . ."

"It does."

"Let's not go through it again. . . ."

She sat up. "I just want to clear the air. . . ."

"Christ!"

"I always had the feeling you wanted me to be someone else. . . ."

"I believed you were someone else."

"And now?"

"You're not that person. . . ."

"So you have no feeling for me. . . ."

"For God's sake, Jane. You walked out on me years ago, when we'd talked about a future and planned for one—and in my mind we were already there. All that's over. We don't have to dredge it up again. There's too much else to worry about. Get some sleep."

She was silent for a while, and then she rolled over to the side of the bed, and in the light from the street lamps I could see her watching me.

"I didn't want to tell you this before, but I broke with my husband two years ago. That night you came to the house—you thought he was there. He wasn't. It was just the girls."

"Why didn't you say this earlier?"

"Because it's not important. Isn't that what you've just been telling me? There isn't anything between us anymore."

In that moment, it seemed we were both dancing the same tightrope. And I was getting up off the floor, climbing in beside her, drawing her close, with her head on my chest—and the sudden feel of a second heartbeat.

It wasn't like Irina, wasn't cold and somehow . . . procedural. And yet I could hold Jane at a distance. This time it would be one short night—and no investments for the future. I thought. . . . I can find the place in my heart that you once occupied and lend it back to you. And in the morning I'll kiss you and reclaim it. No permanence with us, Jane Card. We who run down secret corridors, under parks and lakes, away from people who would seek to do us harm. We will summon up the past—and for a little while we'll call it the present. We can hope for nothing more.

We dressed when it was still dark, in silence—unembarrassed.

"When you said, back in London, that only you could get my mother out, what did you mean?"

"I meant—only I could protect her."

"From the Russians? That's ridiculous."

"No, Edward. From our side. From the British."

Chapter Twenty-seven

The contact was set for a church. Always a church when you can, they would say. Churches are perfect. Come alone or in a crowd—early or late, you can wear what you like—because God doesn't mind—nor do we.

And, even better, you can whisper—and we can hear your confession.

I had picked St. Anne's because I knew it was there—knew the name because I'd passed it, on another kind of journey, many years before. It was about a mile from the hotel—down a narrow alley, lit by gas lamps, flanked by houses with sloping, cracking walls.

As we turned into the street, I felt almost confident. But it's funny how fast your mood can change.

I must have been a few steps ahead of Jane, for I felt a tug on my arm, and she was pulling me sharply up against the wall. For a moment, neither of us moved. As I looked around, I could see we were partially obscured from the rest of the street by the outcrop of the church. Jane was peering beyond me, trying to penetrate the darkness. I had seen nothing, so her senses had to be a lot sharper than mine.

"What?"

"I don't know. There seems to be a truck blocking the far end. I don't like the look of it."

"Leave it, Jane. We meet inside the church—and they take care of the rest. There's nothing more we can do."

I pushed open the main door, expecting it to groan and judder—but it must have been newly oiled, swinging smooth and soundless through its arc. We stepped into a narrow vestibule. A curtain covered the doorway to the nave, and I stood for a moment listening. There was no sound, but even a silent church will echo. Somehow you can hear the voices and the supplications long after they've died away.

We entered the body of the church. In the darkness, there was a lingering smell of incense—a reminder that this is where the living go to make their most personal investments, where hope is encouraged, where men and women raise their voices to chant and sing, and the Lord sits silent—the way He sat that early morning in Poland.

I can't go into a church without feeling guilt—for things left undone, for things I should not have done—how does it go? And as I stood there, waiting for the contact, my sullied conscience was right beside me.

Gradually my eyes adapted to the dark, and I could see the figure at the far end of the church, a presence more than a figure—light coat, motionless. A mourner? I wondered. A troubled soul? Maybe both.

And as I approached, the full lights came on, and I stood in shock at the rows of empty pews, the chandeliers and stained-glass windows and the sight of a woman back there, a simple patterned scarf around her head, hands folded on her lap. And although she sat still, there was about her no sense of peace. She had not come to pray, she sought no inspiration or strength, she had nothing to confess. She might as well have been sitting in a café, or on a bus. There were no concessions to her surroundings. All that lay so clearly in the confidence of her demeanor, in the set of the jaw, the tilt of the head.

"I thought you'd come to God in the end," said Irina in English. And her voice echoed out across the empty, ornate little church, cutting through the stillness. "As a matter of fact," she added unpleasantly, "I've been praying for you."

The church seemed suddenly cold. Irina must have taken away its warmth.

"You haven't introduced me to your friend," she simpered.

"I didn't think I needed to."

Irina turned her attention to Jane. "How nice of you to join us, Mrs. Card. I was a little bit surprised to learn you were going to be here as well—but now, I'm not really surprised by anything. You wouldn't have come in the old days; your masters wouldn't have let you—but now"—she threw her hands in the air—"now anything is possible in this grand new world of ours." She stood up. "It's time we were going."

"You haven't exactly disguised your presence here," I said.

"Bright lights keep the animals away." Irina was walking toward the door, stiffly, painfully, as if the last ten years had not been kind to her. "Unfortunately," she added, "there are plenty of animals around at the moment—British and American, mostly, and one or two others. But we have some old friends here. We can still put on a little show if we have to."

Even before she got there, the door was opened by a middle-aged man in sneakers and Windcheater—one of the old troopers, it seemed, quiet, thick-necked, made in the USSR for export when needed. They had rolled such people off the production lines in the thousands.

Beyond him—the van I had seen earlier, parked with its engine running; and along the street was the kind of show Irina had meant—a small band of plain-clothed security, placed at regular intervals, doing nothing to hide their automatic pistols. They would have been the ones to cordon off the streets around the church. And in a little while they would disappear back into the undergrowth from where they had come.

So the Communists still had their people. They were still a network, a band of the committed and the desperate, still turning out on special occasions to do the business. Only who was now the underdog?

We climbed in the back of the van and sat on the floor. It moved off immediately, riding fast and rough over the cobbles—the engine already hysterical, not built for speed or passengers.

Irina shifted uncomfortably on the floor. "All right, Edward," she said. "You wanted to meet. You made the call. Now you tell me why."

The two thin headlamps picked out the road and then one of them gave up. Maybe a stone had smashed it; maybe the bulb had gone. The driver didn't want to get out and check. Around us the darkness was total—the countryside deserted. No lights of welcome, no beacons, no friendly haven if it all went to hell.

Something ludicrous about running around the Polish countryside in a silly little van with only one headlight. Except the company wasn't ludicrous—and if I knew anything about Irina after ten years, it was simply that she meant business.

Besides, she held the key to my father.

We turned suddenly off the road and started bumping eastward. After a few minutes, the track disappeared completely, and we were crashing over open country, dodging trees and ditches. I looked across at Jane, and if she was worried, she didn't show it. She was gazing out, her eyes on the move, perfectly in control. She had plenty of strength—that one. But I couldn't help wondering what her interests really were—and what would happen when they diverged from mine.

After a few minutes, the road improved dramatically, and we were on a wide strip of concrete that could only have been part of a runway. At one end, I could make out a series of low buildings—like bomb stores, but otherwise it was overgrown and desolate.

The van pulled up, and Irina and I got out. She motioned for Jane to stay where she was, and we walked to the edge of the strip while I prepared what I was going to tell her—what to leave in; more important, what to leave out.

She stopped and turned toward me, and the moon came out, illuminating a face much changed from the one I remembered. The features seemed strangely pinched, the skin not lined but drawn tightly across them. "You know what this place is?" she said.

"Why ask me? Of course I don't."

"As you can see, it was once an airfield, but it hasn't been used as that for a long time. More recently it was a kind of meeting place. Right at the end of the runway is a fence that marks the border between these two great countries—or more precisely," she added, "these two stupid dinosaurs. . . . There were many times over the last ten years when meetings would be arranged here. Little trips across the border, men and women who didn't want to be identified, who needed direct contact in a private place, without microphones or documents, or any of the other petty officials. Just people who needed to talk."

She turned away, and the wind came up, tugging at her scarf.

"So we, too, needed to talk."

I let the wind have its say for a moment. "I've come for my father," I told her.

She didn't look at me, just stayed very still, staring at the moon.

"I would have thought you'd come for your mother."

"I've come for both of them."

"Why should we help you? We don't have the power anymore. We're out, gone. . . ."

"Like hell. Look at the little show just now in Lublin."

"That's all it was, Edward—a little show. You've seen the news—the party is on trial. We're all criminals on the run."

"I want to know where my father is, and I want him out. . . ."

"You're not listening, Edward. . . ."

You wouldn't be here if you didn't want something."

She paused, and I had to strain to hear what she was saying.

"We seem to have taught you well, my friend. You came to us so many years ago—such a tender little student, so anxious and worried." She turned back to me. "But you always had a hard streak in you. You stood up well in Moscow. The others didn't think so. But I did. I sensed it right from the start—a tough little Russian, I said, in British clothes. You looked as though you were wearing your heart on your sleeve, but that was just a show. You were very focused."

"I loved my father. I still do. I'm not going to play games with you, Irina. . . ."

"Regrettably, Edward, we have very little else to do, these days, except play games. . . ."

"I want to know . . ."

"And your mother is a great game player, Edward, if we are to speak realistically of such things. Your mother plays the game most beautifully—or shall I say, most sensitively?"

"What's this got to do with her?"

"Don't be so naive, my friend."

"Don't lecture me, Irina. You're not in a position to do that anymore—or haven't *you* seen the news?"

She walked away toward the van, and I caught up with her.

"Find your mother, Edward, and we'll talk again. Find her, and we will have something to talk about. Otherwise, you can forget the old man. . . ."

I must have grabbed her arm, for she spun around angrily—and for the first time her composure was unsettled.

"You touch him, Irina, just once, you take away his medicine, you deny him his comforts, you unsettle his life to the tiniest degree, and I will hunt you down myself, in whatever filthy ditch you're hiding."

She got into the van, and the driver switched on the engine.

"This is where I leave you, Edward—and you, my dear Mrs. Card. . . ." She gestured for Jane to get out. "This border crossing will open now—and then close again for good. I have laid on a car, and you are to be the last passengers, if that is the right word. It is not considered safe anymore—now that these 'democrats' have come to power—so many of them have used this route themselves. Everyone is so busy plugging old leaks and doorways, the old paths that crisscrossed Europe, the secret traffic that touched us all. . . . When you have found your mother, Edward, you can contact the lawyer. He has the same number as poor Karol in Warsaw—you will recall it, I think. . . ."

"And my father? . . ."

"Your father has been asking for you. Don't keep him waiting."

Jane and I stood together in the darkness, watching the one-eyed van out of sight. And it was only when the noise of the engine had died away that the two headlights came on at the other end of the runway.

It took us four or five minutes to reach the car. The

driver had wound down his window and was extending his hand.

"My name is Yuri," he said, and there was a smile full of gold teeth and a face in its early twenties, and a dark sailor's cap. "Please to hurry. I have instructions to take you to station at Zvenigorod. From there you will catch the train to Moscow."

"But Zvenigorod is in Russia. . . ."

Yuri laughed out loud. "You are already in Russia, my friends. The runway is the border. That is why I waited at this end. This . . ."—and he pointed to the floor of the filthy little car—"this is Russian soil."

We got in, and he started the engine, producing at the same time a brown packet from below his seat. "Here are documents and money . . . not too much, I have to say, because I already looked, but okay, enough to get by. . . ."

"How long to the station?" asked Jane.

"About two hours, dear lady. It could be quicker, but we have to go the long way around, to avoid some of our new democratic friends. . . ." He chuckled. "Russia is a big joke these days. Are you armed? . . ." he asked suddenly.

"No," I replied.

"Good," said Yuri, and laughed again, slapping me on the back with a free hand. "You will need all the weapons you can get. I myself have two guns. It is like . . . we call it the Wild East. Everyone has a gun these days, but you know the problem . . . there is no responsibility. In the old days, it was the state pressing the triggers; now it is the ordinary people, everyone firing all over the place, like crazy people. You want something—you go and shoot the person who has it; then you got it. Just like Chicago. Only no pizza." He laughed again and plucked at my jacket. "How much you pay for coat like this? You want to sell it?"

He lit cigarette after cigarette and kept up the patter for most of the two hours. We stuck to the back roads—maybe there *were* only back roads—and I looked behind at Jane sleeping on the backseat, and the dawn was coming up through the front windscreen—the first streaks of red in a new clear sky.

Through villages, skirting the towns, and now there were people along the roads—peasants, farm workers, carrying their tools, women in black, their hair tied in brightly colored scarves.

Zvenigorod itself was ugly enough to have been built in the dark—muddy tracks for roads, bare buildings and blocks that stood artlessly between chimneys—and everywhere you looked, the great workhorse trucks with their bonnets up and their drivers half-disappeared inside, trying that magical Russian combination of force and faith to get them started.

Yuri said good-bye in a hurry, laughing to himself, as he lit his eightieth cigarette of the day. "Good luck, dear friends," he said, "and welcome to the madhouse. Don't stay too long!"

The station was crowded—just two platforms—and mankind and his boxes piled onto both of them, and we were both hungry and cold and pretty disoriented, pushed and battered by the local travelers.

I found a man who still had the semblance of a uniform—the jacket, at least, and a pocket watch and chain that rested on the outcrop of his stomach and still marked him out as an official of the great Russian railways.

"What time is the train to Moscow?" I shouted over the noise.

"What?"

"Moscow. What time is the train?"

"What train?"

"Oh God."

"What do you want to go to Moscow for?" He was shouting back.

"Quite right," yelled a peasant woman. "They'll kill you and rob you there. Much better stay put"—and she opened a mouthful of gold, similar to Yuri's. "There's everything here," she shouted. "Better food than the pigshit they'll give you." And everyone seemed to roar with laughter at that.

I remember feeling like public property, but you forget that about Russia. Your business is everyone else's business—that's how it is in secretive countries. The government says nothing—so they have to tell their own gossip or make it up.

Mother used to cite that as the reason there were so many informers. "Wait till I tell everyone" was the cry that would go up each night in the land of the communal flats.

And that's what they did. Everyone knew everything about their neighbors—and nothing about anything else.

Two hours later, the train came in, and I suppose we should have been grateful for that. As it was, we had sat an hour in the muddy main street, like stray dogs. When the bakery opened, we bought a loaf and picked at it—and drank some milk from the dairy.

And then we were boarding the carriage. Jane squeezed into a seat and slept for an hour. Later we stood in the corridor and talked, as the train dashed through the tiny little stations and the sun rose higher.

"Of course," she said, "Irina and her people want the files more desperately, perhaps, than anyone else. That's why she told you to find your mother—the documents she has in her possession are the only things that can buy your father out."

"And if Mother won't hand them over?"

She didn't answer, and suddenly we were in a tunnel, and I didn't need her to answer.

When we emerged, the moment and the question had gone. The train was in a narrow escarpment with grassy sides and no chance at all to view the countryside. We weren't going to consider the possibility that Mother might not wish to hand over the documents. Of course she would—once she knew her husband was still alive. Once she knew they would buy us his freedom.

A clear deal on offer—a straight swap. That's why Irina had met us on the border and delivered us into Russia.

We pulled into a tiny station, and some of the passengers jumped out and ran to a tiny kiosk to buy hot bread—the women squealing and shouting at the driver not to set off without them.

And Jane, I discovered, doesn't say much, but she doesn't miss anything at all. "Edward," she said, "tell me about this lawyer we're supposed to contact."

Such a simple question, it was, asked, not in an unpleasant or demanding way, but it traveled straight to the center of the last ten years—as she had, no doubt, suspected it would.

Chapter Twenty-eight

Arkady, the lawyer. Oh yes—Arkady the survivor. Arkady—the honest. With the great hooked nose and the dark eyes that would moisten instantly when he greeted you and when he took his leave.

Arkady, Irina once said, is a merchant of truth. "We use him when we tell the truth. We use others when we lie. And there is still another group who can do both—but Arkady is not one of them. In a country like ours, it is important to know the difference."

To all the descriptions of him, I would add one more—his all-embracing sentimentality, worn like a stripe on a uniform, proudly and for all the world to see.

He didn't mind blowing his nose and wiping his tears away, striding as he used to through the corridors of the Soviet hierarchy, his handkerchief protruding from his left sleeve or billowing from his hand like a sail. If he saw reason to cry, he would cry. If he laughed, you could hear it, they used to say, on the borders of the Union.

Arkady was the messenger so cleverly chosen for me, in my arrangement with Irina and her friends. I assumed they were KGB; I often assumed he was too. But it was never spelled out. Arkady would simply bring me a message and take one back—and we would talk about the world and lament the speed of its decline.

He managed to overcome my disgust and persuade me that the deal was not of his making, that he would do everything he could to humanize it and shorten it, and improve conditions for my father.

"I am what I am, Edward," he would say. "A lawyer in a police state. And the only way I can bear to look at myself when I shave in the morning is that I tell the truth. And I tell it for anyone and on anyone's behalf. I believe that within the confines of this system I have been able to help some people and limit the harm to others. If that is cooperating, then those are the terms under which I cooperate."

I suppose I believed Arkady because I wanted to. Anyone else—a Soviet diplomat or a KGB goon—and I am sure I could never have continued with my own role—not even for my father. But Arkady smoothed my path and took away some of the bitter edges—so I say they were clever to have chosen him.

I asked him once how he knew he was conveying the truth, and he would smile with his old blackened teeth and tap his nose and tell me that if you lived through enough lies, the truth would stand out on its own. "People want to wrap the truth and package it—adorn it and explain it. Only lies need that.

"And I make one another stipulation," he said. "With me the truth goes on a single journey. On way. No return. Passed to one person and then forgotten. I do not hawk truths between different kinds of people. I do not bandy them around. One mouth speaks to one pair of ears—through me. That is all."

How self-deprecating he was—my friend Arkady, the messenger.

About a month after my student trip to Moscow, he telephoned me from a call box in London and introduced himself.

"Irina asked me to send greetings," said the voice full of legal depth and precision; and I could feel on that cold autumn day the same foreboding I had sensed in Moscow. And then . . . "Would you like to have lunch with me? Shall we say Langan's at one-thirty?"

A Soviet lawyer, taking a student to lunch in the fashionable West End—no shady little meeting for Arkady, no miserable, furtive encounter, your heart in your sphincter. He played to an audience—this merchant of truth.

I found him on the ground floor, and I was as anxious to dislike him as he was to please me. Arkady in gray sports jacket and egg-stained tie, garrulous, witty, and oh-so-sharp. In another age, he would have been the court entertainer, wheeled in to entertain the king, to tell stories, to enlighten the influential. Now he was a Russian lawyer, somewhere out there between the black and the white—in the netherworld were justice was handed down on a secure telephone line, or during a meeting in a car park—in conversations that never took place, in places that didn't exist.

"In our system," he would say, "there is no *right* sentence for a criminal, but there are most certainly wrong ones. Always we were given the wrong ones—sometimes because the judge misheard the instructions, sometimes he was too stupid to understand them, and occasionally he lost the papers and released people who should have been locked up for life." He looked hard at me, and the smile left him. "But you didn't come here to talk about that," he said. "I can tell you your father is well. I have good reports from the doctors. The Flutamide is proving most effective. They are confident of moving into a new and . . . uh, beneficial stage."

"How confident?"

"This I cannot answer. I am not sure how much to trust them."

"So there is good news and bad news."

He smiled without humor. "Is that not the essence of life itself?"

I suppose others might have waited for the end of the meal to raise the most unpleasant topics—but not Arkady. Business was always urgent and quick—the thing to get out of the way, before the pleasures of life could be resumed.

"Edward, if I may call you Edward, this has been described to me as a first request from your interlocutors in Moscow. That does not mean it will be followed by others—I simply do not know."

"I do," I replied. "I know perfectly well."

He closed his eyes and appeared to recite his text from

memory. Not a long one, two or three minutes—precise, easy-to-follow instructions—that sounded so ridiculous and trivial that I remember thinking this was something of a joke. People didn't go around doing this sort of thing, or if they did, then there was no rational point to it.

I was to collect a package from a bookstore in Knightsbridge. I was to find a return air ticket inside. I was to travel the next morning to Paris, take a taxi to the city, hand the book to the owner of a café in Montparnasse, and return to London the same day. There would be money for my transport and sufficient for a light snack along the way. "Russians," said Arkady, "are not insensitive to the demands of the stomach," and he stuffed another piece of bread into his mouth.

"Does my father know anything about these arrangements—or any others?" I asked.

"He does not."

"He would never agree to it if he did."

"That is quite possible."

"That," I replied, "is certain."

Arkady shifted closer to the table. "As I understand it, your father believes, simply, that he is able to get messages from you because we have established a channel of communication—to keep him happy, to allow him to continue with his work, and so on. He is, of course, of some value as a scientist. . . ."

"Of great value," I interrupted.

"This I am unable to quantify, Edward."

"I want to see him."

"Once every two years, Edward. That is the advice."

"I want more."

"I will pass on your request, but I doubt if you could arrange it more often and retain the confidentiality of our understanding."

Arkady had a point.

I walked out of the restaurant while he paid the bill, and we didn't see each other again that year. Of course I went to Paris and delivered the book. There were no hiccups, no searches, no one to ask me where I was going or what I was doing. Only my conscience.

* * *

And then I waited. The months slipped past—soon it was December. London had its first snowfall in three years, and I remember looking out of the back window at Stanley Road, remembering how much Dad had loved the snow; how bitterly he had complained about the shortage of it in England; how he had fondly believed he had left all the shortages behind.

In the old days, he had looked forward to Christmas, almost as if it belonged solely to him. Maybe it represented the childhood he had never had. Weeks before, he would scour the streets for decorations and presents, for tinsel and holly. He would buy not one tree but two, keeping the larger in the garden and the other in the living room for us. The decoration lights in our otherwise-frugal household burned incessantly. Turning them off would have been a sin—and Dad would stare out for hours over the back garden, in case a cat or a stray dog interfered with his tree.

"Tree of hope, Edward," he would say. "Tree of hope. This is what we never had in Russia. No tree. No hope."

Only that Christmas, three months after Arkady's mission, there was once again no tree and no further word of Dad.

Gradually the secret life began to weigh heavily on me. It became both a fixture and a burden. I lived in dread of a contact—and yet I wanted one. Because each contact meant news about my father.

In this way, I now believe, the Russians duped us both—me into believing that I was helping my father—and he into thinking they were kinder than they really were. In him they sought to develop a dependence on my letters and on later visits. I was the weapon they could hold over his head.

As for me—they had a hold. They could push my buttons whenever they felt like it. I can't have been of any great value to them. I'm well aware of that. After all, I had no experience. But I was there for the time when they might need me. Just in case. Just in an emergency. They were, after all, the supreme planners.

Late in January a letter arrived from Arkady. It had been addressed to me at the faculty and contained another invitation to lunch.

We met at a crowded Turkish restaurant in Marylebone High Street—he in the same gray tweed jacket—me in my jeans and a filthy mood.

"Why haven't you contacted me before?" I demanded. "I want to know about my father."

"How are you, Edward?"

"Lousy, as I expect you can see. My father . . ."

A waiter approached but, seeing my expression, scuttled away in the other direction. Arkady took a few papers from his briefcase and slid an envelope across the table. There was a photograph of Dad, sitting on a park bench, smiling, holding a newspaper. . . .

"You can verify the date of the paper from the picture on the front page," said Arkady. "Exactly a week ago. The face, I feel, speaks for itself, no?"

I looked again. Dad had clearly put on weight. The stomach carried hints of the old bulge; the cheeks had filled out perceptibly.

"Is there a message from my father?"

"I was given nothing else, Edward."

"It's time I saw him."

"This had been addressed in my instructions. . . ."

"What the fuck does that mean, Arkady?"

The Russian sniffed as if I had offended his sensibilities. "Please, Edward, it is not necessary to raise your voice. I am here to ask you to stand by, just in case your services are required. It is conceivable that you will receive a request for assistance over the next few days. A man, I cannot be more specific, will make himself known to you—perhaps in the street, perhaps at the university or a bar—who can say? He may be in a hurry, he may be nervous. He will ask you to take a small package, and he will tell you where to leave it. . . ."

"And then?"

"And then," said Arkady, "you may come to Moscow and visit your father."

Chapter Twenty-nine

I finished the story as the train slammed into the darkened suburbs of western Moscow. It seemed extraordinary that we had found our way along the unlit tracks and escarpments, across bridges and over the soundless waterways of Russia. Ever forward went that train—and we with it.

As the other passengers grappled with their boxes and shouted at their sleepy children, I clung to the guardrail along the corridor and told her what had happened all those years ago.

Arkady had been right—I was about to be needed. And for a while, at least, things would move very fast.

It broke five days after his visit. A March Monday—lethargy clinging to the corridors of the faculty, overheated, the students underoccupied, months away from any important examinations.

He must have watched me.

For some reason, I didn't emerge with the other students that afternoon. They were on their way to a union meeting, and I wasn't big on university politics. You spent your days being lectured by people who knew something, why go off to smoky little gatherings where they didn't?

I came out to find the afternoon waning fast—car lights already cutting open the gloom. For a moment, the cold sank its teeth into me, and I pulled my scarf tight.

My destination was Dillon's—the university bookshop on the corner of the street—a regular haunt where I could leaf through the new books on Russia, the famous, the obscure. I never knew what I wanted. Some kind of enlightenment maybe, some clues as to what might happen—and end to my own predicament.

The shop was crowded as usual, and I made my way downstairs to the Russian section. My eye was taken by some new Moscow guides on the bottom shelf, and I knelt on the floor to look at them.

He must have moved directly behind me. Quick, agile. He knew what *he* wanted.

As I rose stiffly after a few seconds, brushing the dust from my knees, the figure was right there in a blue anorak—my height and build, yet older—a pointed face, with a brush of reddish hair. I'd had a schoolteacher who looked like him—that's why the name came to mind, "foxy." Only this one had a tiny river of sweat cascading down his left cheek and an eyelid that twitched uncontrollably.

You've been running, I thought, running hard.

I recall standing inanely, hands at my sides, until he shoved a small package toward me—the size of a prayer book.

"Put it in your pocket," he said, the voice was no more than a whisper. "When you go tomorrow, take it with you; leave it on your chair after the last lecture." He turned to go and then looked back. "For Irina," he said awkwardly. And in that instant someone bumped into me from the side—a young woman hand in hand with a child.

"Sorry," she said quickly, and then, "say sorry, Kirstey. You bumped the gentleman. Go on, say it. I'm sorry," she repeated, "Kirstey never says sorry. I've tried, you know. . . ."

I pushed past her, and now there was no sign of Foxy. On the stairs, I felt a sudden wave of heat and nausea, and I ran out into the street, filling my lungs with the cold, damp air. In the darkness, Foxy could have been any one of the backs, walking away from me, either side of the street. I thought I saw him heading toward Bloomsbury, but it was probably someone else . . . a sweaty little figure with eyes that wouldn't hold for long, his nerve snapping even as he stood before me. A man going under. Who are you, Foxy? And where will you run?

As I stood there waiting for my breathing to calm, I could feel the book in my pocket, where I'd shoved it.

Of course I took it home and, after supper with Mother, opened it in my bedroom, drawing the curtains, as if Stanley Road were full of snoopers and spies. It was a small German-English dictionary, and though I turned it upside down and scrutinized each page, I could find nothing unusual about it. No microdots, no added pages, no algebraic symbols. A dictionary. A bloody dictionary.

So was this what spies and agents carried around with them? And was Foxy a British traitor on the run? There didn't seem to be many other explanations. When Arkady had seen me, he must have known the man was getting ready to make a move. They were planning the escape route, planning to make me part of it. And somewhere in this book was the reason.

The next day I left it on my chair in the lecture hall and didn't turn around or go back to watch who took it. I didn't want to see another nervous, sweating face, with little rivers of fear running down its cheeks. Quite enough to look at my own.

"So you went to Moscow, after that?" Jane asked, and the train stood for a moment, waiting for its final green light.

"I went to Moscow. They flew me out there for the weekend. Dad was much better, leading an almost normal life—with the medication. He'd been given a little flat near the Arbat—good central location—and he was working and . . . what can I tell you? It was wonderful to see him. It made it all worthwhile. He became my father again. We talked, we had a relationship, we went out for hours, tramping the streets, talking about the politics. . . . Dad was convinced things were going to change, said the old fear had gone. Gorbachev had done that. And once the fear had gone, you couldn't get it back again. The party was losing control, and they knew it."

"Did he ask about your mother?"

"Of course he did. But we both knew we couldn't tell her. She wouldn't have tolerated the arrangement. And by then she was mixed up in other things. She was getting on with her life. There was Coffin; there were others. It's what Dad wanted. He made me promise not to tell her."

"And after that—you went again?"

"Yes, pretty much as Arkady had said. Every two years. Occasionally I carried a message for them. I handed on a parcel. Little things, very sporadic. But at least I got news of him. And then came the coup attempt—the party was out—and I heard nothing. I became desperate. That's why I cooked up this business trip through Eastern Europe with Harry and his crowd. We were just about to leave when Mother disappeared—and the body was found in her car. And that's where you came in."

Jane shook her head as if trying to clear her thoughts.

"I still can't believe you didn't tell your mother during all those years."

"Then you don't understand much about Russians. We were like all the other millions of families, used and twisted by the system, living life in tiny compartments, hoping they didn't overrun. We didn't want anyone else's secrets—we were scared enough of giving away our own. Years ago when Mother was visited in the camp by her father—he didn't even ask about her trial or the interrogations, or whether she had suffered or been tortured. He was too scared to ask his own daughter if she was okay. Can you imagine what that's like? And then you ask me how I could keep my father's existence a secret from her. It was too dangerous to tell her, dangerous for him and her, for all of us. That's what you learn from the cold war."

"So what happens now?"

"Now we have to get down the mountain—all of us. Everyone's going to have to sit down and make a deal. If one person refuses, we're finished. Mother has to hand over the documents, and we all pretend they never existed. The old Soviets, the new Russians, the Americans—the whole lot."

Jane turned away for a moment watching the sparse city lights. "Do you think they will?"

"I wouldn't bet on it," I told her. "The body count seems to be going up all the time."

As I looked out, the train gave a final heave and seemed to collapse on the track, worn out by the journey.

"This is our great capital, children," said a voice in the corridor. "We have arrived in one of the biggest cities of the world. See how beautiful it is."

She must have been a teacher. A big, blousy blonde, the way Moscow often makes them, with a gaggle of children under her ample wings, declaiming in that tear-laden falsetto all Russians use when they talk about their country.

We let her go first and then joined the masses as they galloped toward the exit, pushing each other with their bags, elbowing their way through.

Jane broke off to the side, and we entered the main concourse. Along one wall a row of ticket counters. Opposite—a snack bar lit by the kind of blue neon bar that stretches in an unbroken line across Eastern Europe.

We bought two glasses of tea and sat at a table.

"I have to contact Arkady," I told her.

"It's very dangerous."

"Of course it is. But if we don't get all the sides together, they'll hunt down me and my mother—and Dad will never get out."

"They may hunt you down anyway."

"The thought has occurred to me."

She swilled the tea leaves around in the bottom of the glass. "I think I should get some backup."

"Then leave me out of it."

"Why?"

"It might be safer for us to split up. Go somewhere I can call you, if I need to . . ."

"If there's time to call . . ."

She went over to the tiled wall, where the telephones hung crookedly, like broken arms. She turned away as she spoke and hung up after a few seconds.

"I hope that wasn't the embassy," I said.

" 'Course not. I wouldn't trust the bloody tea-lady there."

"Who then?"

"A journalist . . ."

"Oh Christ."

"He's been very useful over the years."

"I thought we didn't use them anymore."

"You thought wrong. We use anybody."

"I hope you'll be very happy together."

She laughed and wrote a number on a thin square of napkin.

"He'll be here in twenty minutes. I told him you weren't coming."

"Was he pleased?"

"Promised me a good meal and a bath. . . ."

"Did he offer to wash your back and feed you?"

She laughed again. "Who knows what the night may bring?"

We wandered toward the street, and even in the darkness I couldn't help feeling the shock.

For I didn't recognize the city. In front of me were signs for Mars Bars, a Pizza Hut, General Motors, for God's sake, advertising a dealership. Who the hell buys American cars here? They're queuing for bread. They're out in the street ten deep, selling their underpants. We've all seen the pictures. What is going on here?

I look again. On every side, I see bright hoardings, bright signs, and yet still the same crushed faces.

Like tides meeting off a coastline, there are crowds mingling on the sidewalks, arriving and departing in scenes of total chaos.

An old man pokes a walking stick at me. "You have colossal energy around you," he shouts crazily. "Colossal. I felt it as you went past. A great magnetic field," and he moves off into the crowd waving the stick like a water diviner.

All around are peasant women, stomachs like barrels, legs like tree trunks, jabbering and nodding their heads, judging the world as it moves before them. Russia is in flux this night. No single aim or purpose, but many thousands of them, unleashed to run in all directions. Whatever held together this bazaar they once called a country has gone. You can feel it in the footsteps along the broken concrete. They're moving—after decades of standing still.

Jane spotted the car. A blue Ford by the look of it.

"Stay there," she said quickly, and I thought she was

going to kiss me, but instead her finger came up and brushed my lips, so lightly I could barely feel it. The same pressure she'd used in London. The same gesture of promise.

Jane, you never stop surprising me.

And then she was getting into the car, and I bent down, but still I couldn't see the driver's face. Even as they moved away from the curb, though, he turned, and the blue light from a street lamp must have caught him, for I could feel the instant chill of recognition. A flash second. An instant journey back through time. A terrible realization that was enough to make me yell out and start running after the car, as it pulled away ever faster toward the Ring Road.

Jane, Jane, get out for God's sake. Jane. And about thirty yards away she turned and looked back, only the figure was already leaning across her, and I was running helplessly out into the three lanes of traffic, with hooting cars and people leaning out to scream at me, even as the Ford lost itself in the Moscow traffic.

I have good reason to remember that moment of sickening powerlessness, watching her driven away into the darkened capital of all the Russias.

For the face of that trusted journalist she had called was a face that had once belonged to Foxy, my fleeting contact in the bookshop all those years ago. You don't forget that kind of encounter. You don't forget a face, gripped by fear, with all its rivers of sweat. If Foxy was a traitor then, he was a traitor now—and Jane didn't stand a chance.

That night, the past and the present were well on collision course.

Chapter Thirty

Arkady sat by his window and looked down six stories into the quiet of Tverskaya Street.

"Still out there." He made a face at the glass. "You can't see them anymore. No Volgas, with shaded windows, no men in hats and raincoats—but they're there."

He had come down in his dressing gown and slippers to let me in. A tall, stooping shadow, his face half-lit by the single naked lightbulb in the hall of the apartment block.

"We'll take the stairs," he said simply. "Lift makes too much noise."

For a few minutes, we sat silent in the living room, catching our breath, and as I began telling him the story, he shut his eyes and the color seemed to leave his face—and I thought—even to this man who has known all the fears Russia as ever contained—something has come into this room and frightened him all over again. And that something is me.

He didn't speak when I had finished but shuffled slowly into the kitchen and made tea. He returned with a tray—and I realized that the animated, fun-loving Arkady I had known in London had gone. A sad and much older man had taken his place—tired of the battles, tired of the effort.

"We are in uncharted waters, my friend." He observed

and sat down heavily in the chair. "There used to be rules to what we did. Rules that were broken, yes, that is true—but clear procedures and patterns. Now there are none. This is a jungle with no single group in control—armies within armies, powers that rule in some areas but not in others, police and internal security service loyal to different people, and more frequently loyal to no one. This is the Russia you have arrived in."

Arkady paused. "You would like more tea?"

I nodded.

"Particularly," he went on, "particularly I do not like the hijacking of your friend at the station. I see it as a gesture of impatience. . . ."

"By whom?"

"By the old comrades—the former leaders of our country—Irina and others. They have lost almost everything except the records of their crimes—and that is what they wish to destroy now. They are very desperate people. . . ."

"What will they do with Jane?"

"I don't know. For the moment—maybe nothing. It depends on the larger picture."

"Arkady—what is the news of my father?"

He switched on a tiny lamp beside the chair, as if to shed light into his mind.

"Your father has suffered a relapse, Edward. This I have heard. But no details. I don't know if he is still receiving the drugs. He has left his apartment and been readmitted to a sanatorium. I believe it's in the Moscow area, but again I can't be sure."

"What do you mean . . . you can't be sure? These are your people. You've dealt with them long enough. What kind of relapse? What sanatorium?"

"I have no information. . . ."

"Then get some."

He looked at me calmly, absorbing my anger. "Edward, Edward—I can serve only as a mouthpiece. If no one talks to me, then I have no function."

"To hell with your function, Arkady. What contacts do you still have? What's still operating in this city? Let's lay it all on the line. You're not a messenger anymore, my friend, you're a player. We all are. How do we end this stupidity?"

He looked away, and I could see his eyes ranging around the bookshelves that lined the walls. Arkady and his treasures. Forty years of messages received and delivered and a roomful of books to show for it—a pair of tatty rugs on the bare floorboards, a tray of china. It wasn't much.

All right, Edward." He got up and leaned stiffly against the windowsill. "Let's talk of this just once—and then we will go down the road wherever it takes us. But first I want to be sure you know the cost of this journey. There may be irreversible consequences."

"It's time, Arkady. In fact, it's past time."

"Very well." He rubbed his eyes with both hands. "You ask me to lay it all on the line, Edward. And if that is what you want—I will do it. But lay what on the line?" He opened his palms, and I could hear him suddenly as if he were in a courtroom, lecturing a jury, his voice cutting like a blade through confusion and chaos. "You don't want it all on the line. You want it buried and forgotten. This is what you have really come for?"

"I don't follow."

"I think you do. Whatever your mother has seen—whatever the documents that were taken to London, you imagine she can simply hand them back—and your father will be returned—and we can, as you say, live happily ever after? . . . Is this what you think?"

"Something like that."

"But what do these documents contain, Edward? A liberal sprinkling of Soviet scandals, some peccadillos among the leaders, a few husbands in the wrong beds with the wrong wives? Tell me, Edward, is that what you think?"

"More than that. How do I know? Government secrets. Lies. Deals and accommodations. Enough to rock administrations all over the world. Yes, Arkady—all that and more . . ."

"And it's fine to bundle up these papers, hand them back—and say to the good old boys, as you call them, Here you are, why don't you burn them, then the slate will be clean, you can go about your business—oh yes, and I'm flying back to my nice little apartment in London and Dad's going with me?"

"What would *you* do, Arkady? Tell me that."

"I would find the truth. Russia deserves it—the world

deserves it." And now his voice had gone very quiet. Outside, too, the city was still. It was as if the whole of Moscow were listening. "Seventy years," he went on. "Seventy years of miserable, disgusting lies on a scale so monstrous that few of us can even imagine it. We need our history, given back to us. Take it away from a man, and he becomes a slave. He doesn't know where he comes from or where he's going. We want it back, Edward. Millions of lost souls, tortured and murdered in our country—they demand nothing less."

"You were happy to be part of that system."

"I was never happy, Edward. Like millions of people, I had no choice. All right, I could have been a dissident and spent fifteen years in a labor camp. What would that have served? Or I could have shut up and supported the system. I did neither. I worked within it to help those I could. Would you condemn me for that?"

"It's all in the past, Arkady. We have to think of the future. . . ."

"It is for this reason the truth must be told. Otherwise, there'll be no future. We'll never get there."

"Truth!" I shook my head at him. "You talk as if it's a currency you can spend. It doesn't buy you anything. It's not going to make you better off. . . ."

"No, but it's ours, and it belongs to us."

"So what are you going to do? Tell the world that all the governments were as corrupt as yours, that democracy was a sham, that there never has been an honest, decent administration, and everything that we fought for was a waste of time. . . . You don't have that right."

He smiled at me for the first time. "People always talk of rights when they don't have any. I should know. In the Soviet Union, they were always lecturing us about our rights."

Arkady went and sat back in his chair and turned off the lamp. In the distance, I could hear a train clattering out into the suburbs. And then the city seemed to turn over and go back to sleep. In the block opposite, a candle flickered in a darkened room.

"My friend," he said quietly, "give me a reason why I should help you?"

* * *

So he made me the advocate. And yet I had never thought those thoughts, never reached those conclusions, never tried and tested the logic in my own mind—let alone offered it for debate.

I told him he was right about the truth, and I couldn't argue with that. But the truth would never go away—truth was eternal—and one day someone else would find it and bring it to the surface.

I could do nothing for the millions who had died—and the plight of the millions who were bereaved and wronged. But I wondered if there might not finally be a way to break the cycle.

Human beings were always dying for the sake of a principle—could it be that, just this once, a principle might die for the sake of a human being?

Could I buy the life of my father with the truth—with the documents my mother had acquired, with the evidence of crimes and criminals contained within them?

"If I don't get to my father soon," I told him, "if Irina and her friends prevent me from giving him the care and medication he needs—he will die. You know this, don't you?"

"I know this," he said. "I have known this for a little while. Of course I expected your call. Ever since they threw out the party, I have expected you to appear in Moscow, to ask for my help. As you know, my friend, there is a price for everything—only it seems to me you have already paid it. You and your father—in the choices you were forced to make and the separation you have suffered." He got to his feet. "Long before you came here, I made up my mind to help you—but I felt I should ask for your reasons and give you mine. After all, these are important questions. But I should also pass on a warning, based on my observations over many years. What you are seeking to do has never been attempted before—and I have no doubt that in the course of this enterprise someone will smile at you and give you fine assurances and then attempt to betray you. This is what happens in my country. This is what always happens." He moved toward the door. "And now if you will excuse me for a moment—I will get dressed, and then we must take a little journey." He nodded his head. "It is time you saw your mother."

Chapter Thirty-one

"How do you know where to find her?"

"I don't."

"So where are we going?"

"Down the line." Arkady stepped out onto the landing and locked his front door. "You think just because the party lost power, the underground has disappeared. There are more layers to this society than a Hungarian gâteau." He smiled. "Which I would not object to eating at this moment."

Our transport was Arkady's ancient gray Volga, its windscreen scarred and its bodywork holed and cratered by rust. "No one would dream of stealing it," he said as we got in. "Look—the quality, the sense of style, lovingly built by our glorious socialist workforce, and catastrophically unreliable. I call her Stalin."

And then, abruptly, the joking was over—and I was sitting next to yet another Arkady. A man whose guises and disguises I had barely begun to fathom. One man in London—another in the flat. Whom would he turn out to be this time?

Stalin grunted, jolted, and caused what I now believe to be permanent damage to my lower back. But at least we were moving. Across the Moscow River, along the embankment, through into the quiet of the Oktyabr district.

We passed one Lenin statue—still left intact, and I wondered how they decided which to leave and which to remove. A Lenin here and there was apparently permissible. Arkady gestured at the little man as we drove by. "Finally Vladimir Ilyich has become useful to us," he remarked.

"In what way?"

"As a reminder of how low we could sink. We should be afraid of that. Most people are frightened of outsiders. We Russians should be most frightened of ourselves."

He turned the car into a narrow street and stopped. On one side was a long apartment block, a row of entrances and staircases—on the other a small park, a few swings, wooden hut, straggly trees. A handful of lights burned behind paper-thin curtains. There was mud and rubbish and a line of battered cars. And I remembered that visiting the Russian suburbs is like stepping onto a wasteland, where the buildings crumble unkempt and uncared for, where generations grow up without the tiniest bird crumb of hope. "We have a roof over our heads," they used to say proudly after the war. And now—a decade away from the millennium—that's still all they had. A roof and a wasteland.

I put out my hand to open the door, but he stopped me. "Wait, my friend. For a minute, we sit here and listen."

"Why?"

"I wish to make sure we were followed."

A few moments later, I could see headlights approaching around the corner, and then they stopped abruptly and were doused. No car appeared. Arkady got out and breathed in deeply.

"That's it," he said. "They know where we're going. They don't need to come any closer."

He told me, when we were in the lift, said it was important they knew we were making progress. That's the only reason we were still alive. We were serving a purpose, leading them to my mother, and as long as that continued, they would leave us alone.

"They?" I asked.

"Does it matter?" he replied.

The lift rattled upward.

"When you get in the flat," he said, "don't be surprised by anything you hear. There'll be pencils and paper provided. Make sure you write down anything that is at all sensitive—don't, on any account, speak it out loud. Do you understand?"

We got out at the tenth floor. In front of us—a steel door, steel frame, the wall newly cemented to house it.

Arkady rings the bell.

And suddenly I look at the time, and it's after midnight. I tap him on the arm, pointing to my watch, but he's not interested. And already I hear the bolts sliding back, and standing before us is an old lady, in a quilted yellow bed jacket and thick woolen socks and a presence of sufficient force for me to take a step back along the landing. She's tiny, she's gray-haired, but with a skin of unblemished whiteness, and such a presence—a little bundle of strength, built by hardship and endurance, as only Russia knows how. You can see that with the passage of time her face has come to lean forward, so that the nose seems to peer down at the ground, along with the jaw. She wears glasses, but the eyes are cool and clear and see everything. Arkady is bowing. . . . "Maria Valentinovna, a thousand apologies. . . ."

She raises her hand to silence him. "Thank you, Arkady. I have just got up." She looks at me. "And thank you for delivering our guest. You had better get home now. It is very late."

"I . . . I, of course, Maria Valentinovna. I understand perfectly. If that is what you wish, naturally."

"Good night, Arkady."

"Wait," I say, and then I stop, for I don't recognize the expression in his eyes. Why does he seem to be saying good-bye—his eyes aren't damp the way they used to be—they're bright and shining as if he's just a seen a light in the distance and is about to follow it. Why the hurry? Why the sudden departure? We need to talk and plan. . . .

"Arkady . . ." I'm grabbing his arm. . . .

"Good-bye, my friend."

"I don't understand."

"Don't try to. I have done what I can for you. I wish you luck."

He steps into the lift, and I watch him turn away from me, as if to shield his thoughts and emotions and spare me the sight of them.

"Arkady," I say, "Arkady, I'll contact you. Today, tomorrow . . ." And yet even as I speak the words, I'm certain we have seen each other for the last time.

Maria Valentinovna shut the steel door behind me, and her thin hand gripped my arm with unbelievable strength.

"Three minutes we wait—not a second longer. Count," she ordered, cutting into my thoughts.

You didn't argue with this woman. She brought me into a living room and sat me under a dismal chandelier. Half the bulbs were broken, and the rest seemed to have little enthusiasm for the job. I could hear a clock ticking in time with my thoughts.

Three minutes! She got up and led me toward a cupboard in the wall, only it wasn't a cupboard—it was a doorway into another flat. There were people in the corridor, a child, the noise of a television and the flicker from a screen, another corridor and someone handed her a coat, and the tiny figure in front of me was taking all the doors and passages at the kind of speed old ladies don't normally manage; and she didn't stop for a moment, this soft, silent march through Moscow.

Now I understood. Each flat connected. We were moving down the building unseen from the outside. Flat by flat we were passing beyond the sight and reach of any watchers. The underground had built her an escape route.

Strangely, I found myself still counting as we walked. And then the corridor narrowed and turned. On our left a staircase, and a young man was leading—I could see the back of a leather jacket and short brown hair. But he doesn't speak, she doesn't speak—it's like some ritual they've rehearsed and choreographed a thousand times—only I don't know the steps.

Into a cellar now—lights on. A black Volga is sitting unimpressively in the middle. Leather jacket gets in, old lady beside him. . . . "Quickly," she whispers.

But I've sat in too many cars on nights like this—and I need a question answered before I go anywhere else.

"Why did Arkady leave like that?"

"He went to buy some time. Naturally when they saw his car on the move, they would follow it. A mile or two down the road, they would see there was only one person inside. But by then it would be too late. You and I would have already left."

"And Arkady?"

"They would most likely have forced him off the road. They'd question him, and he would not reply. . . ."

"They can be very persuasive."

She paused for just a moment. "Arkady is dead."

"What? I can't believe . . ."

"He wanted to die. I have known this man for many years. I know his good side and his bad side. I know when he sold his soul, and so did he. And ever since then he lived for an opportunity to buy it back. You gave him that opportunity—and now he has used it."

"So he knew he was going to die?"

"He wanted to help you. He believed in you. He felt you had been wronged and that he had been a party to it."

"I'm sorry. I don't know what to say."

Maria shook her head. "Don't be sorry. Not for Arkady. This night he has peace of mind for the first time in fifty years. There is no reason to be sorry."

She turned away from me, but I had already seen the moisture in her eyes.

We're moving again. That's what happened. It seemed there was no time for all the epitaphs to be written, for all the brave people, for all the senseless dying they had done.

Russia had lost another. So had I.

Chapter Thirty-two

"Where are we going, Maria Valentinovna?"

"To see your mother, of course."

"At this hour?"

"What difference does it make—the hour? Either she's there or she's not."

"Please stop the car."

We were on the Lenin Hills.

They will doubtless rename them soon. But that's where we were, on a damp October night, close to 2:00 A.M.

On one side of us was the gaunt ugliness of Moscow University; on the other, the wide balustrade, with the two ski jumps, and below us the city of Moscow, a faint mist drawn across it.

"You should tell me the story, before I see her."

We stood beside the low wall, looking out.

"We don't have time. Why do you need me to tell you?"

"Because if you know where my mother is—then you know a lot about her. I would rather hear it from someone else—first. I know her—she would give me a few details and leave out all the things that matter. Even if she wanted to tell me the whole story, she couldn't. There's a mental block."

I shivered suddenly from the wind, but the old lady was quite unperturbed.

"It began long before she left Russia," she said, and the voice was firm and clear, and I knew her memory would be exact. "Your mother went to the university in Leningrad. She studied medicine; she wanted to be a doctor. In those days, it seemed like a safe profession, not political—that was before Stalin began killing them off." She sighed. The glasses seemed to have slipped farther down her nose.

"She was bright and clever, studied very hard. The teachers, the professors they were *'v vostorgye'* delighted with her, excited about her talent and her possibilities. But you know for her—for Yekaterina, it wasn't enough."

"What do you mean?"

"She did things she was told never to do, started asking questions and pressing and expecting answers. . . ."

"What kinds of things, explain. . . ." And for a moment I felt a terrible sense of urgency, standing in the middle of the night, looking out over Moscow, not knowing who would stay alive long enough to talk to me.

"Politics, my young friend. Discussions. She is overheard poking fun at the government. Overheard! You know what that meant. People are in labor camps for fifteen years after being overheard. She was called into the political office. . . ."

"In a medical school?"

"Everywhere. Listen to me," she snapped. "Don't interrupt. I know what you need to hear. Anyway, she was cautioned, told she could lose everything, job, freedom—the family too." The old woman smiled. "But you couldn't ever tell Yekaterina anything. You know that too. She always did the opposite. She followed her stubborn nature. Poked into everything she could. You know, I wondered sometimes if she wanted to be caught—just so she could spit in their faces, right up close, where they'd feel it."

A car passed behind us, but we didn't look around. As it moved away, the old woman began again. "She got in with a group. Dissidents, they called them later, started producing an information sheet. A fellow doctor helped her, a man called Sergei, bearded and handsome. And you know what? They fell in love, besotted with each other. Even Yekaterina, who never seemed to have a heart to feel, let alone give—she followed him everywhere. She would have given her life for that man—I have no doubt."

"How long did this last?"

"Six months."

"Why didn't they get married?"

"They were going to. He had already given her a ring—except they had no rings to give—it was more like a key ring, made from silver, but two two halves that could unlock. She wanted him to keep one for himself, but he made her take the whole thing, so that she would know he was always with her. There's a silver clasp—he said it was a reminder that his arm was holding her."

"Go on. . . ."

"One night, the police raided their printing room. Took away the press, took away Sergei, tortured him—demanded the names of all those who'd been involved. He didn't know Yekaterina had been taken the same night. Neither of them named the other. Each confessed to the crime and claimed sole responsibility. . . ."

"What happened?"

"They were in camps for six months before there was a trial. Turned out the prosecutor had been treated by Sergei. Had his life saved. Said he owed Sergei a favor. He needed only one criminal, so Yekaterina could be released, if that's the way Sergei wanted it. And he did. She saw him only once more—she was being released. They met in a deserted house—she was getting out—and he was off back to the camps to do eight years. To soften the blow, he said he didn't love her anymore, never had. She was a whore and a bloodsucker, and she was to fuck off and never think of him again. Lies—all of it. But she went. She had no choice."

Far away in the distance I could see a blue flashing light, but there was no siren, no sound of alarm or emergency. The old lady had seen it too.

"Come on—we have to go."

"Wait." I put out my hand to her shoulder. "Tell me the rest. I need to know the rest."

"Your mother came back here because she was shown some documents. . . ."

"Not just documents. Secrets that half the intelligence services on the planet seem to want to kill for . . ."

"Secrets there may be. I know nothing of them, and your mother would not have told me." She sighed. "I know only of one document, relating to Sergei and proving conclusively that he was still alive. When Yekaterina saw that, she had no choice but to come back."

"Sergei? Here in Moscow?"

"Edward, if I may call you that, your mother returned to Moscow and found Sergei. He was living in a place you will shortly see for yourself. Still a doctor. Surprisingly well, given the suffering he has endured. A quiet man, leading a simple, quiet life."

"Come on." It was my turn to hurry. "We have to get there and find them."

I ran to the car, and Maria Valentinovna walked stolidly behind. I held the door for her, and as she got in, I could see tiredness for the first time in the delicate whiteness of the skin and those clear blue eyes.

The driver turned the ignition, and we moved almost cautiously down the hill toward the city. Easy, slowly, so as not to attract attention.

I could not have been more nervous—as close as I was to seeing my mother again, the end of an extraordinary journey.

But it wasn't the end—not that night.

As we reached the Kievsky station, the driver turned left under the bridge and headed North toward the Foreign Ministry. Behind the building is the maze of old side streets and alleys of the Arbat, where the many wonderful houses have been preserved and restored for the few, who have influence and money to secure them.

The roads, of course, are another matter. Like a moonscape, untouched and untended since time immemorial.

We stopped before a beautiful square villa. In the street lights, it looked yellow, with elaborate white cornicing and stucco walls. A low house behind a wall and railings. Two pillars supported the porch. It was simple and elegant, and all the windows were lighted, as if a party were in progress and the owners were celebrating. "She's supposed to be in hiding. . . ." I breathed.

"Sit still for a moment, Edward," said the old lady. "Before we go in—there is one more thing you should know. Yesterday your mother and Sergei were married."

I looked at her, hearing the words. But I couldn't move, couldn't open my mouth. For a moment, it seemed, the world stopped turning.

CHAPTER THIRTY-THREE

"WHO ARE YOU?"

"Later," she says. "Sit for a moment. Collect your thoughts."

But I have too many to collect. I must absorb the truth of what has happened, the tragedy, and then I have to greet my mother.

None of them knows.

None of them knows my father is still alive.

They all think he died years ago, the way the Soviets told it.

I feel as old as this old lady. We pull each other from the car.

"We have to be quick," she says. "No one must stay in the same place for long. Too many watchers."

She knocks once on the door, and it opens immediately.

This is Sergei. I know that from the smile of welcome, from the beard, from the sense of peace. . . .

We are shown into a corridor, paneled in wood. A living room full of dark cabinets, glass decanters, sepia photos of people who never smile. You wonder why they stood like that, so stiff and unwilling. Was this how they wanted to be remembered? There is, I notice, the obligatory chandelier, semifunctional, crouching low over a round table.

"She'll be with us in a moment," he says quietly.

"Where is she?"

"She wanted to look her best. . . ."

"What the hell do I care what she looks like? She's my mother, for Chrissake. . . ."

He stands there not knowing what to do with my rudeness. . . .

"I'm sorry," I tell him. "It's been a strain."

"I understand," he says softly.

But he doesn't. How could he? He has no idea of the disaster he has let himself in for. . . .

The old lady points to the sofa. "We'll wait here, Sergei," she says. "But we don't have long. Yekaterina too—she must leave tonight as planned. You know that."

"Come with me for a moment," he replies, and leads us by a back staircase into a first-floor room. It's dark and cramped, but I can see two men with headphones and boxes of assorted electronics in front of them. They're sitting on upturned buckets, which looks comical enough, but they pay no attention to us. I'm struck by the pungent smell from an assortment of armpits, a faint hum of machinery—an air of makeshift commitment. Russia.

We back carefully out of the room.

"Who are they?"

"Private security firm," says Sergei. "Big business here these days. The two you saw used to work *'v lyesu'* in the forest."

"What's that?"

"Slang for the KGB. Department Twenty—internal surveillance. Now they do it for real money. They're checking the security frequencies, also the British and American embassies, trying to make sure we don't get unexpected visitors. They know what to look for—nothing's changed."

"You seem to have thought of everything," I say.

Silence.

"Or nothing," replies a voice behind me. "You never know until the end."

She is standing in the corridor, in a simple blue skirt and a white blouse—she looks as though she's come in from a day at the office. A slick, powerful woman—way past forty, way past fifty, but not too old to rule anything out. A woman of substance—a woman who travels, a woman lived in and with, a whole cauldron of passion and emotion; and she's holding out her arms to me, just as she did when I was a child.

"Aren't you going to give your mother a kiss?" she asks.

We stand looking at each other for a moment, without moving.

I try not to feel five years old again, being led by the hand, down the stairs into the living room, where she hugs me, far longer than I want.

"Put me down, Mother. You don't know where I've been."

"I do," she says. "Most of it, anyway."

Sergei and the old lady have stayed out of the room. So it's just the two of us on the sofa, eyeing each other, as if we're buying horses at an auction. She doesn't look like a fugitive. The red hair is luxurious and newly cut. She looks freshly packaged, there's makeup on her eyes, straight black lines drawn in the beauty salon. But there's a hue to her cheeks that hasn't come from a bottle. She's relaxed—what is it? . . . almost younger . . . and we sit there, each trying to dissect the other's thoughts, the way Slavs do, pulling at the heartstrings.

"You're married," I say lamely.

"He means nothing to me." She laughed. "He means everything to me. It is like our destiny. To find each other after thirty years. Maria told you, didn't she? Do you mind very much?"

"I . . . mind is not the word, Mum. I am pleased—what can I say. Of course I'm pleased—but . . ."

"There are other things we need to discuss."

"Exactly."

"All right. I have to get out of here. Sergei is fixing that. They have a safe house for me, a little way out of Moscow. You should get out of sight too. Maria will arrange it. I don't know what I would do without her. You can contact me through her. But it may take time. . . ."

"Mum, I have to know what's going on." I can feel her

slipping away. "I'm shot at, I'm pursued by American and British agents. A Russian businessman—dead in London, and there's a whole trail of bodies leading here. Everyone says you have some incredibly secret documents from the party archives—just stop for a moment and tell me what is happening."

She shook her head. "We don't have time for this."

"Then I'm not leaving here."

"Edward." She got up and walked to the door. "Later I will tell you everything. . . ."

"There will be no later, Mum. People connected with you and me are dying at a pretty extraordinary rate, these days. You can walk away if you want—but I'm finished with this."

"You . . ." Whatever epithet was in her mind was stifled at the last moment. She came back to the sofa and sat down again. But there was no question of giving in. Mother had never conceded anything, least of all victory.

"Two minutes." She looked at her watch. "Then I go."

I nodded.

"In London, the day before your birthday, I get a strange call. Man speaking Russian, very nervous, tells me he has to see me quickly. In town somewhere. We meet. He's in a terrible state. Been in a fight over some girl. I've seen the type before. He's a bureaucrat—a nothing. Corrupt and deeply untrustworthy. The kind of Russian you buy for a bag of seeds. Anyway, this time he has something valuable. 'I'm an archivist,' he says. 'I worked in the Central Committee. I saw everything.' And he holds up his flight bag. 'In here,' he says, 'is the kind of material the world will kill for. . . .' "

"He was right."

"Of course he was. But I said to him, 'I don't care about your material. I want to be left in peace. I want to have nothing to do with Russia.' And then he goes all sly on me and starts grinning. 'There is something about you too,' he says. 'A document that you would very much like to see. You remember Sergei? What will you give me for that piece of paper, dear lady?' Edward, at that point I got mad. I go completely crazy. Sergei I had not seen for thirty years. It was the man I had loved perhaps more than anyone else. I start hitting him, wildly. He's sitting in my car—no strength at all, and I'm smashing his head against the dashboard—

and suddenly"—and I can see a shadow now in her eyes—"suddenly, Edward, he's not there anymore. No resistance. No spirit. Nothing." She wiped a hand over her face. The skin was shiny. Her breathing faster. "Edward—he's gone. Dead in my hands. I . . . To this day I don't now. . . . I used to slap you harder sometimes."

"What happened then?"

"I take the flight bag, and I run like crazy . . . what people must have thought . . . an old hag through the streets . . . and I don't know where I am anymore, somewhere beside the river . . . I see this big hotel, and I go in and sit down. Two vodkas, three—I don't remember. But I open the bag. My God, and I start reading, reading. Top level—you wouldn't believe. Letters between the Kremlin and America's president, the prime minister, Germany's chancellor—cynical, unbelievable letters, trying to keep the cold war alive, all of them . . . my hair was standing, Edward. At nine o'clock that night, I know I have to go to Moscow. Sergei is alive. That is one thing. But the other documents. This was too important. . . ." She looks at her watch. "We have to go. You have to go."

"Finish the story. What then?"

"I ring this creep I know—Russian journalist. Used to be KGB only they dumped him because he drank too much. 'I need a visa now,' I tell him. 'How much?' he says. 'Hundred,' I say. 'Three hundred,' he replies. So I go round there and pick him up, and we drive to some dingy little flat in Bayswater. He barges his way in, as if he owns it, and there's this silly little creature there, secretary from the Soviet embassy, all frills and makeup, I thought I was in a whorehouse. He gives her a hundred, and then we drive to the embassy. She takes my passport and comes out ten minutes later with the visa—all typed. 'It's going to cost another hundred.' She giggles. 'I had to give the security guard something.' I think she gives it to everyone. So I say good-bye to the creep, and next morning I'm on the British Airways flight to Moscow."

"And you had the papers with you?"

"Of course I did."

"You didn't even hide them?"

"Edward, they couldn't care less what you bring in—it's what you take out they want to know."

Sergei is suddenly back in the room. "We're leaving," he

says. "Now. There is unusual movement from the American embassy. They have some units apparently heading for the Kievsky Bridge. . . ."

"What units?"

"Unmarked cars, plenty of men in suits. Now let's move."

And suddenly there are more people in this house than I thought, and a lot of hurried movement. Papers are being swept into bags, footsteps are clumping down the staircase. Mother and I look at each other.

"I need to see those documents."

"Now now, Edward. You heard—we have to leave." She's half running across the living room, down the corridor.

"Just how long do you think you can keep this up?" I shout.

"Long enough. We're going to show the world these papers—and then finally there will be some peace."

We're outside now, and she's in one car, and I'm being pushed pretty forcefully into another. The old lady is next to me, the leather jacket is driving, we're heading fast through the streets—and Mother's car has already gone, turned off somewhere, disappeared. We're into a tiny alley now, barely space for the car to move, strange concrete buttresses, a jagged open tunnel. . . .

"What is this place? . . ."

"Part of the metro system that was never finished," says Maria. "There are holes like this all over the city—if you know where to look."

The driver switches off the engine, and we slide about fifty yards into the tunnel and stop. I can hear water dripping—and the sound of unspecified vermin, clawing and scavenging. Probably the whole structure is unsafe and will collapse on itself. Who knows, and anyway—what does it matter?

For me, it's the safest place in Moscow.

Chapter Thirty-four

"You were going to tell me who you are."

"Was I?" she asked. "You really don't know, do you?"

We're in this tunnel, somewhere under Moscow, half-built, half-thrown away—a perfect model for the rest of the country.

"You don't remember a lady who visited you many years ago. Someone who came from such a long way away. You were so very young, and I must have seemed so very old . . . Stanley Gardens, Stanley Road, I used to take you to the sweet shop on the corner. You were such a strong-willed little boy, ideas on everything, opinions, pain in the neck, if you hadn't been my own . . ."

I look at her in amazement.

"I stayed four weeks. We talked—you remember. In those days, you never asked questions. Yekaterina had trained you well. But you wanted to read everything, came and looked in my suitcase, read even the newspapers that I had wrapped my shoes in, you were hungry for Russian things. . . ."

"And then you left suddenly without saying good-bye."

"You do remember." She smiled. "I had started to care about you. I had started to think like an old fool—maybe I could stay in London, maybe I could have a new life . . . yes, even a stupid creature like me, stupid old Maria from Moscow. Maybe I could go to sweet shops and eat in restaurants and live in a country where they didn't have to worry about the police and the thugs and all the nonsense propaganda. And so it was time to go back. I had started to think England was normal. It was definitely time to return."

"But we never heard from you again."

"From time to time I spoke to your mother." She pats me on the hand. Her fingers are ice-cold.

"So you're my grandmother."

"I'm your grandmother." She tries to smile. "I would welcome you to Russia, but I wish with all my heart that you were in a safer land."

Dawn was an hour or two away when they dropped me at a hotel off Smolensk Square. The driver took me in, because he knew someone who worked there, who knew someone else who could fix the paperwork—and they didn't want me in their safe house—and nor did I.

"Tomorrow," he said. "Six o'clock. Corner of Petrovka Street and Maly Karetny. If not tomorrow—next day. Someone will be there each evening, same time. No waiting."

He's like Yevgeny—this one. Brash and confident and nervous—all at the same time. What did he do in the old days? What did any of them do?

I wasn't going to sleep. I sat on the bed, just to steady myself.

And it wouldn't be long, I thought. They'd come very soon. Irina and friends, the blood of Arkady fresh on their hands.

I have very little time left.

Already, it's been a night of terrible realizations. Mother married again—unaware that Dad is still alive. Who could devise such shattering injustice? How do I tell her? How do I tell her I need the files? All our lives, and all the things that matter to us, are on the line.

Wherever he is—I have to reach Dad. This is what counts most to me. This has been my priority for so many years. I have to find him and get him out, whatever way I can.

That's why I don't wait in a room for them to come. I get out of the hotel, because I will set the venue and the time.

It's cold in that Moscow dawn. Within minutes I'm on the new concrete strip of Kalinin Prospekt, passing the high-rise apartments and the shops that should have been supermarkets and never were. It's a long, straight chunk of urban ugliness, rearing up out of the dark, into the morning clouds.

I turn into the flow, trudging toward the Lenin Library, and now the road has narrowed, four lanes into two, past the House of Friendship, and I can see the towers of the Kremlin in the distance—and Irina will come here to face me. Irina knows where I am.

You see—I haven't come here all these years without learning how the game is played, learned the language, learned what they're telling you, when they say nothing at all.

Take the hotel—the driver never said this, and I never asked. But by checking in—I automatically signaled my presence and my location. I filled out a card that would have gone direct to the former KGB headquarters within the hour. I was followed on my way out of the hotel—I was followed along Kalinin Prospekt. They're with me as I move into Red Square, but I don't know who they are.

I'll go down to the embankment, past St. Basil's, I'll look out over the Moscow River. I'll see the smoky chimneys and the power station that once sported the most idiotic slogan in Moscow—"Communism Means Soviet Power and the Electrification of the Whole Country." Such a catchy phrase.

This is the place to wait. I turn around and look at the faces one by one—especially the couples. The people who seem a bit too much in love for so early in the morning. They're the ones who're putting on an act.

Twenty yards away, left, there's a youngish woman in jeans and sneakers, beige anorak, a hair band. She's quick and lively, gazing at her man and mouthing short, staccato chunks at him. But there's a distinct absence of chemistry between them. He looks far too stupid for her. Square forehead, hairline an inch above the nose. And he's not doing too well. He's in suit and raincoat, carrying a transparently empty briefcase. It's so light that when he put it down for a second, a gust of wind blew it over. And he's wooden—shoulders like a doorframe. He wouldn't work in an office—he'd be more likely to build it.

She's kissing him good-bye now—on the cheek, for God's sake—they don't get paid nearly enough to do it on the mouth—so she's just going off to report my position, while he stands there aimlessly, palms almost scraping the ground.

Not good, these two.

It's starting to rain—so I'll make it easy for Irina. I walk back up to Red Square, where the tourists are starting to make a run for GUM—the color drips from their faces. Someone slips on the cobbles. The police in long gray capes huddle under the trees.

Turn right now. And I'm going to have breakfast at the Metropole Hotel, the one the Finns did up with money *they* won't make back, and the Russians never had.

Outside, two photographers are sheltering with cardboard cutouts of Gorbachev and Yeltsin. Haven't we moved on? Have we? One of them puts a plastic bag over Yeltsin's head and pats it. "Got to look after you, Boris Nikolayevich," he says. "Can't let you get wet in the rain."

Up the stairs now, bar on the left, dining room like a museum—no beautiful people.

I eat scrambled eggs on white china with gold rings. I pay ridiculous prices. And then I sit with a can of beer, waiting for Irina. When the rain stops and the streets clear and she's found out I'm alone—then she'll come.

She arrived on the edge of dusk, when I had wasted a whole day, thought too much, drunk too much.

"Why did you kill Arkady—you and your bastards?"

"I don't set the rules," she said.

"You set the conditions. There are no rules. You murder, you lie, and you extort. And you call those 'rules.' "

"You want me to go?"

She drapes her raincoat over the back of her chair and reveals a white wool polo neck that hugs her breasts and makes me remember that she nearly turned my twenty-year-old head. It's a disgusting thought, given what she's done to me since.

She orders herself a beer and points to mine.

"You shouldn't drink so much, Edward. You could find yourself with an alcohol problem. . . ."

"It's kind of you to worry. . . ."

"And we do, Edward, we do worry." She gulped a mouthful of beer. "How is your mother?"

"How's yours?"

She put the beer down.

"Right—let us review the progress so far. You have met her, I take it. You have discussed the proposition. And now we wish to secure the handover of our rightful property. This is the subject of our discussion. Nothing else. You can do all the moralizing you want at a later date."

"There's another subject—my father. I want assurances about his condition."

"He's holding his own."

"I need to see that."

"When we get the documents . . ."

"Now."

A couple sits down, at an adjoining table, closer than necessary. I recognize them from the morning. But they look tired. Man with briefcase—girl with headband. Only they aren't kissing anymore or holding hands, just sitting sullenly, awaiting instructions.

"when do we get the files, Edward?"

"Within forty-eight hours."

"There can be no going back on this, you understand, don't you?"

"Perfectly."

"Good." She pours the rest of the beer into her glass, and I'm wondering why I've just said this. That's what happens when you sit around all day drinking. I've just promised her papers I don't have, and I've fixed a deadline. I might as well have dug my grave and gone to sit in it.

She gets up.

"One more thing," I tell her.

"Surprise me."

"Jane Card. You have no reason to hold her. Let her go."

"You're quite right, Edward. We have no reason to hold her, and that is why we don't."

"What do you mean?"

"I mean what I just said. We didn't detain Mrs. Card, and I have no knowledge of her location."

"You're lying. . . ."

"I think we're past that stage, Edward. I don't think any of us needs to lie anymore, do you?"

I follow her out into the street. This city is a mask, and beneath it a whole series of different faces. I can't recognize them, can't tell them apart. Which one is hiding Jane Card?

Opposite us the Bolshoi is propped up with scaffolding. Taxi drivers are standing around, touting for business. As we pass, one of them holds his nostril and blows the other onto the pavement.

You know you're abroad here—every minute of every day. Well outside Europe. Outside everywhere.

"Where's the transport?" I ask.

"We'll walk," she replies.

I turn around, searching for the intrepid couple, but I can't see them.

And if you please, we're heading up the hill toward the Lubyanka, right side, keeping clear of the street-sellers, accosting everyone outside the big toy store.

Ahead of us—the plinth from which they plucked the statue of Dzherzhinsky, bearded psychopath who founded the first state security machine. He may have gone—but Irina is following nicely in his footsteps.

We take half an hour to reach the apartment block. It's almost in the road, standing, sinking on a little island—a lone survivor stuck between the six lanes of the Ring Road. It's like crossing hell to get there, as the cars and trucks spray us with damp filth and the yellow headlights seem to hunt us down. The noise is intolerable.

But now I'm hurrying. I see a path through two buses. We're separated, me dashing forward, leaving her shouts behind, the little killer in her raincoat, stuck in the Moscow traffic. I'm into the building, and she's still pinned down out there.

One entrance only. Loose wooden stairs. What is this place? I need to see Dad, need to know what they've done to him.

Second story and there's a distinct shortage of guards

here—unlike the old days. Dad used to be watched by an entire posse, and I had a thug for each of my fingernails. Now I push open a door, and there's just a frosty old concierge wielding a teapot.

"He's through there," she bellows, pointing to a corridor beyond. And as I follow her finger, I can feel my pulse quicken with excitement.

It strikes me I've almost forgotten how to hope, how to feel elated, how to thank God for the kind of surprise that is sitting in front of me.

"Holding his own," Irina had said, and I expected to find a man in a coma. Dad's in bed, but it's as if he's home, and the light is on in every room. There's a book on the covers beside him, a cup of tea in his hand. His jaw is hard and lined like a peach stone. "I'm not finished yet," he seems to be saying.

He isn't, nor am I.

Chapter Thirty-five

I know my dad. Even with all the broken years, I know him.

And while his mind is open and reaching out, his hands are cold and the strength has gone out of them. It's as if he's started to wander away, down a long slope.

I hold him tight. Stop there, Dad, come back. You can do it. I can get you out of here. We can go home.

And yet, when I look at him, he is home. A Russian in Russia—not like me, born and conditioned in Britain. He is strangely at peace in this filthy little room, with the traffic raging around him. No frills, he used to say. No extras. Real life, stripped bare.

I ask how they've treated him.

"They're Russian," he says. "They expect me to suffer. Doctors give out medicine, patients suffer. Each of us has a role, each has to play it."

For a moment, the noise of a siren fills the room. The lightbulb is swinging tiny circles at the end of its wire.

"Mother's fine," I say, hoping he won't probe deeper.

He nods and smiles. "You know I used to carry this picture of your mother in my head. Not real one. Make-believe. There would be a nuclear war. Total destruction. Towns and cities reduced to rubble. And there"—he smiles again—"there, marching through all this desolation would be your mother. Strong and purposeful. The only person who would get through. The one survivor. When everything else had been blown to hell—your mother would be there. She . . . she would be the one to deliver. Strong, so strong, that one . . ." He seems to lose his way for a moment and wipes a hand across his forehead. "I would give so much to see her again . . . I often . . . Edward, tell me, I been thinking so much. . . . I did wrong to leave you and come back here. I know this for a long time already. Tell me the truth. Please."

For a moment, I can't answer. And what, in any case, is the truth to an old man lying sick on a bed in Moscow? An old man who's my father. What is the cost of this truth?

"No, Dad," I tell him. "You had to go. . . ."

"But I left you as a little child. . . ."

"You never left. I always knew you were there. Even when they said you had died. . . ."

"It was wrong decision."

"Why do you say that?"

"Because a man cannot jump from one world to another. I jumped to England—I should have stayed there. . . ."

"It wasn't you. . . ."

"Then too bad. I could have made accommodations. I had a wife and a son—who should have more in life?—and I thought only of myself. Edward, if I tell you how bitterly I regret all the pain. I just didn't know what else to do. I was blind . . . I looked at my life, and I couldn't see you. I didn't know until I had gone. You have to believe me. . . ."

There are tears down his cheek, damp patches on the pillow.

"It's all right." And I take his hand again. "I understand. You were trapped in an alien world. Mother said so. No point of reference. No landmarks. Outside the house it was like a jungle for you. I never blamed you. Nor did she. We understand. It wasn't a world you could live in."

"There was the work. . . ." He coughs and clears his throat. "Edward, I was a scientist, physics, important work. The study of my life. In England it was just not possible. Always I had feeling I was working for foreigners, against my people, against this land I had grown up in. For that, too, I had to leave. Even when I knew of the cruelty and the stupid, stupid decisions, the endless lying—these were my people. Look, look . . . go to the window."

I get up, not understanding what he means.

"Look out," he commands. "What do you see?"

The sky is almost black, but over to the west there are brush lines of crimson, cranes against the skyline, rooftops, jagged and haphazard.

"A Russian sunset," he says simply. "Even when it is dark, the sun leaves its mark in the sky. A sign of hope," he says. "It is not all darkness here. Even when you look out of the window and see the night. You understand, my son?"

He lies back on the pillow and closes his eyes. We never talked like this in the past. We talked about events—not feelings. His childhood, my childhood—the things and the people that made us smile. The way the world had gone and was going.

Now he's trawling through his mind for something else—for the peace he never had.

"What troubles you, Dad? What is it?"

"I also ask this," he says. "It is not the end that troubles me—or the beginning. It is the middle. The middle of my life. This is what is wrong. The beginning and the end you have no control over—someone else brings you into the world—someone else carries you out, bumping your feet against the walls. The middle is where I should have done more. You are the middle, Edward. I would wish to have done more for you. You are my regret. More than I can say."

Irina is in the room. For the first time, I can feel her presence. I get up and kiss Dad on his wet cheek, holding his head in my arms. "I'll come again soon. In a couple of days. We're going to be together now."

And there's an answer from his eyes—a flash of warmth, the beginnings of a distant hope.

We stop by the front door.

"He is as I told you," she says.

"When did the doctor last see him?"

"This morning. He will come again tomorrow." She shakes her head at me. "And in case you have any silly plans—your father will be moved within the hour. We have all taken to moving around this city, rather than staying in one place." She bites her lip. "Safer that way."

I go out and stand on the curb, waiting for my moment to cross.

"Forty-eight hours," she shouts. "Remember that. . . ."

"I'll contact you. . . ."

"No," she answers. "We'll contact you."

I hail a taxi that almost runs me over. I'm shattered by the sight of Dad. But there isn't time to hang around or get lost in emotion. That's what bogs you down in Russia—oceans of wounded feelings, of invalid souls, and neat suffering, like neat alcohol, served out in huge quantities to everyone.

I know what I have to do—and what I can't. I can't tell Dad that Mother has married again. Not here in Moscow, not a few miles from his bed. I know he wanted her to get on with life and grab some happiness. All the same, I won't be the messenger for that.

And there's the other side of it. I can't tell Mother that the husband she thought was dead is dying again. I can't rake her a second time through the pain and the loss, can't burden her with more anguish than she carries already. When this is over, there must be something she can hold on to.

I ask the taxi to go to the Aerostar Hotel—and this is one more gamble. It's the hotel I would have stayed in with Harry and his colleagues. A concrete square of modern Canadian luxury, set back from the Leningradsky Prospekt, the road to the airport. Opposite lies a military barracks and another park of straggly trees, bowed and leafless from the October winds. Just the way I feel.

I don't know if Harry is still there.

But I need his help.

Chapter Thirty-six

Harry is not alone. Harry is drunk. Harry is less than delighted to see me.

He falls off the barstool and slopes toward me.

"See that, Edward." He points to the girl he's just left. "That is my fun for tonight. Got it? Not you, not the boys, not the fucking business—but that little Ninotchka, who is my birthday present to myself."

"Happy birthday, Harry."

"Thanks, Edward. Now fuck off and leave me alone."

I have to admit that in a choice between me and his date, Harry has done the right thing. The girl is truly lovely. Blond, narrow-hipped, large-breasted, and with that air of superiority that would seem to rule out any kind of financial transaction. She would always appear enthralled by her companion, she would feign love, she would feign endless and continuous orgasm. She would pocket the money only in passing, since it just happened to be there. She is Harry's for the night, and he is hers. I couldn't have chosen a worse time.

I approach the bar and order a lemon vodka. Harry's hands are resting on the girl's lower thighs, but his eyes leave her and follow me.

For a moment, curiosity seems to win out over lust.

He comes back over, taking me by the arm, leading me to a table.

"You really pissed me off, Edward, you know that, don't you?"

"Yes, Harry."

"So what are you doing here?"

"I need your help."

"I'm drunk, and I'm going to take Ninotchka upstairs to put me to bed."

"Sounds like fun."

"Fun is what I need, Edward, what I crave. I'll be straight with you—you weren't much fun on this trip. Lots of early mornings and people pointing guns at me—that's not fun, is it?"

"So . . ."

"So before I throw you out, I want to know what you're doing."

And then I see it in his expression. Not just the drunkenness—but Harry really wants to know. Harry has this liking for the odd, the corrupt, and the violent. He misses it. He thinks about it—the good old days when a clunk on someone else's head was far more satisfying than a hundred contracts, signed and delivered.

I look at the sweat marks on his shirt collar. Dear old Harry, pissed as a rat, zip wide open, longing for a chase and a punch-up. The effort of going straight is much too much for him.

I open my mouth to speak, but he's back at the bar, talking earnestly to the girl, giving her something in his hand. Money? A key?

"She'll wait," he says when he comes back. "I told her to go and get ready."

I look up, and she's on her way to the lift, sliding not walking, in one of those midlength black dresses that could be daywear, or evening wear, or nothing-at-all wear, loose, light, with points of entry at every conceivable angle. For a moment, I'm deeply envious of Harry. And then he slumps onto the leather sofa beside me. And all I can hear is his heavy, arrhythmic breathing, as I tell him what I want him to do.

* * *

I spent the night on the floor in Harry's room. Ninotchka had left him about midnight, professing undying love, taking two hundred dollars, just for expenses, "you understand, darling"—not for payment. "What I did was for love."

I had been waiting in the corridor, so I heard the whole thing.

He slept till eight—and now we go downstairs to arrange the day.

Costa and Arthur have also emerged from the sexual undergrowth. They both have a raging thirst and are emptying glasses of orange juice down their throats. Evidently Moscow has exceeded expectations during the hours of darkness.

Last night I actually recounted most of the story to Harry, but he probably doesn't remember it. In any case, none of them seems that bothered.

They've all had enough of paperwork and figures. "Besides," says Costa, "I feel like a bit of action."

At nine we pick up their rental car. The cold is a welcome shock—like a punch in the face. An easterly wind is tearing a wide strip across the city. Harry looks like a red-faced scarecrow, with his coat and his baggy trousers flapping wildly in the breeze.

I suppose we're more or less ready. Between us we have a map and a gun—and I know how to use at least one of them. But that's not really the point. We will issue some invitations, we will do some largely gratuitous intimidation. For afters we'll lie and mislead and then dispose of some stolen goods among a band of thieves. It's all home territory for Harry.

We stop beyond the American embassy, the old yellow-ocher building, flying the flag, still hunting for bugs years after the Russians drew a map of where to find them. In the old days, the Stars and Stripes meant something, billowing above the Ring Road, reminding everyone that there was grass on the other side—and yes, it was greener—but no, sorry, they couldn't have any.

Nowadays it's just a symbol of another cockeyed system, with no one of its own size to play with.

I can imagine the kinds of games they'll have to dream up to stay active.

Harry wants to know what to do.

"You and the boys—stay in the car," I tell him. "If it looks like I'm outnumbered, you might want to come out and glare at a few people."

"Right." Harry doesn't have to think too far back to know how to glare.

The embassy is fronted by low concrete barriers and a couple of police guard posts. But they're not interested in me. They don't care who goes in. The days when they used to bludgeon their own people half to death for even hinting they might want to enter are long gone. Now it's the Americans who want to keep you out.

Inside the door is a glass cage, doubtless bomb-proof, certainly dissident-proof, behind which sits a uniformed marine, his cap pulled well down, and a Colt revolver resting fat and shiny on his thigh. I have no idea if this is going to work.

"Sir." At close quarters, the officer is spotty and hairless—his nose like a miniature blimp. I can see the remains of a suntan. But there's no smile today. America is not putting its friendly foot forward.

"I've come to see Edgar Coffin."

The guard leafs through a folder.

"We have no one by that name, sir."

"I think you do."

"Just a moment, sir."

Every embassy has a procedure for troublemakers. Rudeness, ignorance, comforting, meaningless phrases to fob you off. I wonder which they'll choose. The guard lifts his receiver. "There's a gentlemen here asking for a Mr. Edgar Coffin. I'm not showing a Coffin."

He replaces the handset. "Someone will be down to see you in a moment. Step this way, sir." He presses a buzzer to open the glass door. And if I was an even bigger idiot than I am, I would walk through into the soft, comforting clutches of the embassy, I would sit in a fat armchair, help myself to coffee, and leaf through a two-month-old copy of *The New Yorker.* All of which would give them time to get Coffin, get his sidekicks—and find a suitable room in which to tear off my fingernails one by one and electrocute my genitals.

"Tell him I'm outside," I say to the guard.

Behind him I can see a tiny camera, recording every movement I make.

* * *

Coffin, like many tall examples of the species, has developed a sloping back. Or is it the cut of the brown tweed coat, the set of the shoulders, the attitude?

With him are two immaculate young men, much more fashionable, in calf-length blue coats, one fair, the other dark, with that swept-back hair, showered and blow-dried with infinite care just minutes earlier. Coffin is like a weather-beaten mongrel, beside them. They are professionally unpleasant. They do it for a living.

We come together on the street corner, slow, nonchalant—no jerky movements. Nothing to upset the passersby or the police. Everyone very careful. Walking on glass.

"Edward," says Coffin, experimenting with a smile. "Wonder if you'd mind stepping inside with us for a moment? My friends here will help you if you feel faint . . ."

He breaks off, and I feel their eyes shifting from me to a space behind my back. . . .

"He's not faint at all," says Harry, right beside me. Good boy, Harry. All the old instincts on target. "He's having the time of his bleeding life, aren't you, Edward? Besides, such a pity to go inside on a nice day like this."

Coffin has given up on the smile. Costa and Arthur have joined our happy little group. We all stand around for a moment, contemplating our navels. I like watching Coffin's embarrassment.

"Why don't you and I take a little stroll," he says to me. "Just the two of us." He gives his bluecoats a pointed look.

We move off toward Kalinin Prospekt. Coffin puts on a pair of woolen gloves as if he would like to perform surgery on me.

"You're becoming quite a surprise, my friend," he says.

"So are you. An unpleasant one."

He shrugs carelessly, as if it's all the way of the world. But now that I see him again, I'm suddenly very interested in why this man has changed his colors. I played with him as a child; at times he almost lived in my house. He roamed the countryside exploring every inch of my mother. Now he would kill me. . . .

"What happened, Coffin? Why did all this go wrong? You came to see me in the hospital; you were still a friend. You wanted to help me and Mother. Was it all an act?"

I stop and turn to face him. He looks older each time I see him. It's as if his aging process has accelerated dramatically. So it strikes me that, on this cold Moscow street, these may be the final moments of honesty we will share.

"I wish it weren't like this, Edward." He exhales deeply into the cold, damp air. "But this one is big. Very big. I'm under the kind of pressure I never dreamt of. Threats to me. Threats to my family, even. You have no idea what you've set off. I had no choice. . . ."

"I don't get it. I thought this was the kind of system we've been fighting *against* all these years. What the hell was the cold war about? We were trying to destroy a government that did such things to its people, threatened them, used them, threw them away. Coffin—this has to stop somewhere. . . ."

"Not here, Edward. Not now." He turns away. "They're all the same—the governments—you know that. Okay, the pain thresholds are different—some tolerate the weirdos and misfits; others don't. But when you cross that threshold—they'll lash out any way they can. . . ."

"Can't you just walk away?"

"If I didn't care about my family, if I didn't care about having a home to go back to—maybe I would." He made a face. "Or maybe I haven't got the strength. You'd call it fiber, I suppose. I haven't got the balls to walk away. I'm getting old, and I don't want to be hunted down and shot in a gutter. . . ."

"Who, Coffin? . . ."

"I can't even begin to tell you. Right now our lives are being priced about the same as a bag of beans. If I told you, we might as well lie down under that fucking bus. . . ." He points to a dirty red-and-white contraption, unloading passengers across the road.

"Can't you stop it?"

"Only you can stop it," he said. "You and your mother. Give them the documents they want—the originals. Give them the dirt, and let them bury it—it's the only way."

"And if we don't?"

"You'll die first, and I'll die a few hours later. They don't want prisoners. They don't want tracks. They'll put us in graves where not even the worms will find us. . . ."

"But . . ."

"Good-bye, Edward. I've talked long enough. You see those two boys of mine. Three hundred years ago they'd have been wearing masks and carrying a chopping ax. And you'd have had to tip them to cut your head off cleanly. Same job. Same executioners. Tell me what you have to say—and get the hell out of here."

Chapter Thirty-seven

Harry and I leave the boys in the car and sit on a park bench. I owe him a short discussion. I owe him a final chance to get up and go. He's sitting there quite relaxed, low down on the wooden boards, legs splayed out, eyes closed. But I don't know what he's thinking.

"You should go, Harry. Take the boys, catch a plane, get out of here. It's going to be pretty nasty."

"That's what you said last night."

"I think we've had it confirmed again this morning."

"What, Coffin and those two ponces? Don't give it another thought, son. Not another thought."

Beyond us, there's a row of notice boards where people have stuck scraps of paper and cards, little adverts for lonely hearts, or piano lessons. And Mrs. Authority, in the shape of a cleaner, is tearing them all off and pasting on a giant poster. So you see how bloody hard it is to get anything done here, to make an impression, to even dent the surface.

Harry is watching too.

"Fucking awful place," he says, and then looks at me. "But we're not leaving yet."

"Why not?"

He sniffs. "Because it's not the right thing to do."

"I don't understand."

"Look at it this way. Here's this lad from the East End. Brought himself up, got a nice place on the river and a business that's doing fine. All right—a little aggravation along the way. All right—a lot of aggravation. But I've learned a few things. And I know what I did right and what I didn't."

Harry sits up.

"You know, ever since I came out of jail, I wanted to do something really good. Know why?"

I shook my head.

"I was brought up by my aunt most of my childhood. Parents were killed in an air raid. Dad was home on leave from the army. Took Mum out for the evening, and they went and stood under the wrong bomb."

"I'm sorry."

" 'Course you are. So was I. My aunt brought me up. Mum's younger sister, Doris—gentle, and fair, and no match at all for a stroppy little bugger like me. So I went my way, and she just stood on the sidelines, patched me up when I came home, washed my clothes, and loved me. . . ." Harry stopped for a moment and swallowed hard. "I think she loved me because she never had anyone of her own. Anyway, when I was nicked, it broke her up more than anyone else. And more than I'd ever imagined. She was desperate. She'd come to see me and cry buckets, and all I could do was sit the other side of the glass—and say it was going to be all right, I'd make it up to her, some such bloody nonsense." Harry took out a handkerchief and blew his nose. "Anyway, by the time I got out, she was dead. Died of a heart attack, after shopping in Sainsbury's—must've been the prices. . . ." He smiled for a moment, but I could see the sorrow was quite genuine. "So I made her a promise. You know, stood by the grave and said I'd do something right by her. I'd make it up. I'd go straight and start doing things for people. . . ." He pursued his lips. "It's been a bloody effort, Edward, I can tell you. . . ."

It's my turn to smile.

"So after our little misunderstanding on the train, I kept thinking it was a shame really, 'cos you could have done with a favor, and I could have done something for my aunt at the same time."

"It's become a bit more dangerous now, Harry."

"I know," he says, "I've thought about that too." He digs out his wallet and produces a small photograph in a plastic frame. "That's her, taken about a year before she passed on." It's a woman in a long brown coat and gloves, smiling nervously as if she's on a special day out. Clamped on her head is a hat with a felt flap, hanging limply, like a spaniel's ear. "Aunt Doris . . ." he announces proudly. "She'll look after me. Always has."

At six o'clock, I'm alone. More accurately, I appear to be alone, standing on the corner of Petrovka and Maly Karetny streets, waiting for Mother's contact.

Six o'clock each evening, he'd said, the spiv in the black leather jacket. No waiting.

And nobody ever waited on this corner. In the Stalinist years, Petrovka was the site of the most notorious interrogation center. A jail, although nothing was just a jail—a place of execution. A place where they broke people and threw them away. An underground charnel house, well beyond the borders of any civilization. A land of fantasy trials and accusations, where death was delivered in quotas in the name of the greater good.

Why do they make me wait here?

From an open window, somewhere I hear a bell, the Moscow radio call sign, and a white Lada has come out of the maze of streets behind the prison, pulling in beside me. It isn't the same man. This one is older, more nervous, telling me to get in fast, leaning over and locking my door.

And while he's in a hurry, the traffic isn't. We're crawling onto the Dmitrovskoye Road, and he's pulling off down the side streets, muttering and gesticulating, only to rejoin the logjam farther on.

There's an epidemic of foreign cars. Where the hell do they get the money? They can't all be former party members who salted it away in Swiss banks. What's keeping this country afloat?

The driver has found the road he wants, a great empty tract past a stadium, a railway siding. We're turning now, climbing the concrete sidewalk, up a ramp and onto a flyover that hasn't been finished and in some places has barely been started. The underside of the car is crying out in pain but not enough to prevent us shooting up the wrong side of the road, zigzagging wildly to avoid the holes and the jagged edges. I look over, and the man has acquired a grin as wide as the Winter Palace, because if anything was following us before—it won't be following now. That's the logic.

We come down off the building site, clump around on the pavement, and head sedately back into the city center. I'm trying not to look in the mirror, not to imagine the worst.

When we stop, it's in a courtyard, about half a mile from where the journey began. Opposite side of the Ring Road. Tall pre-revolutionary terrace, tatty and peeling like everything else. But once it had style. Above the main door a pair of gargoyles are sitting on stone balls, to which they seem more than a little attached. There are lace curtains in the downstairs windows. Lace!

"They told me she was going out of town," I say to the driver.

He's still grinning. "They tell lots of things. It is of no consequence. You want to see her or not?"

As I get out, two men are descending the front steps to escort me. I recognize them from Sergei's house. They're from the new security company—only now they've changed into jackets and ties. And it seems to me this is suddenly a city of private armies, doing wonders for the dark-suit industry. Tailors working round the clock. Maybe Harry could do some shopping. . . .

I look back toward the car, as if I've forgotten something, but I have to check. . . .

Out of the corner of my eye, I see a dark Mercedes cross to the other side of the street and go out of sight. And I think to myself, you're very good, Harry Willets. In your time, I bet you were the best in the East End—what with your security gadgets, your radio microphones, and the homing transmitter you put on me a couple of hours ago.

As I take the stairs, I thank God for the memory of Aunt Doris with the terrible hat.

CHAPTER THIRTY-EIGHT

"HOW LONG CAN you run?"

She's more tired than when I last saw her, half-sitting, half-lying on a mattress in a basement room. The neat-pressed blouse has given way to a black pullover. The hair is lank and uncombed. Behind her, a cockroach sets out on the long march up the wall.

"I don't know, Edward. A few days, maybe. And then someone will talk. Whom can you trust? Russia changes with the tides—there is no order. No rule. Each day the sun rises again and the world is reinvented. You were on top today—who knows where you'll be tomorrow."

"How much time do you need?"

"A week, two weeks? The material . . . I mean, it is something quite out of this world. Names that are known across the world—here, there—and on their hands is blood, other people's blood, dripping from each of the pages. I have read nothing like it, my son. I never thought to see such things in my lifetime."

She gestures to the black flight bag beside the mattress. "I have kept it all—just as it was brought to me."

"They won't let you publish it, Mum."

"They won't be able to stop me." She sits up suddenly,

animated. "These are documents that will dominate the headlines from now until forever, years and years. . . ."

"Somehow they'll stop it, stop you. Look at the last few days. Look at the people who've had to die. They have their connections, their people. Believe me. . . ."

"Believe what? . . ." Her eyes are shining black with anger. "I believe this is worth any sacrifice to bring the truth to the world."

"A lot of people have made the sacrifice already. . . ."

"And there will be more."

"Why, Mother? Why, for God's sake? Why should you insist that people go on dying for something that's past? Just because you tell them? Just because you decide the world should know?"

"You're a fool, and you understand nothing. . . . You think I forget the people who have died. It is exactly because of them that I do this. For the ones I have known and the millions I haven't. So that they won't have died for nothing. Why do you think I came to Karol's funeral in Warsaw—at great risk to myself—why? Because he was my friend. We had met in the camps. And there you don't just meet people. You live on top of them, with them, sometimes in them. They keep you warm and feed you, and when you cry out in your sleep, they soak a filthy rag in water and put it on your forehead. Like I did with you as a child."

"I, too, have lost a friend. A lady who helped me—Jane Card. I think maybe you knew her."

"No."

"That's all you have to say?"

"What do you want, Edward? Shall I sing a hymn? I'm sorry for you, for her, for all of them."

I clapped, as if in appreciation.

"If that's not good enough," she said, "go home."

"Terrific, Mum. Well done. You know something . . . you won't be happy until we're all dead. And then what? You'll climb out of the ground and announce to all the bodies that you're the winner?"

I could see her moving toward it, but until it happened, I didn't think she'd slap me—a hard clap of anger from the flat of her hand—and she turns and walks straight out of the room.

I had needed to anger her—to provoke an outburst, get her away.

And I suppose the one thing I have in common with her is that I also believe I'm right. Totally. I haven't the slightest hesitation, seizing the black attaché case, checking the files inside, gathering some others she's left on the mattress. . . .

I'm on the stairs now. Stop a moment. Her voice is coming from another room, loud, tearful . . . she's telling someone what a shit her son is, and how he can't be trusted . . . and she's right about that.

I reach the hall. Bare wooden boards, worn smooth. A row of boots. A mirror cracked and discolored.

Three steps to the door.

Get the engine running, Harry.

Let's get out of here.

And I turn to see Sergei standing halfway up the staircase.

We watch each other in silence in the semidarkness. Light filters in through a dirty pane over the door. I am conscious of every sound—voices, traffic, life passing by outside this building.

Of course he knows. He knows many things that ordinary men can never know. Fifteen years in the camps, lived as an animal and returned as a human being. He has taken his mind to places I could never go—and he has come back.

I would like to sit down with this man. I would like to stare into his eyes—and lift out his past. For there is courage and knowledge that I can never touch.

"What would you say to me, Sergei?"

"Nothing that would change your mind."

"Why don't you stop me?"

"Sometimes there's a certain inevitability in life. It doesn't do to interfere."

"How do you know when?"

"You don't. It's a matter of trust."

"You all right?" asks Harry.

He was there, of course, when he was needed, ready to bulldoze a path through the traffic, break heads . . . I think he was disappointed to see me alone.

We're moving out along Kutuzovsky Prospekt, past the

old government apartments, the Triumphal Arch, right onto the Rublevskoye Chaussée.

"You sure you know what you're doing?"

Harry asks a succession of questions to which the answer is no. But I'm not expected to answer. He's only filling the silence.

Twenty minutes later we have a clearing beside the Moscow River. Someone's fishing in the distance. Someone's always fishing in Russia.

"You want me to photograph everything?" asks Harry.

"The whole lot."

"Have you read any?"

"Later."

"Doesn't look that interesting."

"Never does, Harry."

Eighteen rolls of film, and Harry is nursing his shutter finger. We get out and stand by the riverbank. The tide is well out, and I can see miles of mud and shingle stretching away toward the forests. It's an evil, unhappy sky, the clouds fast-moving and low, the wind plucking at the water, rain close by.

"And now?"

"You get moving, Harry. You pick up the boys. You drive to the airport. You get the first plane going west. Finland, Sweden. Wherever. Don't spend a lot of time, waiting in the lounge. Try to be late and try to be in a hurry. That way the airline girls will hustle you through Customs and Immigration—and there won't be the inclination to check you over. They like to please the girls, when they can."

"What happens when we get there?"

"Harry, listen to me. When you get to London, send the boys home, but you keep traveling. Take the boat train across the Channel, lose yourself on the Continent. A month, two months. Don't go back to your flat, whatever you do. Not now. When you're ready, call me from a phone box. Nowhere that can be traced. Do you understand me?"

"I'm beginning to." And Harry's face is draining its color. He's quiet, and there's a lot of thinking being done.

"What if there's no answer when I call you?"

"Don't come back. The boys will keep the business going. Stay out of reach and stay very quiet. If you can't get hold of me within six months, get the film printed up, make copies, and send the story to the major newspapers around the world—all of them, *New York Times, Washington Post, Daily Telegraph*—the lot. When they start publishing, go home and forget you ever knew any of this."

Harry gets in the car and says nothing. We come back into the city, and I notice that he's already at home here. He has an instinctive grasp of direction, an inbuilt compass. I've watched him handle a map even if he can't read the street signs. It's a gift that will serve him well in the weeks to come.

"You can drop me here, Harry."

"Wait a minute, Edward." He pulls into the side. Some of the color is back in his face, but Harry isn't going to be sentimental. He's not the type. He isn't going to throw his arms around me—or go all wet-eyed like Arkady; he just wants to tie a loose end.

"Edward, what if they don't publish? What if I send off all the pictures and nothing happens?"

"Then the danger will still be there. Then you lose yourself for good. You'll be marked, Harry. Understand that. They'll know who you are."

"Blimey." He lets out a big sigh and pats me on the shoulder. And then the car moves away. I watch for a moment, until the Moscow traffic pushes him out of sight. I hope Aunt Doris is riding with him.

Chapter Thirty-nine

I GIVE HIM three hours to get away.

Harry will need a fair wind, Harry will need luck; and life for Harry, if he keeps it, will never be the way it was.

So I have three hours to read.

I decide on a civilized act—dinner at a private restaurant behind Pushkin Square. They're very obsequious and very grateful because I'm the only person in there, and so I'm assured of privacy. There are four glasses I can choose for my wine—there is a starched white napkin the size of a flag. If I don't see what I want on the menu—they say they'll get it for me.

A young waiter admits they don't know how long they can stay in business.

Nor do I.

When the food and the bearers have gone, I open the case and read.

Five minutes in, ten.

The effect is gradual. It's like slow-acting poison, sinking steadily into the bloodstream, killing silently, routinely, as it travels.

It's a world where treason and deceit seem normal, devoid of drama. No talk of high stakes—no headlines or signposts. One word in front of the other . . . and I find myself wondering who typed this sort of thing—just a secretary, sitting in stockings and a cheap dress, with a bag of shopping on the floor, coat and scarf hung up? And what did she do—go for lunch in the middle, walk home after work; take a bus, watch television, go to a concert? How do you type this kind of thing and then go lead a normal life? At the very least, you'd open the window and jump out; you'd go home and thrust your head in the gas oven. You'd walk under a bus, or garrote yourself on a clothesline. But how could you walk the streets, peopled by humans, carrying such words in your head—as if nothing had happened?

This *is* fantasy land. Letters to and from the leaders of the world—papers written by one fool in one language to be read by a different fool in another.

And I begin to know the truth of my mother's words.

Later, they bring a candle to the table and ask if I'd like a cognac—French or Georgian. They have both. I take the Georgian. It's warmth and it's company for my journey.

I shouldn't be surprised by what I read. Imagine a nightmare, in which all the things you feared and suspected came true—and there they are, double-spaced, without a correction or deletion, in perfect, numbered order.

There are the assassinations, eliminations—there are the bribes and the forgeries, there are the politicians, bought, sold, and discarded around the world. Names, real names—addresses. Grand lies, and small lies, and little seams of truth, like rivers, running into a desert and drying up altogether.

I had to steal these papers from my own mother. I should know.

They opened the record on her when she was eighteen. There's a picture, shrunk to the size of a postage stamp—and even in this tiny image she's different. Her chin is held high, the eyes are alive. The hair is thick and untamed. She laughs at them from the pages of their own file.

Her teacher informed on her first of all.

—Bright girl, clever girl, daughter of workers—has the credentials, could go far.

Her neighbor informed.

—Ringleader for the other children in the block, noisy at night, spilt milk in the corridor, refused to clean it up.

A man from the housing committee informed.

—I don't like this girl—socially regressive, asks questions, questions authority.

And one by one the clouds came to circle above her, closer by the day.

A cousin informed.

—She plays, but she's but interested in the same things as normal kids. She made a joke about Brezhnev. We told her not to do it again.

Boyfriend informed.

—She said she had a dream about the West, and wanted to see New York. On the way back from the cinema, she made physical advances in a side street. I told her this was to be tolerated only within the boundaries of a secure and loving relationship. She insulted me, using socially unacceptable language.

And then the file seemed to take a journey of its own accord.

—KGB, Department Four. Timiryazev region.

A signature I can't read and a comment I can.

—Negative tendencies. Continue observation.

Mother is twenty years old and a sinner, because the paper says so.

I ask for mineral water. But there's no one to bring it.

The lights are out in the restaurant, the waiters have gone home, and the manager sits forlornly at his little desk, head in hands, snoring softly.

Do they all have files like this one?

A professor from medical school informed on my mother.

—Very good student. Worth taking, despite the risks. I have warned her against any antisocial behavior.

A friend informed on her.

—She has met a man called Sergei Kauzov, second-year student, I walked with them in the park. They get on well instinctively. He is quiet; she is noisy. And yet she looks to him for guidance. At one point, we joked about informers, and she said to me, "You won't tell on us, will you?" And we all laughed out loud. So I am certain she knows nothing. I will continue to observe their behavior.

A month later, the friend was reporting again.

—She has begun an affair with Kauzov. When his mother goes out to work, they sneak into the flat. Yesterday, they were there for two hours! When they left, I went up to them, as if meeting by chance on the street. We took the metro to the university and sat around talking. They want to set up a printing press. They say there is no freedom of speech in the Soviet Union—I disputed this energetically. They assessed very negatively the decisions of the last party congress. I think they were drunk.

Days passed, and the friend went ever closer.

—They have met a foreigner—possibly British or American. I don't know how or where. Sergei let it slip. Plans have advanced to the point where printing equipment is to be brought in under cover of a shipment from Poland—electrical goods, I believe. The two of them were talking yesterday in the student meeting room, but they stopped abruptly when I arrived. "What's going on?" I asked. "Nothing," said Sergei. "Everything," she replied, and then laughed. "You'll find out soon enough."

New page . . . and it's all there. Little steps to treachery.

Only now the file has acquired additional circulation points: KGB, criminal investigation. Ministry of internal affairs. Party executive committee, Timiryazev region. State militia. They're all switching in, sensing the kill.

Last entry from friend.

—They tell me to meet them at ten tonight in Chisty Street behind Nevsky Prospekt. I sense something strange in their attitude toward me. I don't think they know anything—I think they're just nervous about the printing press. Tonight I should find out the details. Tonight we should act.

I turn the piece of paper and look around the deserted restaurant. Suddenly it feels cold.

It's only half a page, this report. Just the facts, the barest details. But in my mind I can see the final act of betrayal.

Little Judas on his way in the dark to Chisty Street—how clever he must have thought himself, how well he had done, what would be his reward? Maybe they would open the sack of jewels and let him pick one—a party privilege, a car, a flat—God only knew!

According to the file, Sergei met him that night as planned, took him to a flat the other side of the city. Morskoi Prospekt, filthy run-down area, near the Kirov stadium. Full of women's hostels, workers from the Red Triangle factory. Showed him the printing press, laughed and shook his hand, and told him how he was going to make a difference.

A week later, Sergei and Mother were arrested for anti-Soviet agitation. Mother released after six months, London address/updated twice. Sergei Kauzov—eight years hard labor.

There's a release order for him, dated 1972/ Moscow residence permit 1980/ rehoused 1990. Employed as a translator. Address and telephone number.

Last page.

I finish the brandy, and now I have to read the words twice. This file is different. Different color, different type. Same name at the top: Yekaterina Bell. And this is the mother I never knew I had.

Wait, wait wait.

I read it a third time. And then again.

Now. Word by word.

Mother's name and then a column beside it.

Designation: Long-term penetration agent, London.
Function: Nonoperational.
Product file: Empty
Suspended: July 1991
Record to be destroyed.

You know it is suddenly so silent in here. The traffic outside has disappeared, all those trucks and trains and people everywhere. . . .

I can't judge her.

I don't want to.

The knowledge is enough—why she disappeared to Moscow—why George died in London.

No one had any choices.

I have to believe that.

Mother was a long-term Soviet agent, positioned in Britain, waiting for a call that never came. She never spied for Moscow. She was never asked to. But if they had ordered it—would she have obeyed? Would she? And what were her reasons? Permission to get out? Release of her parents?

Does it matter?

Haven't we all made our accommodations?

And yet, in a strange way, I wish I had never known.

I get up and go to the bar. The brandy bottle is sitting, waiting for me. I pour another glass and return to the table. And I take this last piece of paper and run it through the candle till it catches fire.

Chapter Forty

Two calls into the night.

Irina listens but refuses to speak. It's as if I'm talking to the empty space, where she once lived.

Coffin sounds tired and despondent.

"The journey ends tonight," I tell him.

"Not before time."

"Bring your conscience with you."

"I can't seem to lay my hands on it right now," he replies, and I have a vision of him, putting down the receiver and picking up a gun. He checks to see if it's loaded. It's a practiced gesture. He's good with guns. He won't think too hard before or after he fires.

A street away from the disused metro tunnel, I stand with the flight bag, watching the late evening crowds. Those who move and those who wait. Hard against the buildings you see only the lighted cigarettes, burning little holes in the darkness.

In front of me, a black BMW slows down as if searching for the way. Moscow plates, shaded windows. Chic and expensive. Show and tell, come to Russia. Irina is first.

The car turns off the main street, and I lose it between the narrow concrete buttresses.

Take it slow. Give them time. The only protection is when they're both there.

Three minutes. Four.

What's the matter with you, Coffin?

Beside me a giant television screen is projecting pictures from the Russian parliament. There's a line of teletext, declaring tomorrow's weather will be lousy. You'd know that, wouldn't you?

Watch the street. Stay focused.

City of new cars, this Moscow. They're wearing them instead of coats. Sign of the changing world . . .

Then I see it—American car, turning fast across the road—something with a monster bonnet and a hundred yards of chrome. Nice, unobtrusive little package. I catch a glimpse of the inside—only one head. Coffin is alone.

Another minute passes, but no car follows. Coffin couldn't trust anyone with this. When you get so far down the line, when you start betting the company—you're on your own. You don't know who's been bought and sold and you can't afford to find out now. No witnesses. You do the business your way—because it's your life on sale.

Wait a few more seconds. Count out loud. Just think about Dad. Nothing else matters.

The two cars are pulled up inside the opening to the tunnel, headlights on.

Lights, too, from the windows at the back of a building, tiny squares of yellow on the gravel floor.

It's for you, Dad. This is for you.

They're standing by the cars. Just the two of them. Coffin and Irina, the darkest little gathering in the world.

"Like a funeral," she says as I walk toward her. "Parents are dead, buried. Now the children must settle the estate. Children of the cold war. Do you like that, Edward?"

"I didn't come here to deal," interrupts Coffin.

She laughs at him. "Then you came for nothing. For that's all we have left. The main show is over, Mr. Coffin—there are just a few paltry deals still to be done—here in the backstreets."

Coffin moves away from the car. "My government shared these documents with yours. And yours is gone. Bust open, bleeding. Know how I read that?"

"I don't care how you read that," she says. "We take the files back, and they will be as safe as before. All the arrangements have been made."

Coffin's turn to snigger. "You don't see it—do you? The world has moved on, Irina. Your assurances aren't worth a pigeon's piss. In the old days, you had it all—power, money, control, like no one else, some of us even envied you—but you people blew it. And we're not about to go the same way—just because you can't keep the keys to a fucking archive."

Coffin is breathing heavily. Evidently it's a speech he's had waiting.

"And what about all the other documents?" asks Irina.

"What other documents?"

"Look at the case," she says. "Edward has no more than three hundred pages, maybe less. Do you realize the Central Committee alone had over seventy million files? Million! Do you know how many of your secrets are held in there?"

He looks at her without expression.

"Even if you took these pages, we could leak others, specifically to embarrass your government. But don't you understand—it's not in any of our interests for the information to come out. Not in mine, not in yours. We're all implicated. That was the beauty of the system—everyone involved. Your governments wanted to keep the old system going—same as ours. It suited them. Good for the arms industries. Good for science. Look at all the discoveries that came out of the military budget. Without a threat, there was no incentive, no progress, dear Coffin. That's how it worked. The dynamic in your society was the threat of ours. When you woke up to that—you started moving ahead. Now everyone wants that fact covered up. We live in a new world. All of us."

Coffin takes off his glasses and rubs his eyes. In an upstairs window, a little yellow square goes out.

"So what order do you represent these days?" he asks.

"*Any* order. Russians need discipline. They can't function without it. You give them democracy—it's like giving the wrong medicine to the wrong patient. Every time it's been tried, it fails. But first we look after the past. This has always been dangerous. *We* bury the Communists—we have to bury their possessions with them. Like the ancient Egyptians—then we'll move forward. Try something else"—she raises an eyebrow—"or maybe we'll just try an old trick—do the same as before, only call it something different."

For a moment, there's silence, and I have the impression this furtive little gathering is the last of the superpower summits. Then we all go our ways and pretend it never happened.

"You could certainly shoot us both," she says to Coffin. "You could do it now, take the bag, and hope to make it to your embassy. But you'd never get there, I assure you of that."

"I can't go back without the documents," he says.

"Then don't go back."

"And do what?"

"Run, Coffin. In time they'll leave you alone. When they're certain the papers aren't going to leak out. Just disappear. We can help. . . ."

"They could use my family. . . ."

"I doubt it. Not if you don't contact them. Make your choice, Coffin. Now! We shouldn't be here any longer. Leave the car. Come with me."

The life has gone out of him—this old man. He's punctured, sagging, on his final descent. But I look at him and feel neither pity nor hatred. Coffin was once a friend and a fixture. And now he isn't. He'd have killed me, if he could have. Now he has to run for his own life. There may after all be some justice in this.

"I'm sorry, Edward."

"Coffin."

"Perhaps you'd remember me to your mother, sometime."

"Perhaps not. I don't think she wants to remember you."

As he gets into the car, Irina takes the flight case and hands me an envelope.

"It's the address of a sanatorium just outside Moscow. You can ask a taxi driver. Your father is very weak. Now I must go."

"And Jane Card? What's happened to her?" For a moment, the courtyard is perfectly still. An old man in a string vest comes to an upstairs window and peers out.

"People get lost in wars," she says simply. "Sometimes they're never found. Who can tell?"

"You can tell *me*."

She opens the driver's door and stops as if a thought has suddenly occurred to her.

"You copied those files, didn't you, Edward?"

"What a question."

She smiles and nods her head, and I follow the taillights of her car, as it snakes back through the concrete pillars and out into Moscow.

It's midnight in October, a month away from the winter, and now, for the first time, I can feel the savage, unstoppable cold, seeping in over the buildings, freezing the city where it stands.

Part Three

Chapter Forty-one

I TRAVELED THAT same night to the sanatorium. A crooked old palace that belonged once to the Russian nobility—and seemed to have died in sympathy. Even at dawn you could see the broken chimneys and gables—and smell the decay.

I battered on the door, till a rude young bastard strode out in his vest, told me I was disturbing the patients, tried to force me into a waiting room.

"My father's very sick."

"They're all sick. That's what this is. House of the sick."

"I want to see him now."

"Impossible."

I came close to him and said quietly, "Then I'll return one day and kill you."

He was cowed by my anger, muttering apologies, fumbling with his jacket. . . . "Was only doing his job; if visitors came in at all hours, the place would be run by the wolves . . . he didn't know, hadn't realized, wouldn't have said . . ."

There were endless corridors, like so many last journeys, ill-lit, bare, freezing.

We passed wards and rooms, some empty, some full, without reason or explanation. Stairs and more stairs. And two old men lay end to end on the floor on stretchers, their eyes open, staring at the ceiling.

Finally we stopped by a room with no number. He opened the door quietly, smiled, and beckoned me to go inside.

We must have been at the end of a long wing, for as I looked out of the window, I had a clear view of vast woodlands, coming up in the dawn, and the lights of the city in the distance. Out over a lake crows were circling and cawing.

For the first time since coming to Russia, there was a sense of untroubled peace.

Dad was asleep, on a narrow single bed, his breathing regular, a tiny night-light on the floor beside him. The room was warm and clean-smelling.

"How long has he been here?" I asked the orderly.

"Two days. A woman brought him in a big car, foreign. Said his son would come and take care of things. I know because I was on that night. You must be the son."

He wandered off, and I sat beside Dad as the day appeared, gray and dull beyond the windows. I turned off the light, and he woke up for a moment and stared hard, as if unsure who I was.

"I thought you wouldn't come," he said.

"I promised."

"I know, but so often this country gets in the way of promises."

Later I went in search of the doctor, a woman in her late forties, so tired and pale that she seemed in need of treatment herself. For a while, she ignored me, while she wrote slowly on a file and I wondered if she had already fallen asleep. On her shoulders, her white coat was a patchwork, sewn together from little pieces of cloth.

"I wish to make arrangements to take my father to England."

She put down her pen and looked at me in astonishment.

"That's out of the question, Mr. Bell. He's not about to go traveling the world."

I stood up. "Please have him made ready to leave. It is his wish, not just mine."

"He's not leaving. . . ."

"I don't think you understand. You simply don't have the drugs or the equipment to take care of him. Let him go somewhere where they do. If you won't help, I'll carry him out myself."

She was going to shout at me. But something stopped her. By now we were both standing, glaring at each other across the desk. And then her face seemed to soften.

"Do you drink tea, Mr. Bell?"

"I . . . yes. Yes, thank you."

She gestured to the chair, and we sat down again. I could feel the anger dissipating.

In the corner, she boiled water on a small gas ring. When it came, the tea was black, with the leaves floating at the top.

"I am sorry to have spoken as I did," she said.

"So am I."

"It has been a long night, you will appreciate—it is the start of winter, and many old people are brought here because their flats are too cold. This year, for the first time, much of the city's heating has been turned off. It is one crisis after another. You were right to be concerned about your father—and I was wrong."

"I *do* want to take him home."

She sat looking at the tea leaves for a while and then reached for a file on her desk.

"These are your father's medical records, Mr. Bell. As you may know, his condition has developed in phases. There have been periods of remission, helped, I must say, by a rare Western drug." She raised an eyebrow. "This is not one of those periods. If you insist on removing him, I can't stop you. But if you wish my advice . . . I would wait a week . . . the journey might be . . ."

She stopped in midsentence and looked down at the desk.

"I'm very sorry, Mr. Bell."

I knew then what she had really told me.

I stayed with him those last days. They gave me a mattress, and I slept at the foot of his bed. We took meals together, and once I bribed the orderly for a small bottle of vodka and a pot of caviar.

But sometimes he didn't know me. And when he couldn't talk, I talked to him. About books I'd read and films and plays. Often I made them up, just to have something to say.

Frequently, though, a bad night would be followed by a

day of calm, a day without pain. And then we would recall the things we had done together, the sights of London, the little bars of chocolate that crumbled in their cellophane. There were no tears. I laughed, and so did he. Can you understand when I say it was a happy time?

It was about six in the evening when he died. I had been watching the birds above the lake, and I realized suddenly I was alone. My father had quietly left the room and gone his own way, and I kept staring out of the window in the hope that I would see some sign of him, or hear some final word.

I didn't notice the doctor tiptoe in and cover him—not until she had finished. She came over and stood silently beside me.

"I wanted to take him home," I told her.

For a moment, she didn't answer. When I looked around, she was crying softly into a tattered old handkerchief. "I know you did," she said. "But maybe he was home already."

Dad was buried on the edge of those woods, in a little graveyard where the first snows of winter came to cover him.

A priest arrived from thirty kilometers away on a tiny motorcycle, loud enough to wake anything except a cemetery, and he laid a hand on my shoulder and bowed to the doctor, as if she were God—and maybe in this place she was.

When it was over, he took me aside, and I was struck by how young he was beneath the long beard, speckled with snow.

"The stonemason says you have forbidden him to engrave the date of death," he observed. "It is not customary."

"I know," I told him. "Sometimes we have to break with customs."

"But . . ."

"It was a very dignified service, and I want to thank you for that."

He stood among the gravestones looking perplexed, and then ran up to me as I was about to leave. The snow had begun to fall more thickly, and my father's grave was already covered.

"What do I tell people if they come and ask when he died?"

"No one will come," I replied, and shook his cold, shivering hands. "Don't worry. I doubt if anyone will ever come."

Chapter Forty-two

"Has my mother forgiven me for taking the papers?"

Sergei shook his head. "But she hasn't forgiven me either. Says we're both related to the Devil—and destined to enjoy his close attentions."

"I think I already have."

He took my coat and hung it in the hall.

"Will you be staying, Edward? Please . . . as long as you wish . . ."

"Thank you, but I must get back to England. . . ."

"Your mother will be here soon. . . ."

"I saw her leave. I waited."

He nodded and beckoned me into the living room. I had, in fact, waited two days before coming to his house on the Arbat, tramping the winter streets, seeing them for the first time as a free man, realizing the place no longer had a hold on me. Never again would it be able to wrench my gut close to or from far away. It was once more a city—not a nightmare.

"Did I do the right thing?" I asked him when we'd sat down.

"You mean—giving back the files?" He sighed. "No, you didn't do the right thing. But you did the only thing you could. You broke the cycle."

"I broke my relationship with my mother."

"I don't think so. You may not be her favorite son at the moment, but you are the only one she's got. She knows that."

Toward evening we heard the key in the door.

"The markets were full of food," she announced from the hall. "But the prices are completely ludicrous. Completely."

She came in the doorway and stopped in her tracks.

"I expected you days ago," she said. "I worried you might turn up in a zinc box, and then I would have had all the trouble of getting you home."

"I'm sorry, Mother."

"You are a little bastard," she said.

"Your little bastard, though."

"That is no consolation."

She sat down in the chair I had just vacated.

"You know why I gave them the files, don't you Mother?"

"Sergei said we would never get any peace unless you did."

"More than that. It was time to bury the past, not add our names to the casualty list."

"You are fools to think this. You cannot appease dictators, and you cannot forgive their crimes." Sergei leaned over and took her hand. "But, anyway, I am tired of arguing."

"You're mellowing, Mother. Could this be the start of graceful middle age?"

She mouthed an obscenity at me—but I was amused that she wouldn't say it out loud in front of Sergei. Mother wasn't a mother in the loving, caring sense—although in her own way, she had been that too. But she was an institution in my life—rough, permanent, immovable. She was like the sky. You could walk away, but she'd still be there.

And, like Dad, she, too, had come home. Oh, she would hate the place, turn complaining into a new art form, live out her life, biting and carping—but she wouldn't go anywhere else. The life in Stanley Road was over.

"I'll sell the house. . . ." I said.

"You don't want to live there?"

"Too many memories. I'll go and look at it from time to time. That'll be enough."

"Don't let the agents rip you off. Always you know there are people who will cheat—and you are not that good with money. Listen, buy a new suit, Edward, you look terrible." It was my old mother back again, tough, opinionated, the way she had always been.

"I'll send you a check if there's anything left over."

I got up to leave. "You know, I still haven't heard anything about Jane Card. I don't suppose she's crossed your path, has she?"

"I made enquiries," said Mother. "Nothing. Not even rumors." She shrugged. "But this is not uncommon. People are like old sweets. Often they fall down the side of the chair, and you find them months later. She may still turn up, my son."

We went into the hall, and she put a scarf around my neck, and tied it tight.

"Edward—tell me. . . ."

"Yes, Mother . . ."

"Did you read the file you took from me?"

"There wasn't time," I said. "But I hope you'll let me know what was in it sometime."

She kissed me on both cheeks and took a step back. "I must do that," she replied. "Next time."

For a moment, there was silence between us, as if to mark the things we could never tell.

Chapter Forty-three

So . . . BACK TO a normal life?

London seemed tamer now and more civilized. Thank God, the cleaner had been to my flat. She left a note telling me I'd forgotten to leave the money for her. Again. So nothing had changed.

My prize plant was holding on to life by a single stem—there was a new damp patch on the outside wall. A letter from a company in Wigan inquired if I could help open markets in Eastern Europe. The sum total of my contacts with planet Earth.

On the first morning back, I awoke to see the sun, and everyone else on the river. It was the kind of day that motivates me, points me forward. So I set about disposing of Mother's house, ringing agents and placing ads. I decided to sell fast and cheap, knowing that whatever I did would be wrong.

I suppose I made the mistake of wanting a happy ending.

After a few days, I tried to get news of Jane Card. Maybe she'd slipped back into the country. Maybe there was a ministry that knew her name. Maybe. But no one would admit to it.

I even drove to South London and found the house she

lived in. The place was deserted. Neighbors knew nothing. Curtains were drawn. Britain can be very like Russia when it wants to be.

And yet, I felt as if two steel claws had been released from around my neck. After all these years, I was free to pursue just one life, not waiting for secret contacts or phone calls, or sweaty, fearful little faces to cross my path. It was time to move on.

I wrote back to Wigan and said I'd take the job.

A week later Mother's house was sold. Even I knew it was a miserable price; she would doubtless have her customary heart attack—so it was some consolation that I couldn't get through to her number in Moscow to tell her the news. Not that day. Not the next either.

And then, as they used to say in Communist countries, there was a knock on the door.

"Did you think I'd gone to heaven?"

Jane Card, very much alive, makeup-free, newly dressed, stood on my doorstep and smiled her way in.

"Good God, Jane . . . I don't believe . . ."

"I know," she said. "I don't really believe it myself. Listen, Edward, it's a beautiful day. Let's go for a walk somewhere. I've got the girls outside in the car. Come on—be fun . . . and then we can do a lot of talking. . . ."

"What now? I thought you were dead. I tried everywhere to find out about you. . . . I simply can't. . . ." I held out my arms, but she didn't move forward, didn't hug me. You'd have thought . . .

"Come on," she said, and laughed. "I'll tell you all about it." I pulled on a jacket and followed her out, muttering things like, "This is extraordinary" and "How long have you been back?" As we went down the corridor, I could hear the phone ringing, and I hesitated for a moment. I didn't want to miss my calls. I still hadn't heard from Harry.

"Wait," I said. "Phone . . ."

"They'll call back."

And then as I listened, the ringing stopped.

"See, I told you."

Her two girls were sitting outside in the car in striped dresses and white socks, little studies in middle-class England—hair bands, freckles, lots of pleases and thank yous, their teeth enmeshed behind the standard steel wire, as if to stop them biting strangers.

"Thought we'd go to Primrose Hill," said Jane. "Give the girls a nice view of the city. That's if an old man like you can make it up there."

"I can still do a turn," I replied.

"I know." She glanced at me sidelong and blushed.

We parked, and the girls dashed away, shouting at each other. All around us the autumn leaves were being blown from the trees; the grass was damp. On the hillside, I could see bright-colored kites, bobbing against blue sky.

Moscow might never have happened.

"You go first," I told her. "When I saw you get into the car with that guy, I thought that was the end of you. . . . I'd seen him once before."

"I know. I suppose I can tell you now, but he was one of ours—from the old days. Somebody we allowed the Russians to recruit over here many years ago. We then made it look as though he'd been betrayed and had to escape in a hurry back to his Soviet masters. That's when you came across him."

"So what happened when he picked you up in Moscow?"

"That was the end of my role, Edward. I couldn't tell you any of this, but my function was to get you safely to Moscow—after that the Americans and Russians were going to sort out the documents."

"So I was to fend for myself. Was that it?"

"Pretty much, I'm afraid. There was nothing more I could do for you."

It was an effort climbing the hill, but worth it. The air was cold and clear, and you could see right across London to the southern counties, where the clouds played on the horizon. We were both breathing heavily. I couldn't help remembering it wasn't the first time.

For a while, we threw tennis balls to the girls, laughing as they missed them and chased them down the hill. I kept looking at Jane and thinking how odd it was that she should show up on my doorstep with no warning—and nothing resembling a plausible explanation. And yet I was enjoying the afternoon, didn't want it to end. Given the chance, I, too, would have liked a slice of that "normal life."

"I suppose we should make a move," she said eventually.

"Come back to my place for tea," I suggested. "Nothing in the cupboard, but we can get some things along the way. You're not in a hurry, are you? . . ."

And suddenly I was aware that she had fallen behind me. As I looked back, she had stopped on the path and was holding the girls tightly to her.

"Jane . . ." And something in her eyes told me it was over, told me she was saying good-bye.

I glanced down the hill—and there was a car at the bottom, four or five men lounging around it. A black official car, anonymous, like a hearse.

"Why, Jane?" I shouted back to her. "Why? You got the documents. It's over, isn't it? Is this the kind of world you want your children to grow up in?"

"They're in it already," she said. "It's too late. We have to go on, Edward. The world doesn't want to know about the past. They don't want you to know about it, either."

"So why wait until now?"

"See if you were contacted by anyone. See if you were the last."

"And Mother? I couldn't get through to her by phone."

"I'm sorry, Edward, I can't tell you. . . ."

She was hugging the girls ever more tightly, pulling their heads so they wouldn't look at me. . . .

"What about the killing, Jane? You went along with all that?"

"I didn't think there was going to be any. I mean it. But then the Russians began shooting at Dover . . . Coffin's crowd in Warsaw. I don't know why, Edward, it got too big, it seemed to have its own momentum. And then when you and I were together in Poland, a deal was done at the highest levels . . . over my head. Somehow they'd all talked themselves into it . . . agreed the leaks had to be plugged."

I turned away from her, and I didn't have to think for long. I set off across the park, faster than I'd ever run in my life, under the trees, across the damp grass, south toward the zoo and Regent's Park, with the sun going down fast on my right, and the shouts of the people behind me. . . .

And all I could think of was that Harry had the copies, and Harry would make it.

One of these days when all our fine governments were sleeping peacefully, fondly believing they'd got away with it—then dear old Harry would emerge. Harry the ex-con, Harry watched over by gentle Aunt Doris.

Harry would tell the story.